Carbon

Elise Noble

Published by Undercover Publishing Limited

Copyright © 2017 Elise Noble

v6

ISBN: 978-1-910954-50-8

Edited by Amanda Ann Larson

Cover art by Abigail Sins

www.undercover-publishing.com

www.elise-noble.com

A diamond is just a piece of carbon that's handled stress exceptionally well.

CHAPTER 1

EVER HAD A dream come true?

I have. Four times, and this evening, I was hoping for a fifth.

"More champagne, miss?" a waiter asked.

"Yes, please."

I held out my glass. Tonight, of all nights, I needed the courage it gave me. Or, as my mother would argue if she found out what I'd been doing for these past few months, the stupidity.

All around me, partygoers danced and chatted, their faces covered by masks ranging from plain to ornate while they noshed on canapés and knocked back the free booze. At the back of the ballroom, I spotted my mother stumbling into Sir Arnold Hall, inventor of a revolutionary...uh, I forgot. Something to do with aeroplanes. Of course, the masquerade ball had been her brainchild—she'd use any excuse for a party and tonight, celebrating the launch of her daughter's latest romance novel, she'd certainly pushed the boat out. We even had a flipping orchestra in the corner.

There was a slight flaw in her plan, in that few of the guests would recognise the author herself, but Mother didn't concern herself with such trivialities. If I were a gambling woman, I'd bet most of the partygoers hadn't read the book and didn't care that it even existed.

Emphasis on *most*. One of the regular attendees certainly had read Sapphire Duvall's offerings, or at least her previous release, and he was the only man who mattered to me tonight.

Was he here?

I pulled my phone out of my clutch bag and checked the screen for a message—the hundredth time I'd done so in the last hour, even though I'd have felt the vibration if one arrived.

Please, say he's here. Mr. Midnight, the object of every one of my dirty dreams for the last month. He hadn't promised to come—he'd never promised anything—but during Mother's last four shindigs, he'd texted me by ten.

My twin sister Angelica waltzed up, resplendent in a red ball gown quite at odds with my dark blue one. She revelled in the attention whereas I'd deliberately matched my dress to the curtains in a desperate attempt to fade into the background.

"Enjoying yourself?" she asked.

"Not really."

But *she* clearly was. A glass in her hand, a man on her arm, and those who recognised her under the jewel-trimmed mask congratulating her on yet another bestseller.

"Lighten up, Gus," she said. "Won't be long until you can go back to your own world."

She didn't mean to sound cruel—she never did—but tact wasn't her strongest suit. Her words stung, a harsh reminder that I didn't fit in here. As if I needed one.

I mustered up a smile. "Two hours and counting."

Angelica drained her glass and whispered

something to the man at her elbow, lifting his wrist with delicate fingers to check the time. He wore a Patek Phillippe watch. Expensive. His mask covered most of his face, but I didn't miss the curve of his lips or the heat he exuded. Clearly, he liked whatever suggestion my sister had just made.

"See you in the morning," she said, giving me a little wave.

Three guesses as to what she planned to do for the rest of the night. Once, I'd have been depressed and maybe even slightly jealous over yet another of her conquests, but tonight I forgot her almost instantly as I snatched my phone out of my bag again. Nothing.

Had he got bored with our game already?

Three months ago, Midnight's first message had come out of the blue as I pretended to enjoy my mother's St. David's Day party. No, nobody in my family was Welsh, and we lived in rural Oxfordshire not Wales, but little things like that never stopped her. When I said she'd use any excuse for a party, I meant it.

Unknown: Meet me at midnight. The summerhouse by the pond.

At first, I thought the message was a joke. It had to be. Because *Meet Me at Midnigh*t was the title of Sapphire Duvall's latest bestseller, a bodice-ripper set in Victorian England where the object of Lady Anne's affections asked her to—you've guessed it—meet him at midnight. First in the summerhouse, then behind the chapel in the grounds of her family's country manor, even in the stables.

And what they got up to made my mother splutter her tea and hastily flip the pages until Anne was safely laced into her corset once again.

Augusta: Surely you're not serious?

Ten rather sweaty minutes later, as I stood with my mother and sister pretending to listen to their conversation, the mystery man replied.

Unknown: Only one way to find out...

No, I couldn't. I mean, the idea was preposterous. Yes, Lady Anne had gone, but Anne was a fictional character, not to mention a lot braver than me. Back in her day, the world wasn't full of serial killers and murderers like England nowadays. Okay, so Jack the Ripper lived in the nineteenth century. And Burke and Hare. But that was completely different.

I poured myself another glass of garish yellow fruit punch from a daffodil-patterned jug and sighed. Angelica would go, but Angelica had more courage than I did. People always expressed surprise when they found out we were twins, seeing as we weren't identical, and I quite understood why—I was the mouse to her lioness, the water to her fire.

The "other" daughter. The one without fame and all the trappings that went with it.

The one who'd never stepped out of the box I'd carefully constructed around myself as a schoolgirl.

"Angelica," my mother bleated, interrupting my thoughts. "You simply must tell Petronella about your new book. And, Augusta, be a dear and bring us another bottle of rosé."

Fine, so I was the waitress to Angelica's lioness.

Why did Mother make me go to her flipping parties? I hated every second of them. And at a quarter to midnight, while Angelica dissected the plot of Sapphire Duvall's debut novel and got several key points wrong, I was sent to the wine cellar for my sixth trip that evening. And that time I kept walking. Right out of the house, across the lawn, past the swimming pool and the tennis court, through the rose garden, and as far as the pond.

I hadn't planned to go there. I hadn't even thought about it. Okay, so I had *thought* about it, but not seriously. I mean, the whole idea was crazy, right?

But my feet walked me across the estate until the summerhouse I'd played in for hours as a child stood in front of me. Of course, since my mother had a hand in the design, it wasn't simply a wooden hut. No, its hand-finished oak walls had been built by a master carpenter, and a sought-after designer had furnished the roomy interior. Three or four times a year, Mother would sit there and read a book for a morning before she got bored. Not one of Sapphire's—Mother preferred memoirs.

The rest of the year it lay empty, except when I borrowed it in the warmer months. Or possibly this evening. Did Mr. Midnight really exist?

Before I could slap myself over how insanely stupid the whole idea was, I tapped in the combination to open the door, and the creaking hinges reminded me how little use the place got.

Now what?

A minute ticked past, and my toes began to get a little chilly. I still had time to leave. But the part of me that actually believed in Sapphire's stories kept my feet planted next to the floral chaise longue, my whole body trembling in the dark.

At least, until the nearby screech of an owl brought me back to reality. Had I lost my mind?

Lady Anne might have found love on her foolhardy jaunts, but that was hardly realistic, was it? In my twenty-seven years, I'd been touched by love twice—the childhood crush I'd never quite grown out of and my husband. And look how both of those episodes ended. The boy I used to sit next to at school moved to a different county, and my husband died.

I desperately wanted to believe it would be third time lucky, but the realist in me came to the fore, and my feet finally came unstuck. What was I thinking? I should have been heading for bed with a mug of hot chocolate, not hanging around wishing for fantasy sex with a stranger.

Oh, but it had been a really, really long dry spell. Seven years. Seven long, long years.

Halfway to the door, the soft crunch of footsteps on the gravel path outside stopped me dead in my tracks. Was it him?

Lady Anne grabbed the back of the chaise longue, and her knuckles turned white as her heart beat so hard it threatened to burst from her corset.

"Identify yourself," she said. "Who goes there?"

Me? My knuckles turned white, all right, but I choked on my words, and when I did force them out, the high-pitched squeak was plain embarrassing. "Hello? Is someone there?"

A silhouette appeared in the doorway, lit from behind by a sliver of crescent moon. I squinted in a bid to identify the man, but the darkness veiling his face gave me nothing.

"You know who it is," he said, voice low.

"I'm quite sure I don't."

He stepped forward, closer, closer, until I felt the puff of breath on my cheek. "Turn around."

"Why? What are you going to do?"

"You know that too."

Lady Anne gasped as her mysterious suitor trailed a finger along her cheek, a light touch, but not an innocent one. That single digit promised forbidden delights, sweetness and scandal if she did not stop him that instant. She reached up to bat his hand away but instead pressed his palm against her cheek.

"Sir, what are your intentions?"

The scoundrel clutched her skirts in one hand and lifted them slowly, oh so slowly. Only the thin cotton of her bloomers stood between the lady and her honour. Her breath came in short pants, bosom heaving as his hand rested on her thigh.

"We should not be doing this," she whispered.

"Then I bid you to walk away."

Walk away? Her knees trembled so much she could barely stand. Instead, she bent from the waist over the chaise longue, lost in ecstasy as the stranger had his wicked way.

Was that what Mr. Midnight wanted to do? Have me bend myself over the furniture while he got his rocks off? Talk about forward. Because the idea was...it was...uh, kind of hot, actually.

Augusta!

No!

I didn't know who the man was, anything about him, or worse, where he'd been. But hang on, wasn't that the whole point of surprise, illicit sex?

He trailed one finger down my jaw, and according

to the script, sorry, the book, I should have clasped his hand to my cheek. But instead, I turned my head so his finger slipped into my mouth, then sucked. Heat shot through me, right from my eyeballs to my hoohah. Or my velvet glove, as Sapphire would have called it.

Say something, Augusta. Tell him to stop. Tell him this is totally inappropriate and you need to get the wine from the damn cellar and go back to being bored out of your mind at the party.

His other hand slowly lifted my silk skirt, leaving a burning path along my thigh as it got higher, higher...

"I don't have a clue what I'm doing," I blurted.

Oh, way to go, Gus. You sure do have a knack with words.

He answered with a throaty chuckle as one finger slid under my knickers. Not bloomers but boring white cotton bikini pants, ten pounds for a pack of five from Marks and Spencer. Tomorrow, I'd burn every pair I owned.

"Miss Fordham, your body knows exactly what it's doing."

Really? I'd had sex precisely twice in my life, both times with my husband and neither could be described as awe-inspiring. Romance novels spoke of shattering into a thousand pieces, of fainting with sheer pleasure, but when Rupert rolled off to the side, I wasn't even sure whether he'd come or not. I certainly hadn't.

"My body's lying."

"No, your mouth is lying."

Dammit, he was right. You could have fried an egg on me, such was the heat coursing through my veins. I'd probably scorched him.

"Do you... Do you have protection?"

I felt rather than saw his smile. "I came prepared."

Well, at least one of us did.

Before I could back out, he nudged me forwards over the padded chintz, and I grabbed onto the edge of the chaise longue. The hand under my dress continued its lazy exploration while his other arm wrapped under my breasts, lifting them upwards in a way no bra ever could. Soft lips kissed their way up the side of my neck until I twisted around to meet them with my own.

He tasted faintly of mint with a hint of wine over the top. Had he drunk it for courage like I did? There was certainly no way I'd have been in that position sober.

A thousand sensations washed through me, from fear to euphoria, from heat to goosebumps, but when he pushed my knickers to one side and gave me all of him, I got the strangest feeling of...of rightness. Like my entire life—every thought, every decision, every success, and every tragedy—had conspired to lead me to this moment. With him. A perfect stranger.

"So fucking tight," he whispered.

There was a good reason for that, but I managed to refrain from letting it slip out.

Instead, I bit my tongue as he showed me that each love scene I'd imagined and each lover I'd dreamed of could all roll into one and come true with the right man beside me. Or rather, inside me.

"Why did you send me that message?" I whispered when he slid out of me and smoothed my dress down.

"Because it was written in the book."

"But why me? Why not my sister?" After all, she made no secret of the fact she moonlighted as Sapphire Duvall.

He leaned in closer, nuzzling me with his lips. "Because your sister didn't write that story. You did."

I stiffened in his arms. How the hell did he guess that? Only three people knew my secret—me, my sister, and our accountant. Even my parents didn't have a clue who was really behind Sapphire's novels.

"You're mistaken," I tried, but even to my own ears, my words sounded hollow.

"Again, your body tells me otherwise. Was it everything you hoped?"

And more, so much more, but I didn't want to stroke his ego. "You missed the part where he teased her with freshly picked strawberries."

His muscular arms dropped away, leaving me bereft. "We need to save something for next time."

"Next time?"

He paused halfway to the door. "What? After tasting your sweetness, you didn't think I'd abandon you to some scoundrel, did you?"

"Uh, I... I don't... I didn't think..."

Two seconds, and he'd closed the distance between us again, but this time he picked up my hand and pressed his lips to the back of it in a chaste kiss. "Until we meet again, fair lady."

As his feet crunched away on the path, I gathered up my scattered sanity. Next time?

Would I be crazy enough to do this twice?

Who was I kidding? Of course I would.

CHAPTER 2

CLICK. CLICK. CLICK. Ten hours after Mr. Midnight left me speechless in the summerhouse, Angie snapped her fingers in front of my face.

"What's up? I know you daydream a lot, but you've been staring at the same spot on the wall for half an hour. That's weird, even for you."

She wasn't wrong, but I'd never been taken from behind by a stranger in the early hours of the morning before. That sweet spot between my legs still ached as a reminder. "Just pondering a new plot line."

Or even an old one—the way my impetuousness had combined with alcohol and a sexy stranger to bring one of my scenes to life. At least, he'd felt sexy. For all I knew, he could have looked like Frankenstein's monster crossed with an Orc. It wasn't as if I saw his face. What on earth had I been thinking? Oh, that's right, I hadn't.

"Well, ponder faster. I need you to take a look at cover designs for *The Dark Night*, help me with some interview questions, and take a few photos of me for Sapphire's blog. And don't forget Mother's expecting you for lunch at one."

"She is?"

"I put it in your diary last week and reminded you yesterday and the day before."

She motioned to my MacBook, sitting on the desk opposite hers. My calendar stared back at me, filled with all the appointments I tried to ignore in favour of my precious writing time.

"What's she got planned? Tell me she hasn't brought that colour lady back again."

Three weeks ago, my mother had asked me to join her for afternoon tea, only for an overly enthusiastic lady who looked like a packet of Skittles had thrown up over her to try and force her dubious fashion choices upon me over scones and crustless sandwiches. Apparently, Mother thought the jeans and jumpers I tended to live in weren't appropriate for a lady.

"She was a bit cagey about the reason, but she said you need to dress up."

"Are you coming too?"

"No, I told her I had to go out."

"Couldn't you have said I needed to go with you?"

"I tried, but she gave me that look. You know, the one where she summons Satan and channels him through her eyes."

"Yes, I know it."

Somehow, Angelica got away with more than I did. Her exuberant personality combined with the way Mother favoured her firstborn meant she'd always been granted more leeway. As the second twin, the one who'd popped out by surprise after a trainee midwife missed me on the ultrasound, I'd been playing catch-up to my mother's expectations my whole life.

Father, on the other hand, adopted a more hands-off approach to parenting. As long as we didn't bother him, he mostly left us alone. I say mostly, because it was he who'd decreed that any children of his would work for a living no matter how much money we happened to have.

The day after his colleague's daughter maxed out her credit card and threw a tantrum at the office when it got declined in Harvey Nichols, he'd sat Angie and me down for a little chat.

"No child of mine is going to sit on her backside while the rest of the world slaves away. You both need to get jobs."

It was a fair point, seeing as we'd graduated from university six months ago, but Angie acted like Father had ordered her to become a cat food tester or a shark wrangler.

"But, Daddy, I'm so busy. I've got tennis lessons, and lunches to attend, and I promised Mariella Huffington I'd help organise her wedding."

"And all those things cost money. Who pays for them?"

"You do, Daddy." She plastered on the smile that usually got her anything. "And I've always been grateful for that."

"So grateful you almost got thrown out of university for turning up drunk to your lectures. No, you've got to get a job. Full time, part time—I don't care, but you need to learn some responsibility."

"But—"

"No excuses. You've got three months, and then I'm turning the bloody tap off."

When he strode out of the living room, Angie sat down on the couch and groaned. "This is the worst idea he's ever had. Is he trying to ruin my life?"

"He's kind of right. And besides, we might find something we enjoy."

Even as the words left my mouth, I crossed my fingers at the lie. Not only did I hate having to speak to strangers, which meant the mere thought of most careers sent me into a panic, the writing time I'd grown to appreciate after university would vanish. Three months. I had three months to finish my book before it became ten times more difficult.

So, the next morning, I set to work.

"What are you doing?" Angie asked two weeks later. "You've done nothing but type for the last fortnight."

"Uh, filling out job applications?"

"What kind of jobs?"

She sidled around my desk, and I grabbed at the mouse to minimise chapter thirty-seven of *He Called My Name*, but instead of switching to the copy of my CV I'd knocked together, I accidentally played a rather dirty video of Michael Douglas in *Basic Instinct*.

Angie hooted with laughter. "You filthy woman!"

"It's not what it looks like. This is...er...research."

"Research? Into what? Are you finally going to try dating again?"

"No!"

"Don't sound so shocked. It's a reasonable question." She crouched beside me, and her voice softened. "It's been two years since Rupert died."

"I know, but that's not it."

"What, then?"

How did I explain my worries that any man I found wouldn't live up to the ideals I'd created in my head? "I'm just not ready; that's all."

"So you're using Mr. Douglas as a substitute? You know, to...? Because I'm not usually one to judge, but in the middle of the day with your sister in the room..."

Her voice dropped to a whisper. "I can get you something to take care of that problem."

Could I go any redder? "I told you; it's research."

I had fingers, thank you very much, and I knew how to use them.

"Research for what?"

"I'm writing a book, okay?"

"On what? Porn?"

"If you must know, it's a historical romance. I was just watching for...uh...pointers. Since it's been so long, as you kindly reminded me."

"A book?"

"That's what I said."

"I know; it's just... I guess I'm surprised."

"I did spend the last six years studying English."

"Do Mother and Father know what you're doing?"

I stifled a laugh. "Of course not."

My father only read non-fiction, while Mother stuck with women's magazines and the occasional memoir. The idea of them reading the naughty bits and realising they came from my head? Yes, I'd rather walk across glowing coals.

"Come on then, let me have a look."

The mouthful of tea I'd just taken almost flew across the keyboard, but I managed to choke on it instead. Angie thumped me on the back until the coughing subsided.

"What was that all about? Me reading your book? What's the point in writing it otherwise?"

"I guess I figured the only people who might read it wouldn't know me. That I could stay anonymous."

"Are you planning to publish it?"

"At the moment, I'm just trying to finish it."

"But then what?"

"I haven't thought that far ahead, okay? The bit I enjoy is the writing."

Angie sat down at her own computer in the little lounge we shared upstairs, the one that had been our playroom as kids, and I thought she'd lost interest. But the next day, she dumped a huge pile of print-outs on my old walnut desk.

"What's all this?"

"More research."

I stared at her, then glanced at the pile, expecting to see a picture of a stripper after my excuse yesterday, but the top page was filled with tiny print.

"Research on what?"

"Publishing. I did it for you." She shrugged. "Sure beat ringing around friends and begging for a job to keep Daddy happy."

"Uh, I'm not sure..."

Truth be told, the idea of publishing scared the crap out of me. Sure, I had the goal of finishing this book, but I'd poured my heart into those pages, and I didn't want my nearest and dearest to see inside.

"What's not to be sure about? You've written a book; now it's time for other people to read it. Two options—get an agent and a traditional publishing deal, or go the DIY route. Personally, I think that one looks more fun. Nobody telling us what to do, and we can sort out all the publicity ourselves."

"Publicity?" My heart sank at the thought. "And what's this 'we' business?"

Angie shoved the papers aside and perched on the edge of the desk. Her smile worried me, and that gleam in her eyes? She only got that when she came up with one of her brilliant ideas—the ones that always ended in disaster, apologies, and when we were a few years younger, getting grounded. Like the time when we were ten, and she wanted a puppy. Mother said no, dogs were dangerous, so Angie decided we'd prove otherwise by borrowing our old caretaker's Great Dane and taking it for a walk. It knocked Angie over, then I got my hand tangled in its lead while it rampaged through Mother's rose garden. After that, we weren't allowed so much as a goldfish.

And now her grin grew wider.

"Daddy wants us to get jobs, right?"

"Right."

"So, you become a writer, and I'll be your assistant. Daddy's always harping on about how important it is to have a good grasp of the English language. It's perfect."

No, no, no, no, no. A thousand times no. "No way. I mean, most writers don't even make money."

"Augusta, Augusta, Augusta." She placed both hands on my shoulders. "This isn't about earning money. It's about keeping access to the money we already have. Just think about it—you get to carry on doing what you love, and I'll... Well, I can post stuff on social media for you. Answer your emails, that sort of thing."

My heart gave a little flutter. In a way, her crazy plan made sense, and the thought of being able to write all day rather than actually speak to people filled me with a sense of relief. Apart from... "I don't want people knowing that story came from me."

"Why? Aren't you proud of it?"

After two rewrites and the mountain of advice I'd got from the editor I secretly hired? "Well, yes, but..." I lowered my voice to a whisper. "It's got sex in it. Mother would look at me all funny."

Angie giggled. "It's not like you're a virgin. You were married, for crying out loud."

For all of three days. "That's different."

Angie rolled her eyes, suggesting the difficulties were all in my head. "Okay, new plan. We'll tell her I wrote the book, and you're my assistant. She already spends her life moaning about my serial dating habit, so she'd totally believe it."

"But what about everyone in the village? Your friends?"

"My friends will love the idea of me being a writer. I can sign books for them and stuff. And the people in the village talk behind their hands every time I walk into the pub, so what's new? You never know—one of the old biddies might read your smut and have a heart attack."

"It's not smut!"

She waved at the screen. "Really? Michael's naked backside?"

"I toned it down a bit."

"Come on, if we're going to do this, you have to let me read it."

Okay, so it wasn't the worst idea she'd ever had. No, that honour went to the time seventeen-year-old Angie snuck out to a party late one Saturday evening with the lead singer of a local band Mother had banned her from seeing. I'd got a panicked phone call the next morning, whereupon I had to drive a hundred and fifty miles to pick her and her tattooed beau up from Manchester, still drunk. Mother caught us sneaking in, with Angie dressed up as the Green Absinthe Fairy complete with half a bottle of the vile green concoction, and we both got grounded for a month.

A tiny white lie regarding the true origins of *He Called Her Name* seemed tame in comparison. Besides, it wasn't like I'd sell many copies, would I? If nothing else, I was a realist about my chances of success.

Only it didn't quite turn out that way.

Fast forward five years, and twenty-seven-year-old me still hadn't found herself a boyfriend, but I, or rather Sapphire Duvall, had become a bestseller nine times over. It turned out sex really did sell.

Too bad I still wasn't having any, apart from that one glorious night with Mr. Midnight. Mother kept attempting to meddle in my love life, just as she always had, and Angie had never stopped chasing anything with two well-muscled legs and a six-pack.

And now Mother expected me for lunch. If it was just the two of us, I'd be amazed.

"Are you sure you don't want to join us?" I asked, no, begged Angie.

"Sorry. I'm meeting the events planning guy for the launch of *The Dark Night*. You know, for the masquerade ball?"

A sigh escaped. "I forgot."

"I'll be back by five. We can catch up before my date this evening."

"Another date?"

"So many hot guys, so little time."

CHAPTER 3

I MADE THE effort and put on a frock for lunch, not because I wanted to impress whoever Mother wanted me to meet, but because it simply wasn't worth the earache she'd give me otherwise. Knee-length and floral, if I was lucky, I'd blend into the Laura Ashley sofa.

Mother looked pointedly at her slim gold watch as I walked into the garden room, and she checked the clock on the wall behind her for good measure. Only a minute late, for goodness' sake, and Dorothy hadn't even served the bread rolls yet.

Rather than eating in the formal dining room, Mother always preferred to have lunch overlooking the back lawn, presumably so she could check the gardener was doing his job properly. Despite having a beautiful garden designed by a gold medal winner from the Chelsea Flower Show, she barely set foot outside. I glanced over at the table—four places. Who were they for?

"Didn't Angelica give you the message about dressing up?" she asked.

I risked a look at myself. Yes, I was still wearing Cath Kidston's finest with a pale pink cardigan and my late grandmother's pearls.

"I did."

Her sigh said it all: where did I go wrong with this one?

I held in my own exhalation as she motioned me to take a pew next to her. Chilly air from the open French windows wafted up my skirt, but it did nothing to cool the fire still burning in my core from last night's encounter with Mr. M. I crossed my legs and forced myself to breathe as I waited for Mother to explain who we were expecting for lunch.

"Mrs. Fitzgerald from the tennis club will be joining us shortly," she informed me.

Mrs. Fitzgerald... Mrs. Fitzgerald... Which one was she? All the ladies from the Sandlebury Lawn Tennis Association looked the same to me—perfectly coiffed hair, a touch of Botox, white skirts more suited to a woman half their age, and enough jewellery to dazzle their opponents to distraction. Angie still kept up a membership, but I'd cancelled mine years ago. On the rare occasions I still picked up a racket, I played against my sister on our own court.

"Lovely." I forced a smile. "Is she bringing a friend?"

"Her son. You remember Gregory? He attended the fencing club with you until he went away to boarding school."

Ah, fencing—something else I wasn't very good at. Ben, the boy I'd sat next to in English and French, convinced me to start classes, but he was far better at it than me. I only went along because Mother said I had to go to ballet otherwise, an activity I took to with the grace of a grasshopper and the enthusiasm of a sloth.

And yes, I did remember Gregory, particularly the time he'd laughed at me when I put my fencing jacket on the wrong way around. Even though Gregory was two years older than us, I'd still had to stop Ben from doing something unsportsmanlike with his épée.

And now Gregory was expected for lunch. Hurrah. "Yes, I remember him. But why is he coming here?"

I had a horrible feeling I knew the answer.

Mother rose from the sofa with an elegance I'd never mastered and glided over to the table. "Where's Dorothy?" she muttered. "I'll need to have a word about her timekeeping."

"Mother, why is Gregory coming?"

A tiny frown creased her forehead, then she smiled. Her expression told me I wouldn't like what she had to say.

"Gregory's just moved back from California, and his mother says he's ready to try dating after his divorce. Of course, I thought of you. It's about time you made the effort again."

"Effort to what?"

She gave her head a little shake. "To get married, of course."

"Mother, I don't want to get married again."

Truth be told, I hadn't wanted to walk down the aisle in the first place, but I'd given in to the pressure—from her, from Rupert, from his family. And after last night, emulating Angie and her penchant for no-strings sex held a certain appeal.

"Nonsense, darling. You're almost thirty, and your biological clock is ticking away."

"So is Angie's."

"Yes, but at least she dates. It's not her fault it's so difficult to hold down a high-pressured job as well as finding an eligible bachelor."

I wanted to scream at the injustice of it all. Angie didn't date; she just had a whole series of one-night stands. And that high-flying career? That was my bloody job. Angie spent most of her working life on social media, which although necessary for Sapphire's reputation, wasn't exactly taxing.

"Please, Mother, I'm not—"

"Here they are now." She pricked her ears at the sound of the doorbell. "Smile, Augusta. You look as if you're about to eat lunch at a homeless shelter."

Quite frankly, I'd have preferred that. I'd also have preferred if my mother stopped being so judgemental—I'd volunteered at a shelter last Christmas and met some really lovely people. But that was my mother. She'd go to the grave criticising the vicar's choice of footwear.

Dorothy showed Mrs. Fitzgerald in, then scurried off as Mother tapped her watch. I wished I could have followed her.

"Sandra, how lovely to see you," Mother cooed.

Air kisses followed while I stared awkwardly at Gregory. "Uh, hi."

This was why I preferred to write all my words rather than speak them. My tongue tied itself in knots, and I never knew what to say. Except with Midnight. Words had been unnecessary, but my tongue sure had loosened in his mouth. Since my encounter with him last night, I'd checked my phone over and over for another message, but he'd been the silent one.

"Good to see you," Gregory said, leaning in to kiss me on the cheek. "It's been a long time."

His tan spoke of warmer climes than England, but when he got close, I gave a subtle sniff and stifled my giggle. Yes, that delicate bronze colour came from a spray booth rather than the sun. I'd smelled the same strange aroma on Angelica. At least I could eliminate the possibility of him being Mr. Midnight—his sexy musk had been all man.

"Yes, it has been a long time. Fifteen years?" More than half my life. Honestly, what was Mother thinking?

"So kind of you to invite us around today." He placed a hand on my arm. "Although next time, you don't need to send your mother with your invite. I won't bite."

Ouch. His overly white teeth hurt my eyes when he grinned, and I clenched my own together. Mother told him this was my idea?

"I'll remember that."

"Anyway, how have you been? Have you stayed in Sandlebury all this time?"

Of course. I wasn't brave enough to escape its clutches. "Yes, I still live at home. Angie and I share the annex. How about you? Mother said you lived in California?"

"Since I finished medical school. Met a girl from LA in my final year, and we moved there when we graduated."

He'd become a doctor? That surprised me—he'd never seemed the altruistic type as a child. "I didn't realise you'd gone into medicine. Which field?"

"Cosmetic surgery." He showed me those teeth again. "Always happy to offer a discount to old friends."

Well, that was generous of... Hang on. "You think I need work done?"

A little of his colour faded, from burnt umber to a disturbing shade of orange. "So sorry, I didn't mean it the way it came out." He ran his eyes up and down my body, and I wished I'd never asked the question. "No, you're absolutely fine as you are."

Fine? Fine? Last night, Mr. Midnight had made me feel desirable, sexy even, but Gregory had undone all that with one sentence. Still, Mother was watching me, so I swallowed the remains of my pride.

"That's good to hear."

Mrs. Fitzgerald clasped my hands in hers. "So nice to see you again, Augusta."

"And you."

Please, palms, stop sweating.

"I hear you're working as your sister's secretary."

"Something like that."

"Wonderful, wonderful. Not all girls are career-driven, you know, and that's the way it should be. Far better to work for a few years and then stay home with the children while your husband climbs the ladder." She pinched Gregory on the cheek, and he rolled his eyes. "Luckily, my Gregory has a good job."

"Mother, stop scaring Augusta. We're only having lunch."

I shot him a grateful glance, but his comment rolled off her.

"Nonsense. The two of you aren't getting any younger. Now, why don't you sit next to each other while we eat?"

My mother flashed a smile and slid into a chair opposite. "What a wonderful idea."

Gregory pulled my chair out before settling next to me, and to give him credit, he looked about as comfortable with the situation as I felt.

"How long ago did my mother extend the invite for

this little get-together?" I whispered to him after the main course.

Both of our mothers were ignoring us in favour of a discussion on flower arranging, and we'd more-or-less exhausted the small talk on current affairs and the weather.

"She suggested it a couple of weeks back, but I'm afraid I've been too busy with my job up until now."

He'd told me all about his new position at the private hospital in the next town, specialising in breast augmentation. I'll admit the thought of dating a man who spent every day with his hands on other women's boobs made me cringe.

"Well, today was the first I heard about it."

"Oh dear. I was under the impression you were rather keen, just a bit shy."

"Not exactly."

An awkward silence followed as Dorothy cleared the plates away. After the slightly uncomfortable start, Gregory had proven to be less unpleasant than I feared, and a far cry from the bratty boy I'd detested. With fifteen years having passed, I guess he'd changed, even if I still felt like a ten-year-old child intimidated by his proximity.

"With all the time I spent overseas, I forgot how meddlesome Mother could be. Until I went to university, she was forever trying to run my life."

"I sort of wish I'd gone away to university, but as I attended Oxford, I was close enough to catch the train into town each day."

"I didn't realise you were an Oxford girl. Congratulations. Went to Cambridge myself. We probably shouldn't be speaking after your boys thrashed us in the boat race this year."

A giggle bubbled up before I could stop it. "Mainly because your team's boat nearly sank. The wind was terrible. I'm so glad I only watched on television."

"I stood on the banks of the Thames one year, in the rain, but I don't remember much about it due to the pub crawl afterwards."

"Aren't doctors supposed to act responsibly?"

"Ah, but I wasn't a doctor then, merely a student."

Chatting with Gregory came more easily over dessert, and when I glanced at the clock, I was amazed to find two hours had flown by, even if half of that time was taken up by me reliving last night with Mr. M while Gregory waffled on about a recent medical conference. I'd successfully wasted most of the day, and I needed to get some editing done if I was going to meet my next deadline.

"So sorry, but I'm afraid I need to excuse myself. I promised to update Angie on a few things before she goes out this evening."

Mother dabbed at her mouth with a napkin and gave Mrs. Fitzgerald a knowing look. "So lovely to see you two getting along. It's a good thing Gregory's coming to my Black and Red party a week next Saturday."

Gregory raised an eyebrow. "I am?"

His mother fixed him with a hard stare. "Yes, Carolyn invited us both last month. Don't you remember?"

He turned to me and shrugged. "Looks like I'll see you a week next Saturday, then."

"Looks like you will."

Weirdly, I didn't hate the idea as much as I thought

I would.

Chapter 4

A WEEK AND a half passed, and the frequency of my phone checks had waned to every two hours. Not a peep from Mr. Midnight, but someone had given Gregory Fitzgerald my number, and he'd messaged to say how much he was looking forward to the party this evening. Or at least, somebody using his phone had messaged me—I wouldn't have put it past his mother to step in again.

"The hairdresser will be here in two hours," Angie said. "How's the editing?"

"Done. Finally." I'd typed "The End" on *The Dark Night*, and usually that would free my mind to turn one of the hundreds of ideas floating around inside my brain into a tangible plot line. But not tonight. No, tonight all I could think of was how Mother's last soirée ended—with me bent forward over a chair while Mr. Midnight ploughed into me from behind.

Angie mistook the flush of my cheeks for something else and smiled. "I heard you and Gregory Fitzgerald got on well at lunch the other day."

"It was okay. He's not as bad as I remembered."

"Oh, don't play coy. You've gone all pink."

Yes, but Gregory couldn't have been further from my mind. "It's nothing."

"Nothing to do with the fact that Gregory's coming

tonight?"

"No, honestly."

She just laughed. "You don't fool me."

Well, as long as she thought my blushes were over Gregory, I could deal with that. Far better to believe I'd got the hots for a well-to-do doctor than a faceless hunk who'd shown up once to shag me senseless.

"Have you decided on a dress?" I asked, changing the subject.

Angie's raised eyebrow told me she knew what I'd done, but she humoured me anyway and turned to the four possibles hanging from the wardrobe door, all bright red and all more risqué than I'd ever have dared to wear.

"I'm thinking the one on the left." She looked me up and down. "Unless you want to borrow that one?"

"No!"

While Angelica had been blessed with a naturally slim figure, every cake I ate went straight to my bottom, and I had to wear a bra at all times. I'd fall right out the top of that dress, and then there was the colour. Mother had decreed we wear either red or black to fit with her party theme, and my choice would most definitely be the latter. Long, dark, plain—I envied those ladies in the Middle East who got to wear a burka every day.

"I've already chosen my outfit," I said.

"Where?"

I pointed across the hallway, through the open door to my bedroom. "There."

Angie squinted at my bed. "You do know this is a party, right? Not a funeral?"

"Yes, I'm well aware of that." And I didn't want to

give Gregory the wrong idea, or anybody else either. Unless... Mr. Midnight had mentioned a "next time." Was he being serious? I mean, I hadn't heard a peep from him, but what if...?

No.

I mustn't get my hopes up, and besides, now I'd had time to think about that night, I realised I must have been suffering from temporary insanity. Honestly, skipping off to meet a stranger for sex again would be a terrible idea.

Crazy. Awful. An idea so bad it made me ache between my thighs just considering it.

"You've got that look again," Angie said. "Still daydreaming about Gregory?"

Damn my flipping face, betraying me like that. "I'm going to change."

Her laughter followed me out of the door.

"Can I get you another drink?" Gregory asked.

He'd worn a tuxedo with a red bow tie as a nod to Mother's theme.

I glanced at my champagne flute—half empty, but it was my third glass, and I was wearing heels. "Better not, but thank you for offering."

The evening had turned out less painful than most of Mother's parties, mainly because by hovering near Gregory's elbow, I'd avoided duty as a glorified waitress. Plus, she hadn't introduced me to any random strangers as her "other daughter, the one who doesn't write the books."

Gregory's company had been...nice, I guess. It

reminded me of the parties I used to attend with Rupert, in those years when every conversation didn't start with, "Augusta, I was so sorry to hear about your husband." I hadn't needed sympathy; I'd needed to sit on my own and cry.

But now? Enough time had passed for people to forget that I'd been widowed at the age of twenty, and Gregory certainly commanded the respect of Mother's social circle. He fitted in perfectly.

"Yes, I do believe I'm free next Sunday," he said to Mother's accountant. "Eighteen holes?"

"Nineteen, old chap. Can't pass up on a drink afterwards."

I stifled a yawn at the golf discussion, a favourite topic of that crowd, along with planning policy, British-made cars, and the state of the economy.

"Tired, Augusta?" Gregory asked.

"A little," I admitted.

Tired of small talk, tired of strangers, and tired of wearing shoes that made my feet ache.

"It's carriages at midnight, so only two hours left."

I pulled out my phone. No, two hours and nine minutes. Nine minutes that had the potential to stretch into eternity if that bloody accountant didn't stop talking. I looked around, ready to play my usual game of making up stories about the party guests in my head, when my phone buzzed in my hand.

Instantly, I stiffened, then forced myself to relax as Gregory's eyes cut my way.

"Okay?" he mouthed.

"Great. I just need to visit the powder room," I muttered, then speed-walked out the door. Or rather, speed-tripped, but a passing waiter caught me. Damn those heels.

Safely locked in one of the downstairs cloakrooms, I looked down at my phone, praying it wasn't just another one of those bloody sales messages from ambulance-chasing solicitors. "Have you had an accident, trip or fall?" No, not unless you count throwing my phone against the wall in annoyance.

Mr. M: Meet me at midnight. Behind the guest cottage.

Beads of sweat popped out on the back of my neck. Behind the guest cottage? Not inside it? Okay, so in my book Rufus met Lady Anne behind the chapel, and we didn't have a chapel, but the idea of doing anything outside terrified me. What if a stray guest walked past? The cottage wasn't that far from the main house, after all.

No. I should text him back and say no.

But the very thought of that made my heart plummet, where it landed among the butterflies swarming in my stomach at the prospect of another Midnight-induced orgasm.

Maybe I could meet him, then convince him to go somewhere a tiny bit more private? Like the summerhouse again. Yes, that would work.

Fingers trembling, I typed out my reply.

Augusta: Okay.

One word, and as soon as I sent it, I regretted it. It seemed so...so...inadequate. I was supposed to be a writer, and I'd used one of the blandest words possible. Bleurgh. I needed to work on my communication skills.

Ten minutes passed with no reply, and I needed to leave the toilet because otherwise someone would be sure to inform Mother of my bowel problems. Think that wouldn't happen? Well, it did after Rupert died, and she booked me a colonoscopy.

Back in the ballroom, Gregory's conversation had moved from golf to squash. I'd only ever played once and the bruises took weeks to fade, so I didn't feel qualified to join in. Instead, I tried to block the filthy thoughts going through my mind as the hands on the clock ticked closer to the witching hour.

Only at a quarter to midnight, Gregory was still yacking, and I couldn't figure out how to politely excuse myself.

"I'm feeling a little tired," I said. "I might go and lie down."

The slack-jawed banker Gregory was talking to laughed, one finger tugging at his overly tight shirt collar. "Don't skip out on us, dearie. Only another fifteen minutes to go and then you can take your man for a bit of night-time entertainment."

My face turned the colour of Gregory's bow tie as they carried on with their conversation. How could I get away? I was racking my brains for a better excuse when another of the tennis club ladies teetered up.

"Dr. Fitzgerald, may I have a quick word?"

"Of course, Alicia. What can I do for you?"

She stepped closer, and I strained to hear her words. "It's a professional matter." Her cheeks turned a delicate shade of pink, and she glanced at the cleavage spilling from the top of her dress. "Perhaps we could go somewhere more private?"

A boob job? She wanted to chat about a boob job? How much bigger did she want them to be?

Gregory turned and shrugged. "Sorry, Augusta, but work calls. I'll be in touch during the week."

And that was it—dismissed. At least I knew where I stood, and at least I was free to make my escape. Dumping the dregs of my wine on the nearest waiter's tray, I dashed off like Cinderella, only I was heading towards my Prince Charming rather than away from him.

Okay, so not Prince Charming, exactly, but then I was hardly the stuff of fairy tales either.

I checked my phone as I slipped out of the side door. No more messages, and five minutes left to get to the guest cottage. I'd hoped to change my shoes because my feet were killing me, but would Midnight wait if I was late?

I couldn't take that chance.

My breath puffed into the cold night air as I rounded the corner of the cottage, balancing on tiptoes. He hadn't thought this through, had he? Lawns and stilettos certainly didn't mix.

"Augusta."

A whisper from beside me made me jump, and I whipped my head around in time to see his silhouette step from the shadows by the back porch. He'd picked a moonless night again, but I could just about make out the white "V" of a shirt under his suit jacket. So, a party guest?

I wobbled on my heels, and he reached out to steady me, one hand on each of my arms. Even that innocent touch through my velvet dress made me tingle all over.

"I'm here," I whispered back.

His lips slammed down onto mine as he kissed me with an intensity bordering on painful, a clash of teeth and tongues that had me melting at his feet. No, not melting. Sinking. Sinking into the damp earth at his feet.

"Shit," I muttered. "My heels are stuck."

This never happened to Lady Anne.

I felt him smile against my mouth, and a quiet chuckle escaped his lips. "Ever consider flats?"

"I'm quite short enough already, thank you."

Angie and my mother were both five feet eight, and my father four inches taller still, but by some fluke of genetics I'd ended up at five feet four with most of the other debutantes towering above me.

Midnight's response? He dropped to a crouch and ran his hands up my legs, lifting my dress with them until it bunched around my waist. Only his hands on my ass cheeks preserved any kind of modesty because the black lace thong I'd worn didn't leave much to the imagination. My plain white undies were now stashed firmly at the back of my wardrobe. He drew my bottom lip into his mouth and sucked as he lifted me clear of my shoes and carried me towards the cottage, pressing me to the wall next to the back door.

"Wrap your legs around my waist," he commanded, and I was only too happy to comply as his hard cock rubbed against me through the thin layers of material. The friction of the lace drew another gasp from me as he gently bit down on my lip. I might even have moaned.

"What's with this dress?" he asked. "It leaves everything to the imagination."

"Uh, I could take it off?"

"Not in this temperature, *mon cœur*, and not with those bricks against your back."

"We could go inside?"

He grinned against me. "Where would be the fun in that? Besides, I like the dress. It means none of the lecherous bastards at that party got a good look at you."

"It means you can't get a good look at me either."

"I don't need to. Not when I can feel you." He dropped one hand and ran a finger between my legs. "And I can feel you spent the last two hours getting yourself worked up."

"I..." I couldn't lie. "I totally did."

I loved the sound of his laugh. Rich and deep, it sent vibrations through my core. "Want to know a secret?"

"Uh, yes?"

His lips brushed my earlobe. "So did I."

Oh my... I tightened my arms around him as my pussy throbbed. "Then hurry up."

"You'll need to lend a hand, because I don't have enough of them." He used his weight to hold me against the wall while he fished something out of his pocket. "Unzip me and put the condom on."

I froze in his arms, and not because of the late winter chill. "I...uh..."

"What is it?"

Oh, shit. I could either confess or run into the night. Both would result in mortal embarrassment, but one would ensure I didn't get the pleasure of Midnight's cock. "I don't know how to do the condom thing," I whispered. "I've never had to before."

"None of your men have ever asked you to?"

"Man. And even if he had, it was seven years ago."

It was his turn to still. "Seven years? You haven't had a man in seven years?"

"Not until you."

"Fuck me."

"I'd like to." I couldn't keep the hopeful note out of my voice.

He laid his forehead against mine. "And I bent you over that chair and screwed you like an animal. *Mon cœur*, I'm so sorry." He took my weight and stepped back. "I'll walk you to the house."

"No! Please don't. I... I want this. No, I need it."

"I shouldn't have—"

"Do you know how many people have handled me with kid gloves since...?" How much did he know? "Since my husband died. All of them. Every single one. You're the first man to treat me like a woman, and I don't want you to stop."

"He died? Oh, hell..."

Midnight didn't know? That meant he was a newcomer to the area. It was only in the last few years that people had stopped gossiping about Rupert's death. I'd heard the whispers, even though Mother had banned the household staff from mentioning it right after the funeral. But that was my past, and Midnight was my present.

"Please, stop talking and do whatever you planned to do."

He ran his free hand through his hair, and I wished I could see the expression on his face, but all I got were dark shadows from his nose and eyes. He could have been hideous for all I knew, but I didn't care. Not when he made me feel this way.

"Are you sure?"

Not exactly, but I wasn't about to admit that. "Yes, I'm sure."

He kissed me again, more softly this time, but the

sentiment was no less intense. I lost myself in him until he gently pulled back an inch.

"Reach between us and undo my trousers."

It took a few fumbles but I got there, and he sprang free. This was the first time I'd handled a man's cock, and the smoothness surprised me as well as how hard it felt. And how big. He let me explore for a minute while he kissed his way down my jaw, then he pulled back a little.

"Now the condom. Can you get the packet open?"

I gave up with my fingers and tore it with my teeth. "Done it."

"Squeeze the bubble at the end to keep the air out while you roll it onto me."

That was easier than I thought, and I gave him one final stroke when I'd finished. "Okay."

No more words were necessary as he moved my knickers to the side, arched his hips, and slowly pushed inside. Finally.

"You fit me like a fucking glove," he murmured.

"I'm waiting for the fucking part."

"Your books don't reflect your filthy mouth, Miss Duvall."

"You've read more than one?"

"All of them, but I prefer the reality. This is gonna be fast and hard, Gus. I don't think I'll be able to help myself."

I clenched my muscles around him, and it was his turn to groan. "Do your worst, Midnight."

He wasn't kidding about either part, but my orgasm built as quickly as his. Thank goodness for the cool air, because by the time I shattered around him, I was a hot mess. One final thrust and he followed me into oblivion and leaned into me, holding us both up against the wall. I nuzzled into his neck, inhaling the scent of male and something else. Lime? Did he use lime shower gel?

A minute passed, maybe two, before either of us spoke.

"I need to reunite you with your shoes, *mon cœur*."

"I'm not sure I can walk."

Another chuckle. "I wish I could carry you home, but that wouldn't work."

Feeling brave, I cupped his face with my hands. A hint of stubble scratched my palms. "Why?"

"Because I'm not the sort of man you take to meet your mother."

I'd kind of worked that part out—after all, I wouldn't wish my mother on anyone. But my heart still ached at the thought of going home alone.

"Can we do this again?"

Soft lips brushed my temple. "Yes."

He freed my shoes, then held my hand until we emerged from behind the cottage. Before our fingertips parted, he lifted my hand to his mouth and pressed one last kiss to the back of it.

"Until midnight."

Then he melted into the darkness.

CHAPTER 5

THE NEXT MORNING, I soaked my blisters in a hot bubble bath as I relived Midnight's visit with equal parts pleasure and embarrassment. Confessing I had no idea how to put on a condom? He must have thought I was a complete moron, but even then, he'd been so damn nice about it. And the sex? Honestly, I had no words. My thoughts were best summed up in a series of moans, grunts, and incoherent ramblings.

"Taking the day off?" Angie asked when I perched on a stool at the breakfast bar.

"I need to do one final read-through of the manuscript before it goes for editing." That was always the part I hated most—by that point, I'd read the damn words so many times I hated them, and I was racked with enough self-doubt I wanted to delete the entire book.

"I've got a video conference with the merchandise people at eleven. Did I tell you we got offered a deal for our own line of condoms? They want to print 'Meet me at midnight' on them with space for a phone number."

I spat my orange juice across the table. "No, you most certainly did not."

She threw me a roll of paper towel, and I blotted up the mess.

"Well?"

"Well, what?"

"What do you think? Should we take it?"

"It hardly screams historical romance, does it? Besides, Mother would have a fit." I had another thought. "Did they send any samples?"

Angie grinned at me. "Why? Do you want to use them with Gregory?"

I quickly shook my head, perhaps more emphatically than Gregory deserved. "Just curious."

"They're on my desk next to the mock-up of the masks from *The Dark Night*. Oh, and Petra called yesterday afternoon."

"What did she want?"

Although we'd self-published all our books, Petra, our agent, had helped to negotiate foreign translation rights and our two movie deals.

"She reckons you should write a contemporary version of *Meet Me at Midnight*. You know, update it for modern times with extra filth. Now, that would fit with the condom range."

Palms sweating, I gripped my thighs at the thought of publishing anything half as grubby as my adventures with my Midnight. Hang on—*my* Midnight? We'd done very bad things twice—that hardly gave me a claim on the man, did it? Although if I recalled my high school French lessons correctly, he did keep calling me "my heart," which made mine beat madly every time the words left his lips.

"I think for Mother's sake we'd be best sticking with the historical themes."

Angie pouted at me. "You're no fun. Get Gregory to give you a good roll in the sack, then you might change your mind."

"I'm not sure Gregory's that sort of man. He reminds me of Rupert a bit."

"But you loved Rupert."

"I know... It's just I'm not sure I want that kind of relationship again."

"What do you mean? You and Rupert were perfect for each other."

Yes, so everybody said. Eventually, we'd even believed it ourselves, hence the over-the-top nuptials in a marquee on the banks of the trout stream running through our estate. Rupert was safe. Rupert was dependable. Rupert was...quite boring, if I was honest with myself.

"I'm a different person now."

Inside, I longed for adventure, but every time I contemplated acting on my urges, I chickened out. Probably because my one and only attempt at being that carefree girl had culminated with six weeks in a Thai prison—an experience, yes, but not one I cared to repeat.

"Perhaps I could set you up with one of my friends?" Angie offered. "Crispian's hot and single."

Crispian also dabbled in drugs and treated women like objects, but for some reason, Angie still liked the man. "Honestly, I'm happy with how things are."

With Mr. Midnight bringing a little excitement into my life, as well as spectacular orgasms.

"When's the next party?" I asked Mother three hours later. I'd joined her for lunch, much to her surprise.

"Four weeks, darling. Don't forget your father and I

are going for a break at the villa first."

Dammit, I *had* completely forgotten. They headed for our place in Barbados twice a year, once at the end of winter and once in the autumn, which meant a whole month before Midnight would be back. One hand drifted up to my lips, where his touch still lingered, and I forced it back to my lap.

"Oh."

"You sound disappointed. Why don't you simply call Gregory? I'm sure he'd love to take you out for dinner."

"It's not about Gregory." Whoops, shouldn't have said that.

She looked up sharply. "Then what *is* it about?"

"Er, I just had a fun time talking to everyone, and I, uh, I really liked the canapés."

A smile flickered across her lips. "Those mini orange soufflés?"

I quickly nodded.

"I'll ask cook to make some for you, but don't eat too many or you'll ruin your figure. And if you're finally enjoying my soirées, perhaps you could assist with some of the organising?"

Hmm, like the guest list? "I'd love to do that."

Flowers. I got flowers. No, not as a gift, but to organise. Mother decided on a theme that left the local florist rubbing her hands together in glee, and I was supposed to select the vases and ensure they found their way to the right locations.

And more disappointingly, my casual enquiry about

the attendees was met with a, "Don't worry, Gregory will be there," before Mother swanned out of the door followed by the housekeeper, the caretaker, and the cook, each wheeling two of her matching Louis Vuitton suitcases.

Wonderful.

Then it got worse. Gregory called and invited me to dinner, and without sufficient warning to come up with an excuse, I found myself agreeing.

"I'll pick you up on Saturday at six," he said.

"Where are we going?"

"The Riverside Inn."

He tossed the words out casually, and with a standard eight-week waiting list for a table, I should have been impressed. But all I could think about was the posh dress I'd have to pick out, and the heels I'd have to squeeze my feet into, and the fact that I'd need to beg Angie to do my make-up.

"Wonderful. I look forward to it."

"You look awesome," Angie said as she added one last layer of mascara to my eyelashes.

I peered past her into the mirror. "You don't think this dress is a bit short?"

"It's three inches above your knees."

"Exactly."

She sighed. "No, it's not too short. Now, don't do anything I wouldn't do."

"That doesn't leave much out."

Angie winked. "Yep, you're good for everything up to a rabid public screwing up against a wall."

I froze halfway to the door, feeling a little faint as the blood drained from my head. Did she know?

Behind me, her chuckles drifted through the air. "Relax, I'm kidding. I know you'd never do anything like that."

"Of course not."

Downstairs, Gregory's chauffeur waited by his town car with the door already open, and as I slid into the backseat Gregory glanced up from his phone, eyes widening.

"You look...radiant."

Was that really such a surprise? Oh, who was I kidding? Most of the time I looked more like the household help than Carolyn Fordham's daughter.

"Thank you. That's very kind of you to say."

I watched the dark countryside fly by outside the car window as Gregory returned to his phone, and my mind drifted back to Midnight. What was he doing this evening? And if he were in the car beside me instead of Gregory, what would we be doing right now? I bet it wouldn't involve emails.

A giggle escaped at the thought of emailing Gregory to start a conversation. Would he get off on that?

He glanced up. "Did you say something?"

"No, just a tickle in my throat."

At the restaurant, Gregory rested one hand on the small of my back as he held the door open for me to go through, forever polite. The maître d' rushed over to take my coat.

"Mr. Fitzgerald, Ms. Fordham, how lovely to see you. Let me show you to your table."

I'd imagined Gregory would have got the primo spot by the window, but a couple was already sitting there. Still, the maître d' headed in that direction.

"The man on the left is Phillip Jefferson, consultant anaesthetist," Gregory whispered. "I'm hoping to work with him in the future, so it's important this dinner goes well."

Wait a second. He'd brought me to a bloody business meeting? I clenched my teeth as Phillip rose to greet me with a kiss on each cheek, cursing myself for being made a fool of once again.

"Augusta, this is Phillip and, er..."

"Phillippa, my fiancée," Phillip helpfully put in.

Phillip and Phillippa? I swallowed down the laughter that threatened as Phillippa pulled me into a hug. Well, at least I wouldn't forget their names.

Nor did I forget the manners Mother had drilled into me as I made small talk over the starter and smiled blandly between mouthfuls of the glazed salmon Gregory ordered for my main course. But when he passed on dessert in favour of a cheeseboard, I struggled to maintain my façade.

"If you'll excuse me, I need to visit the ladies' room."

The men stood up as I put my napkin on the table and pushed my chair back, and when I glanced behind, I found Phillippa following. What was this? A group outing?

She started gushing as soon as the door clicked shut behind us. "Wow, this is so exciting! I mean, you and Gregory? And isn't your sister that famous author?"

"Yes, Angelica writes books."

"I've read, like, every single one. Do you think you could get her to sign my copies?"

I managed a tired smile. "Yes, no problem."

"Ooh, you're amazing." She clapped her hands together. "And lucky—I mean, the way Gregory looks at you."

Huh? "How does he look at me?"

"Like he wants to take you shopping and invite you to the opening night at the opera."

Really? All I'd picked up was mild interest. "I'm more of a rock music girl myself." When my mother and Angie weren't around, I cranked up Bon Jovi and danced around the lounge.

Phillippa nudged me with her shoulder. "You're so funny. But seriously, any girl would kill to marry Gregory. I mean, look at his ex-wife—he gave her bigger breasts, a new nose, and a facelift, all for free."

The idea of going under the knife made me shudder. "I'm not sure that's for me."

"Oh, don't be silly. He could smooth out all those little wrinkles." She pointed at my forehead. "Botox doesn't work forever, you know."

"I actually just came in here to use the toilet." Not be insulted by a wannabe Barbie doll.

"Sure, sure. I can talk through the door."

Wonderful. I tried to pee quietly while Phillippa dished the dirt on Gregory's ex, their divorce, and his return to England.

"Apparently it was irreconcilable differences, which we all know means she had an affair. Her personal trainer, I heard. My friend Belinda said Gregory's wife complained he wasn't meeting her needs, which is ridiculous because he bought her a new Mercedes coupé only a month before they split."

"Maybe there's more to life than money?" I said, muffled by the door.

Phillippa let out another peal of laughter. "Augusta, you're so hilarious."

And of course, when Mother arrived home the week before the floral party, she'd heard all about my "date."

"How lovely that Gregory took you to The Riverside. He must think very highly of you."

"I'm not sure about that."

I seemed to be more of a convenience. A girl with enough manners drummed into her that she wouldn't embarrass him by using the wrong fork for the starter.

"Nonsense. He asked whether you'd be at the party on Saturday, you know."

"He did?"

"Yes, and Mrs. Fitzgerald thinks the pair of you would make a wonderful match."

Much like Mrs. Mulcaire had with Rupert. Swap him out for Gregory and my life had barely changed. Maybe the universe had conspired to give me another chance at a relationship, with the hope I didn't mess it up this time?

Except fate had thrown in the added complication of Mr. Midnight, and that confused the hell out of me.

Midnight, Midnight—with three days to go until the party, I thought of little else. Would he be there again? I was going crazy not knowing.

Why couldn't he have told me in advance? Honestly, would it have been so damn difficult? I mean, wasn't communication key in any relationship? Not that we had a relationship, but still... He'd been balls deep in me twice and that should count for something, right?

Angie had gone out, and I paced our apartment obsessively on Friday evening, glass of wine in hand. Who the hell was Midnight?

By ten o'clock, I could take it no more—not the wondering or the walking, because I'd got more than a little tipsy. How dare he leave me so frustrated like this? It wasn't...it wasn't gentlemanly.

Snatching my phone up off the desk, I did something I should have done ages ago and called his bloody number. This little game couldn't be all one-way.

"You have reached the Vodafone voicemail service for oh-seven-nine—"

I hung up in disgust and dialled back with the same result. Asshole. Didn't he know mobile phones were there to be answered? Obviously not. I slumped down into my chair, beyond frustrated.

Now what?

With anger and passion chasing the alcohol through my veins, I did the only thing I knew how to do —picked up the cheap plastic fountain pen I'd treasured since I was an eleven-year-old girl and began to write.

CHAPTER 6

IF MR. MIDNIGHT followed the book, if indeed he turned up at all, tonight's escapade would be in the stables. With the floor made from old stone slabs, I figured I'd be safe enough in heels, so I'd avoided Mother's wrath and gone with stilettos for the floral party.

With the flowers in place, the buffet set up, and the waiters hovering with trays, the ballroom looked magnificent if I said so myself. Now all we needed were the guests.

They began trickling in at seven, starting with the nouveau riche and those determined to curry favour with my parents. Anyone who was anyone would arrive later to make an entrance, Gregory included, it seemed.

Angelica strutted up beside me, making a rare appearance at a family do.

"Didn't you have a better offer?" I asked.

"Rumour has it the Viscount Northbury's attending tonight, and he's..." She made a fanning action with her hand. "Incendiary."

"I thought he'd got engaged?" Or was that another rumour from the tennis club?

"Until the wedding ring's on her finger, he's fair game."

"I'm not sure..."

"Look, I'll just test the waters. Besides, you've got Gregory to attend to your needs."

I pinched the bridge of my nose and closed my eyes briefly at the thought of Gregory in bed. He'd probably keep his socks on and bring his laptop. When I opened my eyes again, Angie had disappeared, replaced by Mother, who wore a black look on her face.

"Augusta, you ordered lilies!"

"Uh, yes?" They were pretty.

"Serena Cunningham is allergic to lilies. She sneezed all over the hallway, and I've had to take her through to the drawing room. Go and help her, for goodness' sake."

"I'm sorry, I didn't realise—"

"Just go."

How was I supposed to know about Serena's allergies? I only saw her a few times a year, and she'd never said anything but hello. Still, I took a deep breath and trudged off.

By the time I'd packed Serena into a taxi with a box of tissues and a thousand apologies, Gregory had arrived, looking admittedly handsome in a dark grey suit. He smiled when he saw me, and I took a glass of wine from a passing waiter as I headed towards him.

"Augusta, have you met Dr. Sorensen? He specialises in orthopaedics."

"Lovely." Whatever that was.

"Knees," Dr. Sorensen clarified, shaking my hand. "I fix knees."

While he spoke to Gregory about some new kind of artificial cartilage, my heart skipped a beat as I caught sight of a dark-haired newcomer. Tall and well-built, even from behind, and the way he moved exuded sex appeal. Surely that couldn't be...? He was about the same height as Midnight, and they both had muscles. Then a petite blonde slid under his arm, smiling, and Angie caught my eye from across the room.

"Viscount Northbury," she mouthed, just as he turned around.

Of course. I remembered now.

Okay, so he wasn't Midnight. I confess to being a little disappointed. I watched as Angie's eyes drifted to his right, where another rather tasty man had arrived. With a lighter build than the viscount, his twinkling eyes and sexy smile meant Angie made a beeline right for him.

A spasm of jealousy rocked through me at the sight —what if he was Midnight? I forced myself to take a deep breath and think through what I knew. Midnight was strong—he'd proved that in the effortless way he'd held me against the wall, and he sure had muscles. I'd felt most of them, from his taut butt to his six-pack to his hard biceps. And even in my heels, he'd dipped his head to kiss me, which put him... I glanced at Gregory... No, Midnight was taller, which put him at six-foot plus. Definitely more like the viscount than his friend. Okay, Angie could have the other dude.

But it did leave me with the burning question: Who the hell was he? I tried to keep it subtle as I gazed around the room, searching for men who fit the criteria. By the time I'd got through my second glass of white, I'd narrowed it down to one man other than the viscount, and I was plucking up the courage to wander over and introduce myself when my clutch bag vibrated.

Was that Midnight?

Because if so, it ruled hot guy number two out—with a wine glass in one hand and the other gesturing as he spoke to an older gentleman, he couldn't have sent a message right then.

"Will you excuse me for a moment?" I whispered to Gregory, and before he got the chance to reply, I hurried from the room.

Three women were queuing for the downstairs toilets, so I slipped into the TV room just along the corridor. Then left rather hurriedly at the sight of my sister getting it on with the brown-haired guy from earlier.

"As you were," I muttered, cheeks burning, but I wasn't sure she even noticed my presence.

Desperate for privacy, I shut myself into the coat closet, sank to the floor, and pulled my phone from my bag, keeping my fingers crossed as well as my toes.

Mr. M: Meet me at midnight. The stables. Last loose box on the left.

I couldn't resist sending a message back.

Augusta: Are you going to bring your riding crop?

A minute passed, then two. Shit. Would he see the funny side? What if I'd overstepped the mark and he was freaking out about the prospect of a bondage session? Should I—?

"Miss Fordham? What on earth are you doing in there?"

I blinked in the glare of the chandelier as Dorothy stared down at me.

"Uh..."

"Are you all right? Should I call somebody?"

"No! I'm just a little...tipsy. Please, please don't tell Mother." Indecision marred her face as I scrambled out into the hallway. "Look, I'm fine, honestly. It's all good."

"You should lie down, miss."

"Great idea."

I shot up the stairs as the phone vibrated in my hand, and I didn't stop until I reached my childhood bedroom, still decorated with the pink ruffles I'd hated so much. Slamming the door behind me, I looked at the screen.

Mr. M: You'll have to wait and feel.

I flopped back onto the pink counterpane, feet hanging off the end of the bed. How could one line of text turn me into a mushy mess?

The sound of Mars from Holst's *The Planets* suite made me jump, and for a brief moment, I was tempted to send my mother to voicemail. But if I did that, she'd send out a search party.

"Hi."

"Augusta, where are you? Dorothy said you weren't feeling well."

Thanks, Dorothy. "I just came over a bit faint, but I'm fine now. Could you tell Gregory I've gone to bed?"

"Shall I get Angelica to come and sit with you?"

Probably Angie wouldn't appreciate that, especially if she was going for a second round with the brown-haired guy. "No, I'll be fine. I think I just need some sleep."

No, I needed a certain dark, mysterious stranger before I lost my damned mind. Shoes in hand, I snuck down the back stairway and scuttled around the house to the annex door—at least Angie and I had a separate entrance or we'd never get any privacy.

Should I change my dress? I'd gone with another

long gown for the party, but the idea of Midnight peeling me out of my clothes tempted me to borrow something more risqué from Angie's closet. Would she have anything that fitted?

When I said Angie's closet, I of course meant the third bedroom in our little pad. She'd adopted it for her clothes soon after we moved in, right after she'd outgrown the two wardrobes in her own room. Surely I must be able to find something?

Too short, too long, too tight, too loose. I tried on a Lycra dress and stood in front of the mirror. Nope. I may have been a lady of the night, but that didn't mean I wanted to look like one. Hang on, what was this? A knee-length black number, plain with a bit of stretch, but that wasn't what made it stand out. No, I was attracted to the zipper that started at the neck and went all the way to the bottom hem. Easy access.

Please, let it fit.

It was a tad tight across the chest, but I could live with that. Besides, if Midnight delivered, I wouldn't be wearing it for long, anyway. Perfect. With ten minutes to spare, I pulled the pins out of my hair so it tumbled around my shoulders in loose waves. I'd always considered the light brown colour dull, but in the dark, it didn't matter. All I wanted was Midnight's fingers tangled in it. Five minutes left, and I dabbed perfume behind my ears and quickly brushed my teeth.

Okay, I was ready.

CHAPTER 7

THE PATH TO the stables was shrouded in darkness, and for a moment, I wished I'd brought a torch, but I suspected Midnight wouldn't appreciate that. He chose darkness for a reason; I just didn't know what it was. Silence reigned. We hadn't kept horses since Angie and I turned nineteen, when the last of our childhood ponies died and neither of us had the inclination to look after another. Horse riding had been Mother's idea, anyway. Just one more skill every eligible young lady should have under her belt whether she liked it or not.

The door to the barn creaked as I pushed it open, and I forced thoughts of rats and spiders from my mind. Midnight was all that mattered. I'd expected inside to be pitch black, but a single candle flickered in the draft from the doorway. A tea light, small and flat, giving just enough light for me to avoid tripping over the wheelbarrow parked in the aisle.

The last stall, he said, and if he'd lit the candle, he must be there already. Heart hammering, I tiptoed forwards, right into his arms.

"You came," he whispered.

"You thought I wouldn't?"

"I worry every time."

His confession gave me confidence. "Trust me;

there's nowhere I'd rather be."

I melted against his chest as he kissed me, and with no danger of sinking this time, I stood on tiptoes and gave as good as I got. The man made me wild, so wild I felt like a character from one of my books, not plain old Augusta.

It was Midnight who broke the clinch, but only to run his hands down my body.

"Tell me you didn't wear this to the party?"

"You weren't there?"

"Not this time. I only came here to see you."

A shiver ran through my body. Me. He'd come to see me. I tried to kiss him again, but he pulled back.

"You didn't answer my question."

"No, I didn't wear it to the party. I borrowed it from Angie's wardrobe afterwards."

His fingers found the zipper and lowered it an inch. "Good girl."

"You like it?"

"I like what's inside it."

The faint sound of him opening the dress all the way to the bottom was the loudest noise in the stables as I held my breath. He did too, I think. Then his hands were on me, running up the bare skin of my stomach until they closed over the lace cups of my bra, leaving a trail of goosebumps in their wake.

"Perfect," he breathed, running one thumb over a nipple.

It hardened under his touch, and as I pressed forward with my hips, I found it wasn't the only hard thing between us.

Midnight tugged me forwards, and a soft thunk echoed in my ears as he sat down.

"On my lap," he ordered, half lifting me as he pulled me further towards him.

My knees hit one of the old wooden storage trunks, covered with a soft blanket. He'd come prepared again. I straddled his legs, taking the opportunity to grind myself against him, but he held my hips still.

"Not yet, *mon cœur*."

"But you're having all the fun."

He let go with one hand, paper rustled, then I felt something at my lips.

"Bite," he said.

Strawberries. He'd remembered the damn strawberries. And not just any old fruit—these were fat and juicy and covered in dark chocolate, bitter against the sweetness. A dribble of juice ran down my chin as I chewed, and he swiped it away with his tongue, finishing with a long kiss that made my toes curl.

"Another?" he asked.

I nodded, then realised he couldn't see. "Yes, please."

Boy, I was glad I'd skipped dinner because I wanted to eat what he offered me all night. I'd certainly never look at Dorothy's fruit cocktail in the same way again. Leaning forward, I reached behind Midnight until I found the box filled with individual paper cases, plucked a strawberry free, and held it to his lips.

"Your turn."

He bit into it then sucked each of my fingers in turn, sending a bolt of electricity straight between my legs. The fruit lost a little of its appeal.

"Are we nearly finished with these?" I asked.

"I thought you liked strawberries?"

"I do, but there's something else I want more."

Feeling wanton, I rubbed against his cock to emphasise my point.

"Good things come to those who wait."

"I already waited. Over two bloody hours this evening, and don't even get me started on the last month. Can't we meet at eleven next time? Or ten?"

He chuckled. "Mr. Ten Thirty hardly has the same ring to it. What would Lady Anne think?"

"I'm pretty sure Rufus didn't have a chest like yours, and speaking of which, why are you still wearing a shirt? It's hardly fair."

"You got me there."

He used one hand to drag his T-shirt over his head, leaving me free to explore his rippling muscles. The rough denim of his jeans served as a contrast, rubbing me to distraction while moisture soaked through my knickers. Too much. This was too much.

Before I could stop myself, I reached for his belt buckle, and this time he didn't try to stop me. Instead, he dipped his head and sucked one nipple into his mouth through the lace of my bra, groaning softly as I reached inside his trousers and freed his length.

"Condom," I said, not wanting to look like a complete pillock this time.

"Yes, ma'am."

The idea of being on top, in control, made me more nervous than I wanted to admit, but as Midnight gripped my hips and lowered me over him, all my worries flew into the darkness. With him, my body instinctively knew what to do, and the animal that had slumbered inside me for twenty-seven years took over, writhing and mewling until we both collapsed back onto the trunk.

"Think I squashed the strawberries," Midnight said. "Oops."

After our last two trysts, I thought he would help me back into my dress and disappear, but instead he held me close against him, his breath whispering across my cheek. The faint aroma of lime shower gel tickled my nostrils again, and I vowed to go out and buy myself some to serve as a daily reminder. Yes, I'd gone quite dippy over him, hadn't I?

He twitched inside me as he kissed me softly, first my cheeks, then my eyelids, and finally my mouth. "How tired are you?" he asked.

"What did you have in mind?"

He dropped one arm to the side of the trunk, and a few seconds later cool leather trailed over my exposed bottom.

I gulped. "Is that a riding crop?"

"It was your idea."

"Uh, I'm not sure whether I was serious."

"So I'm Mr. Midnight and you're Miss Indecisive?"

"Will it hurt?"

"I'd never hurt you, *mon cœur.*"

"Why do you call me that? It's French, isn't it? For *my heart*?"

He shrugged underneath me. "I spent a bit of time in France, and it seemed appropriate."

"Does that make you mon cock?" Holy cow, I couldn't believe those words just left my mouth! "Sorry. Inappropriate."

"Try '*ma bite*' instead."

"Can I?" I whispered. "Try it, I mean."

"If you say things like that, I'm gonna be Mr. One O'clock, Two O'clock, and Three O'clock."

"Put your money where your mouth is."

"Right now, I'm tempted to put my mouth somewhere else entirely."

"Then do it."

He groaned and sat up, and for one awful second, I thought he was leaving.

"You play havoc with my self-control, beautiful."

Beautiful? "You have an unfair advantage. You know what I look like."

"And that's the way it's got to stay."

"Why?"

"Like I said before, I'm not the type of guy you take to meet your mother."

Well, I knew he didn't have piercings all over his face or a punk hairstyle, so why would he think that? "Do you have tattoos or something?"

"A couple. Just trust me when I say the good lady of the house would *not* be happy if you invited me over for dinner."

"Where?"

"Where what?"

"Where are the tattoos?"

He took my left hand and moved it to his upper arm. "A grenade with seven flames here." Our hands reached to the left side of his chest. "An infinity symbol here." And to the top of his back. "The last one I got was a Chinese symbol after I'd had too much to drink *avec mes amies* one night. I don't know what it means, and I don't think I want to. How about you? Do you have a secret tattoo somewhere?"

I spluttered out a laugh. "No way. Mother would go mental if I did that."

Even Angie didn't dare.

"Do you ever do anything because *you* want to do it?"

His words gouged deep. Until his first message had lit up my phone on St. David's Day, I'd never contemplated stepping out of the comfort zone I'd hidden inside for my entire life. But now? He made me see things differently, even if I couldn't see him.

"I'm doing you."

Fire surged through me once again as his lips met mine, but the kiss didn't last long. He was already getting hard again when he slid out of me and lifted me to my knees on top of the box.

"Hands and knees, *mon cœur*."

"Why? What are you going to do?" I asked, but even as the words left my mouth, I was already leaning forwards.

"You wanted a taste, and I'm not letting you kneel on that dirty floor."

Oh! Freaking heck, I needed to make another mortifying confession. "Uh, I've never…"

He brushed my hair away from my face and fisted it into a ponytail behind my head. "It doesn't matter."

Okay, I knew the theory. I'd read enough books, and if I cared to admit it, which I didn't, possibly watched the odd naughty video as well. I could do this.

Well, firstly he was bigger than I thought. Barely a third of his cock fitted into my mouth, if my hands were to be believed, and when he hit the back of my throat, I gagged.

He stroked my cheek. "Easy, Gus."

Right, don't panic. I tried licking the end, and his groan suggested I was doing something right. The salty, musky taste of him overwhelmed my senses as I found a rhythm, licking and sucking until...

"Why did you stop me?"

"Because I'm not going to come in your mouth for your first blow job. Besides, it's your turn."

Midnight didn't seem to have a problem kneeling on the cold flagstones himself as he laid me down in front of him on the blanket. I gripped the fleecy fabric tight as he ran his tongue along my centre, then sucked at my...

"What's clitoris in French?"

He choked out a laugh against me as I clapped a hand over my mouth.

"I really need to think before I speak, don't I?"

"No, you don't. Your complete lack of filter is just one of the many things that make you so damn sweet."

"I'm not always like this. It's you. My brain gets all jumbled when you're around."

"Clitoris is *clitoris.* Or *clito.*"

"Oh. I thought the French would have some sexy word for it."

"Let's go with *chatte,* shall we?"

"Cat?"

"Pussy."

He sucked again and all thoughts of language disappeared, replaced by an incoherent series of moans as he took me to heaven and then held me while I floated back down to earth.

"You okay, *mon cœur?*"

My legs trembled as he helped me to sit up again. "I'm more than okay, but what about you? You didn't finish."

"How about you get on your knees again?"

With pleasure. He arranged me with my knees on

the very edge of the box, and I heard the rip of foil before he plunged inside me. The sweet, reverent man from earlier disappeared, replaced by passion and fire as Midnight thrust his hips. Waves of bliss crashed through me until the sting of the riding crop on my ass made me yelp.

"Too hard?"

No, bloody hot, actually. "Keep going. You just caught me by surprise."

Another orgasm built as he trailed the leather end down my spine, then swatted my butt cheeks again. I'd always classed three in one night as a work of fantasy, but now it looked like I was about to experience a Midnight-induced climax once more.

"Fuck," he bit out, slamming into me one last time as I willed my elbows not to buckle. As if he understood my struggle, a strong arm snaked around my waist and held me against him.

Words seemed unnecessary as he arranged me on his lap and wrapped us both up in the blanket. Five minutes passed, ten, fifteen. Silence and darkness reigned equally. Then Jack Frost joined the party. I tried to draw my feet in closer, but Midnight straightened up.

"You're cold, and I've been selfish. I need to let you get to bed."

"Why don't you come with me?" Bold words, and desperate too. I didn't want to let him go. "We can sneak in. Angie'll be asleep by now, and even if she wasn't, she wouldn't care."

"I can't."

"Why?" My breath hitched. "Don't you care about me in that way?"

He laid his forehead against mine, our breath mingling. "I care too much. I haven't got a good grip on my self-control at the moment, and if I spent any more time with you, I'd lose it altogether."

"Is that why you didn't answer my call yesterday?"

He nodded against me, and hair tickled my eyebrows.

"So that's it? You're leaving?"

"It has to be this way." He lifted me effortlessly to my feet and knelt to zip up my dress, bringing a depressing end to the most amazing evening of my life. "Do you want me to walk you to the house?"

I wanted every second I could get with him. "Yes, please. What time is it?"

He pressed a button, and his watch face illuminated. "Looks like I'm Mr. Three O'clock after all."

His hand engulfed mine as he led me into the pitch black. The candle had long since gone out. A sliver of moonlight outside let us see the path, but I couldn't make out more than the silhouette of his face as we crossed the lawn.

"Stop here," he said, thirty yards from the house. Right before the sensors would have flicked on the security lights. Dammit. He'd certainly done his homework, hadn't he?

"Are you coming back?" I asked.

"I can't stay away."

Thank goodness. I rummaged in my clutch until I found the sheaf of papers I'd stapled together at some stupid hour this morning. "I wrote something. My agent wants me to try writing contemporary romance, but I didn't know if I could do it so I had a go, only I was drunk and..." I was babbling. "Here." I thrust the papers into his hand. "In case you want to read it."

"Gus, I always want to read your writing."

"There's probably typos."

"I don't care." He leaned down and touched his lips to mine. "Until midnight."

Then he was gone.

CHAPTER 8

OH, HOW I wished I'd never volunteered to help Mother with the floral party, because not only was Midnight conspicuous by his absence, she naturally assumed I'd love to help with her Music in May event too. A string quartet, a classical singer, and a pianist would be joining us for an evening of cultural celebration. At least that was how Mother described it. I knew they'd be joining us for an evening of alcohol and small talk, just like every other event she ever held.

No longer trusted to organise the flowers after the lily debacle, I'd been demoted to furniture—chairs specifically, plus those little tables people abandoned their drinks on. Oh, and could I find a piano tuner for the Steinway grand? Sure, I knew hundreds of them. What next? Cloakroom duty?

Over the past two and a bit weeks, all I'd managed to do for work was write out two loose plots for historical romance novels and a whole bunch more dirty scenes like the one I'd pressed into Midnight's hands before he ran out on me again. Two weeks, and I'd heard nothing. Despite what he said about his self-control, I thought the contents might have at least warranted a text message.

The pent up sexual energy combined with my inability to find a bloody piano tuner available at any point before Saturday left me brimming with frustration.

I was sitting at the piano in the ballroom, googling piano tuners from as far away as France when my phone trilled, not with a message, but with Beethoven's fifth, the generic tune I'd set for unknown numbers. Please, let this be good news.

"Hello?"

"This is Althea Warlingame. Is that Augusta?"

"Yes." Althea was the pianist Mother had booked. Maybe she'd know a piano tuner, although I wasn't sure I liked her tone. She sounded a little...worried.

There it was, a nervous giggle. "About the party—I'm afraid I won't be able to make it. I tripped over walking the dog yesterday, and I've fractured one of my fingers."

I gritted my teeth, then forced myself to relax before I cracked my jaw. "I'm so sorry to hear that. Your finger, I mean. I hope it heals up quickly."

"Eight weeks before it's fully functional, the specialist says, but I'd be happy to play at any events after that."

"Wonderful. I'll let my mother know."

Bloody hell. It was all I could do to keep from throwing the phone across the room, preferably towards the caretaker who was polishing the floor on the far side because the quiet hum of the machine he was pushing back and forth was grating on my last nerve.

"Hey, you!" I didn't even know his name.

Nothing.

"You, with that polishing thing."

A second or two passed before he turned and

peered at me from under his battered baseball cap. "Me?"

"Yes. Could you stop that for a few minutes? The noise is driving me crazy."

He shrugged and turned the machine off before pulling out a tin of wax and a rag and setting to work on the edges. Great—he probably thought I'd inherited Mother's bitchy tendencies, and I tried so hard to avoid behaving like her.

I chewed on my bottom lip as I considered my options, idly playing the first few bars of Für Elise. On the plus side, if I didn't have a pianist, I wouldn't need a piano tuner, but realistically if I told Mother we were a musician short, she'd allocate me the washing up next time. Gah! I slammed my hands down on the keys, then regretted it as the hideous noise made the caretaker jump in alarm.

Just when I thought things couldn't get any worse, a voice came from the doorway.

"Is everything okay?"

Oh, marvellous. Gregory was here.

I tried to muster up a smile as he strode across the room, looking dapper in a pinstripe suit.

"Fine, thank you."

"Are you sure? You're giving yourself frown lines."

I bit back my snarky comment about him being able to fix those. "It's this bl...this party."

"Music in May? I'm looking forward to it."

"At this rate, you'll be listening to the Women's Institute choir."

"I'll be sure to bring my earplugs—Ethel Bainbridge is tone deaf." He perched on the edge of the piano stool, and I shuffled over to accommodate him. "What's happened to your mother's usual brand of entertainment?"

"The pianist's broken her finger, and I can't find a piano tuner between Newcastle and Paris who isn't booked solid for the next three days."

"Nothing like leaving it to the last minute."

"Mother only told me it needed tuning yesterday morning."

"That reminds me of the time my mother informed me the day of her winter ball that it was a themed affair. Finding a dry cleaner to get the Chateau Petrus stain out of my white tuxedo with four hours' notice gave me palpitations."

I smothered a giggle. At least I wasn't the only one to suffer in the name of entertainment. Gregory squeezed my hand, and his sweetness in my hour of defeat made me lean into him and rest my head on his shoulder.

"Anything I can do to help?" he asked.

"Not unless you happen to know a concert pianist."

"As it happens, I do. Stéphane and I went to school together."

I watched from the piano stool as Gregory stood by the window on the phone, speaking first in English and then in French. For a moment, I thought of Midnight, but Gregory wasn't him—of that I was certain. While Gregory showed a kind side, he didn't make my insides go all funny like Mr. M, and I couldn't imagine him getting experimental with chocolate strawberries or a riding crop.

But today, Gregory became my hero.

"Stéphane will play for an hour at eight, and his piano tuner owes him a favour."

"He'll come here?"

"At some point tomorrow. I'll confirm the time when Stéphane calls back. While we're waiting, would you care to accompany me to lunch?"

After the good turn he'd just done me, I'd have accompanied him to a burlesque club if it took his fancy. "I'd love to. That's very kind."

Gregory held out his hand, and I slid my sweaty palm into it, wishing I'd had the chance to wipe it on my jeans first.

"Where to?" he asked. "La Rive?"

If he wanted to go French, I'd have preferred french fries and a juicy hamburger to nouvelle cuisine, but I could hardly say that, could I?

"Sounds wonderful."

The caretaker glanced sideways at us as Gregory led me across the ballroom, no doubt glad he'd be able to get back to his cleaning. Should I apologise for my earlier outburst? I'd just opened my mouth to say sorry when the faint smell of lime hit me.

Gregory held me up as I tripped over my feet and fell against him, and with my nose buried in his chest, I sure as hell knew the aroma wasn't emanating from him. Nor was it me. Yes, I'd had Dorothy buy me my very own bottle of lime shower gel, but I hadn't opened it yet. Which left...

I snuck a sideways glance at the caretaker, but he was fiddling with the floor-polishing machine. Could it be...? No, no, it was probably just a coincidence. After all, lime shower gel was most likely available at the supermarket along with strawberries, chocolate, and condoms.

The caretaker stretched forward, his overalls

tightening against his buttocks, and I gasped. If the way the fabric lay taut against them was any indication, he could have had a second career as one of Sapphire's cover models.

"Are you okay?" Gregory asked, concern radiating from his eyes.

My head bobbed up and down of its own accord. "I thought I was going to sneeze."

As he wrapped one arm around my waist, I took one last glance back at the caretaker as we exited the room. The man kept his head down, eyes fixed on the floor. Shyness? Disinterest? Or a fear I might recognise him?

Dammit! The caretaker. Could I have slept with the bloody caretaker?

If so, he was right about one thing. He definitely wasn't the kind of man my mother would welcome at the dinner table.

"Dorothy, have you got a moment?"

The housekeeper smoothed out the sheet on Angie's bed and straightened. "Of course, ma'am."

"Please, call me Augusta. Or Gus." I'd asked her a thousand times over the years, but she still shook her head.

"Mrs. Fordham won't allow it, ma'am."

Damn my mother and her snooty tendencies. "Never mind. My reading lamp has stopped working, and I'm not sure if it's the bulb or the fuse. Do you think the caretaker might be able to help?"

Despite being in her late fifties, Dorothy blushed

and averted her eyes. "I'm sure he would, ma'am. Beau's very capable."

Beau. So that was his name. I'd asked Angie earlier, but she hadn't had a clue, and Mother most probably called him "Hey, you." Much like I had in the ballroom, in fact. I cringed at the memory.

"Do you know where I might find Beau?"

Dorothy glanced at her watch. "He usually rakes the gravel on the drive before lunch. Speaking of lunch, would you like something to eat?"

Lunch? Even the thought of food made me feel ill. Yesterday, Gregory had been surprisingly attentive on our date to La Rive, probably because he didn't have anyone more interesting to talk to, but I'd been so distracted by thoughts of Beau's bottom I'd barely been able to eat. I'd stomached the starter, then given up halfway through the main course, citing a headache.

And what did Gregory do? Carried on his charm campaign by passing me a packet of paracetamol.

I'd felt terribly guilty as he handed over his credit card to the waiter and then drove me home—guilty enough to agree to dinner with him next Tuesday, a move I regretted because if Beau was Mr. Midnight, and if he found out I was seeing another man, he'd most likely think I was a bit of a slut. And I couldn't blame him.

"I'm not hungry at the moment, thank you," I told Dorothy.

"Well, just you let me know if you change your mind. Cook's prepared a lovely quiche."

Rather than go outside, I climbed the stairs to the third-floor landing where a window overlooked the fountain in the centre of the drive. Sure enough,

Dorothy was right. Beau leaned over to pluck a weed from the gravel and then resumed raking, something Mother insisted on to keep up appearances with the neighbours.

Even from that distance, there was no mistaking his muscular physique. The moment my suspicions were aroused, my first thought had been *how dare he?* How dare he, the caretaker, encourage me into doing those filthy things with him? But later yesterday evening, when I'd purged Mother's prejudices from my mind, "how dare he" turned into "thank goodness he did."

That's assuming he truly was Mr. Midnight. Beau didn't have the monopoly on a tight butt and solid thighs, although admittedly they were in short supply around Sandlebury. Believe me, I knew. Angie had spent the last decade searching and enjoyed updating me on every sordid detail.

Gah! I had to find out. I needed to speak to the man, but I could hardly just walk up to him and ask whether, by any chance, he'd happened to bend me over a chaise longue and take me from behind, could I? Would I recognise his voice? Probably not. Midnight's words had been half whispered, and my mind hadn't exactly been concerned with memorising his speech patterns.

No, Operation Midnight required a subtler approach, and maybe, just maybe, another night-time romp—purely for research purposes, you understand.

CHAPTER 9

"BEAU?"

HE TURNED in the hallway, the peak from his baseball cap shading his eyes. His gaze remained firmly aimed at his feet.

"Yes, ma'am?"

Wonderful, Mother had got to him too. "Augusta, please."

A smile tugged at the corner of his lips. Lips that had kissed mine? I sensed a certain familiarity, unless my overactive imagination was playing tricks.

"Not allowed to call you that, ma'am."

"Okay, sir." I stressed the second word. Two could play at that game. "I'd like to get some more bookshelves installed in the study I share with Angie. Is that something you can do?"

"I'm sure I can."

Beau's accent sounded pure English, without a hint of the sexy French lilt Midnight slipped in on occasion. And he had a beard. It may have been a short beard, and neatly trimmed, but Midnight definitely didn't have a beard at all. Not even stubble. Could I have been mistaken?

"Really? I wasn't sure how good you were with your hands."

That got me a proper smile, even if he did try to

hide it behind his fist. "Rest assured, I'm very good with my hands, ma'am. I'll measure up early next week."

The way he said that, confidently with a touch of humour, belied the shyness exuding from his exterior. Oh yes, Beau was definitely hiding something.

"Thank you so much. A girl can never have too many books."

As I walked off, a plan formed in my mind. If Beau was indeed Midnight, and he met me after the party on Saturday, surely he'd come clean-shaven like the other times? So, all I had to do was find him on Sunday and see whether he was still sporting a beard.

And if his face was smooth? Well, I'd have a lot of thinking to do. If I convinced him to bring this...this thing between us out into the light, I'd have my parents' disapproval to deal with, not to mention being the talk of the village. Girls like me just weren't supposed to date the household help, no matter what Lady Anne might have done with Rufus.

Saturday night, and I breathed a sigh of relief. The piano tuner had done his thing, although my ears couldn't tell the difference, and Stéphane the pianist was talking to Gregory while the string quartet played a Vivaldi medley. Even my mother was smiling, and the grudging "well done, darling" she'd given me earlier was high praise indeed.

I'd gone with a navy blue silk dress tonight, knee length with a flared skirt, chosen not for its glamour but for easy access. Yes, it was official—I'd turned into a brazen hussy. The mere thought of wrapping my lips around Midnight's unmentionables left me salivating.

"See something you like?" Angie's voice in my ear startled me.

"Huh?"

She nodded in Gregory's direction, and I belatedly realised I'd been staring towards him while my thoughts were elsewhere.

"Oh, er, yes. I guess so."

"He likes you too."

"Does he?" Apart from a brief hello and a peck on the cheek, he'd barely been near me all evening.

"Definitely. I heard it from Susan, who heard it from Chloe, and Chloe's always right about things like this. Rumour has it Gregory's going to invite you on a mini-break to the family cottage in the Lake District."

I should have been excited, but instead, my heart sank. With Midnight dominating my every waking thought, heading off for a cosy weekend with another man was the last thing I wanted to do. I took a long gulp of champagne, then coughed as it went down the wrong way.

Angie thumped me on the back. "Are you okay?"

"Yes," cough, "fine."

"Ooh, look. Here's Gregory to take care of you. I'll leave the pair of you alone."

Hooray, he'd come over just in time for my eyes to start watering. I imagined mascara running down my face as I attempted a smile.

"Can I get you a glass of water?" he asked.

"I'm good with the wine, thank you." Spoken like a true alcoholic.

"Perhaps if you tried drinking it a little more

slowly?" He took my arm and guided me over to a seat. "Stéphane's about to play. I thought we could listen together."

As I hadn't seen any sign of Beau, I didn't have a good reason to decline. Although memories of Midnight wearing a suit the first time I met him and a tuxedo the second still niggled at me—what reason could a caretaker have for owning such garments?

"Canapé?" a waiter asked.

I squinted at the pastry cases filled with white dollops on his tray. "What are they?"

He looked panicked. "I'm not sure, ma'am."

Gregory picked up one of the offending morsels and bit into it. "Some sort of cheese."

Nope, I definitely didn't want stinky breath when I met Midnight. "I'll pass."

I fidgeted through half an hour of small talk and sonatas before my phone vibrated against my thigh, sending my pulse into a frenzy.

"Would you excuse me a moment?"

Gregory reached over and squeezed my hand—a small gesture but a proprietary one coming from a man who didn't seem to be the touchy-feely type. "Of course."

Luckily, I didn't have to resort to the cupboard this time, and I dashed into the nearest cloakroom and locked the door. What did he want?

Angie: So bored by this music. Yawn. Gone out for a drive with Andreas. Don't wait up.

A long sigh escaped my lips. All that build-up and it was only my sister heading for another one-night stand. Normally, she didn't bother to tell me, but she'd been chasing Andreas for almost six months, so I guess she wanted me to congratulate her.

Me: Well done. Think of me while you're off having fun.

Angie: My head will be full of other things. And my mouth.

Too much information. I'd written out half a snarky reply when my phone vibrated again, and this time my heart deserved its palpitations.

Mr. M: Meet me at midnight. I'm sure you can guess where.

My story—he'd read it! Which meant in two and a half hours I'd be off for a romp in the back of my grandfather's vintage Cadillac, a beauty he'd spent ages lovingly restoring, but which had barely been driven since his death eight years ago. I missed him so much. Of all the people in my family, he and Angie were the only ones who hadn't been blessed with a sense-of-humour bypass. Perhaps that was another reason I enjoyed Midnight's company so much. He had wit as well as a delicious cock.

But before I could sample his wares again, I had to spend another two hours in purgatory.

Under normal circumstances, and by normal, I meant where I wasn't screwing a stranger on a regular basis, I might have been happy with the attention Gregory paid me for the rest of the evening. At one point, he even gave Lord Wordsworth the brush-off in favour of accompanying me to the cocktail bar my mother had set up in one corner. I needed the alcohol to calm my nerves.

"Augusta?"

A voice came from behind me, and I turned to find a friend of my sister's making the most of the free drinks. He had one in each hand. Where did he think he was—a university piss-up?

"Good evening... I'm sorry; I don't remember your name?"

"Giles." His gaze dropped to my chest and lingered there. "Have you seen Angie?"

"No, I haven't."

"Never mind. Fancy coming back to my place? We're having an after-party with better music."

Gregory's arm wrapped around my waist, his hand settling on my right hip. "No, she doesn't."

Giles swayed like an oversized Weeble, and wine sloshed over the side of his glasses. "Wasn't asking you."

"He's right. I don't want to go to your house."

Giles gave me one last lecherous sweep with his eyes and then stumbled off, much to my relief. I thought Gregory would remove his hand, but his arm only tightened.

"Would you care to dance?"

At least if I was dancing, I'd have something to concentrate on other than the ticking hand of my wristwatch. I nodded, and as the string quartet struck up a waltz, Gregory led me to a corner of the ballroom commandeered as a makeshift dance floor.

He was an excellent dancer, hardly surprising when, like me, he'd have been fitted for a pair of dance shoes the moment he learned to walk. As he whisked me around in perfect time to the music, I wondered about Midnight's dancing ability. Did he know ballroom? Or merely two-left-feet-while-drunk-in-a-club? If his horizontal tango gave any indication, he was probably a Latin champion.

"Did I tell you how stunning you look in that dress, Augusta?" Gregory asked.

Not once until now. "No, but thank you."

"How very remiss of me. You always look wonderful, but that outfit complements your eyes. It really brings out that gorgeous blue."

Dammit, why did Gregory have to turn on the charm tonight of all nights? If not for Midnight, I'd most likely have been flattered, but now all I felt was...confusion. On paper, Gregory ticked every box for a girl like me—handsome, wealthy, well-respected—and most importantly, he came with my family's seal of approval. Then there was the loose cannon, Midnight, complete with magic balls.

At the moment, neither of their intentions were clear. And my feelings? Well, they weren't clear either.

Gregory seemed slightly put out when I declined his offer to walk me back to the annex just before midnight, but I was running late.

"I'll see you for lunch next week," I said. "I'm looking forward to it."

He gave me a half smile. "Do you have a preference on the restaurant?"

"Maybe somewhere a little less posh than last time?"

A puzzled look crossed his face, then he laughed. "You do amuse me, Augusta."

"How about pizza?"

"Are you serious?"

"Yes."

Hey, it wasn't as if I'd suggested a roadside kebab van.

"Pizza." He rolled the word on his tongue like it was a foreign language. "All right, I'll arrange a table at a pizzeria."

I shoved Gregory to the furthest recesses of my mind as I hurried towards the six-car garage at the back of the estate. Father kept his collection there—the investments he rarely drove. The everyday vehicles—his chauffeur-driven Bentley, the Jaguar, and the Land Rover—all lived in a smaller garage at the side of the house, while my Volkswagen Polo and Angie's Beetle were relegated to the carport.

As I got closer, my steps slowed. Although Beau would most likely know the key code, he couldn't use it without giving me a big clue as to his identity. No, he'd wait outside.

"Augusta?" The words from my side were followed almost immediately by an arm wrapping around my waist.

"It's a bit late if I'm not."

His throaty chuckle rumbled through me. "I felt you coming."

"Doesn't that happen later?" I blurted.

I couldn't help joining in as he burst out laughing. "Most certainly does, *mon cœur*." His voice dropped to a whisper. "On my tongue and around my cock."

Every muscle in my belly clenched, and I trembled against him. Thoughts of the mystery surrounding his identity fled, leaving just me and Midnight, two souls with an insatiable hunger for each other and a penchant for dirty sex.

"I need to get the door open."

He swept my hair to the side and brushed his lips across the sensitive skin on the back of my neck as I fumbled with the door code. In the dark with finger shaking, I struggled to get the damn numbers right.

"I keep getting it wrong," I muttered.

The light from a torch made me jump as Midnight helped me out by illuminating the keypad. I snuck a glance sideways at his face, but it remained in shadow.

The code was 1-8-0-4-2-3-0-9, my parents' combined birthdays. The lock clicked and we fell inside, slamming the door behind us. Midnight shone the torch around, pausing for a second on my father's Ferrari F40.

"Nice. Which one?"

"At the far end. Father doesn't bother to lock it."

He took my hand and led me towards the 1962 Cadillac, and I realised he'd picked up a bag somewhere along the way.

"What's in there?"

"A blanket. I don't want you getting cold."

"There's no danger of that."

Midnight opened the back door for me, his hand resting on my bottom. "Your chariot awaits, Miss Fordham."

I ducked under the canvas roof and half sprawled across the bench seat. So much for being ladylike. Still, it didn't matter because as soon as I'd wriggled onto my back, Midnight was on me, supporting himself on one elbow as his lips met mine.

While I'd attended the local private school followed by an elite university for the best education money could buy, I very much suspected Midnight had studied for a degree in kissing followed by a PhD in sex—the man was a master when it came to making my body sing. He left me well and truly breathless as he moved his hands downwards, pausing where my cleavage peeped from the top of my dress.

"You like the outfit?" I asked.

"No, I hate it. Take it off."

Fabric ripped as I struggled to obey him, and he took pity and gave me a hand with the zipper. Luckily, he'd gone with a T-shirt again, so it only took me a second to drag it off over his head, then we were skin on skin. I reached for his belt, but he stopped me.

"Not yet. I'm having fun with you first."

"But—"

"Shhh. Patience is a virtue."

"I'm about to shag a stranger in the back of a car. Do I seem very virtuous to you?"

"Fair point, Miss Fordham, but you wrote the story, and I'm following your plot."

He dipped his head and sucked on one nipple, causing it to pebble in the cool night air.

"Can't I change it?"

"No. Besides, your body isn't complaining."

Okay, it wasn't. Meanwhile, my brain was trying to analyse his voice. Did it sound like Beau's? Difficult to tell, seeing as we'd barely spoken. I thought Midnight sounded huskier, with a hint of a French accent creeping in occasionally, but then his mouth moved lower and I gave up trying to think at all. By the time he plunged inside me, I'd gone mushy from two orgasms and was well on my way to a third. No matter how creative I got, or how many times I turned to the thesaurus, I'd never be able to put into words how good he made me feel. My books were a poor imitation of the real thing.

And now I clenched around Midnight and fell over the cliff once more as he gave a long groan and filled me with his heat.

"No other girl will ever make me feel the way you do, *trésor*."

Now I was his treasure as well? "But you barely know me."

"I know enough." He reached outside the car, coming back minus the condom but with the blanket in his arms. "Here, I don't want you catching a chill."

He manhandled me so I was lying half on top of him, half on the seat, then covered us both with the blanket and tucked an arm around my waist. After his abrupt departure following our first encounter, I was grateful to have this time with him, this closeness. I reached up and traced the contours of his face with one finger—his straight nose, a pair of high cheekbones, that strong jaw. Was he Beau? He felt similar to how I'd imagine Beau feeling, minus the beard of course, but I couldn't be sure.

And if he was Beau, what did our future hold? A series of anonymous yet spectacular trysts or something more? My mind drifted back to earlier in the evening, to my time with Gregory and the way we'd fitted together on the dance floor. He'd been different tonight—kinder, more attentive. And he certainly had the means to give me every material thing I could wish for.

Not only did he have a good job, but he came from money and understood the way my world worked. Did Beau? Did he know his Chateau Petrus from his Chardonnay? His Brahms from his Beyoncé? And did I want to find out?

CHAPTER 10

"FUCK! WHAT TIME is it?"

Midnight's curse bit through the air, and I stirred from my slumber, face plastered against...hell! I'd fallen asleep on his chest. Please, say I hadn't drooled.

"I don't know," I mumbled.

It was still dark, but rather than being pitch black, the sky was a dark grey through the corner of the garage window.

The screen of his watch glowed an eerie green. Almost four a.m.—we'd been dead to the world for at least two hours.

"My leg's gone to sleep," he said, stretching it into the footwell.

"Other parts of you haven't." And right now, his cock was twitching against my hip.

A zing of electricity shot straight to my *chatte* as he nibbled my earlobe. "That's because I was dreaming about you, *trésor*."

"That makes two of us. Not about me, about you," I hastened to clarify. "Can we...?"

He glanced towards the window, and I knew what he was thinking. Would he get away before dawn broke? Part of me longed to tell him I already had a good idea of his identity, but my head overruled. Making a decision in the heat of the moment had the potential to end in disaster—I needed to confirm for certain and then have a long, hard think about my future.

"It'll be fast."

"What are you waiting for?"

One rough digit stroked between my legs before sliding inside me. "I see you're ready. Guess you weren't kidding about that dream."

"No, I wasn't."

"And what was I doing to you?"

Oh, *merde*, why did I start this? Writing my filthy thoughts down was one thing, but voicing them to the man who caused me to have them in the first place? "Uh, it doesn't matter." His finger stilled deep inside me, and a whimper escaped my lips. "Please."

"Tell me."

Even in the dark, I still closed my eyes. "Fine. I was bent over my desk in the pool house."

"Is that what we're doing next time, then?"

He was already planning a next time? My head warned me I shouldn't be getting in so deep, but my body, on the other hand, thought it was an excellent idea. "If you're up for that?"

"I'm always up when you're around."

With a bit of shuffling, he manoeuvred us so he was on top, and the rip of foil told me he'd sheathed himself. Seconds later his cock nudged at my entrance. Despite his insistence to the contrary, he took his time as he slid inside me to the root and then paused while I stretched to accommodate him.

"Perfect fit," he whispered.

And at that moment, lying on the backseat of an old Cadillac, I could almost believe we were.

It may have been a quickie, but the orgasm still made me tingle from my fingertips to my toes, and from the way Midnight stiffened as he came, the feeling was mutual. But all too quickly, he pulled away.

"We'd better get home," he whispered, and my heart sank. Would it always be like this?

I reached out to caress his gorgeous muscles one last time before they disappeared under his shirt, then I wriggled back into my dress. "Where are my knickers? Have you seen them?" I realised what I'd said. "Or felt them?"

"No." A strong hand reached under my dress and cupped my ass. "But I prefer you without."

"Be serious—I can't leave them lying around in my grandfather's car."

The torch flicked on, pausing on my chest for a second before Midnight swept the beam around the Cadillac. Ah, my errant thong had draped itself over the back of the passenger seat. I hastily finished dressing while Mr. M rolled up the blanket.

A minute later, the magical night came to an abrupt end as he kissed me by the edge of the lawn.

"Until next time," he whispered, his fingers sliding out of my grip.

"Good night," I whispered, but even as I said it, my insides churned. How much longer would my heart allow me to keep doing this?

I took my shoes off just inside the front door so I didn't wake Angie as I crept across the parquet floor downstairs, but it was pointless.

"Where the bloody hell have you been?" Her voice coming from the dimly lit lounge made me jump.

Busted. "I forgot about the time."

"You're not kidding, but that wasn't my question."

"Er..."

She walked over, now wearing a dressing gown rather than her party frock. "What happened to your dress?"

I glanced down at the torn seam on the shoulder, unsure how to answer as she took a delicate sniff.

"Flipping heck—you reek of sex." Her jaw dropped. "You've been with Gregory!"

"No, I haven't."

"Well, you've been with somebody. I haven't seen you this doolally since Ben Durham kissed you on the cheek in primary school when you were ten years old."

Dammit, Angie knew me too well to fall for a lie. "It wasn't Gregory."

"You picked up another man at the party? Wow, that's...brazen."

"It didn't happen like that. My liaison was kind of...prearranged."

Angie's whoop of delight made my head pound at that time in the morning. "Hang on, you lined up a man for a shag? Gus, I'm shocked. And pleased—it's about time you lost the chastity belt. So, who's the lucky guy?"

"Nobody you know."

"Try me. I know every eligible man in the county."

"It's not quite as simple as that. I don't exactly know who he is either."

"Huh?"

I sagged back onto the sofa, and Angie took a seat next to me as the story of Midnight came tumbling out, minus the graphic details. I also left out my suspicions as to his true identity. At the end, Angie shook her head.

"I can't believe you did that. Have you secretly turned into me?"

"You've met a stranger for sex in the dark?"

"No, but if a hot guy offered, I'd seriously consider it. And you're sure you've got no idea who he is?"

"I'm ninety percent sure I'd never spoken to him until that first night. Just from our encounters, I get the impression he doesn't fit in our social group."

The smile fell from Angie's face, and she gripped my hand. "Then you're playing with fire."

"You think I haven't already worked that out?"

"No, I mean it. Mother will be furious if she finds out."

"She's always disappointed in me. What's new?"

"She'll be worse than disappointed." A sadness that I'd never seen before came into Angie's eyes, and she wiped away a tear. "Do you remember Mark Anderson?"

"Didn't you date him in our first year of uni?" That was her longest relationship ever—six months, while the rest could usually be measured in hours. It was after Mark that Angie had taken up her wild lifestyle. "And dump him because you didn't want to be tied down?"

"That's what I told everyone, but it wasn't true. Mother found out about us—I never did find out how— and told me that if I kept seeing the son of a welder, I could kiss my inheritance goodbye."

A chill ran down my spine. "She really said that?"

Angie nodded and wiped at her face with a sleeve.

"We're not having a commoner marrying into this family, Angelica," she mimicked, and another tear rolled down her cheek. "Your books aren't like real life, *Sapphire*. We can't all be Lady Anne and marry the chimney sweep's son, then live happily ever after."

I didn't want to believe my mother could say such a thing, but at the same time, I knew Angie spoke the truth. "I'm so sorry."

"Why do you think I party so much now? As long as I only fuck men with money, she can hardly tell me to stop, can she? I think she's secretly hoping one of them will stick."

I pulled my sister into a hug, shedding my own tears, both for her ending with Mark and my relationship with Midnight. Because if Mother had hated Angie's economics student, she'd surely hate me cavorting with the caretaker. Damn her and her outdated ideas about breeding and class.

"What am I supposed to do?" I whispered.

"I don't know, but you also need to think about Gregory. The man really likes you."

"At first he treated me like an inconvenience, but the last few times I've seen him..." I suspected Angie may be right.

"Look, from what you've said, your stranger won't ask to meet up again until Mother's next party. Why don't you get to know Gregory a bit better in that time? You might find he can offer you more, plus he gets Mother's seal of approval."

"Are you happy with your life now? Did you make the right decision about Mark, or do you look back and wonder 'what if?'"

Angie gave a not-so-ladylike sniffle. "Of course I do.

But it might not have turned out a fairy tale. I could have ended up sitting in a council flat living on baked beans and jacket potatoes, praying for my lottery numbers to come up."

"Or you could have ended up falling asleep next to the man you loved every night, working as an economist like you once wanted to."

"Well, it's too late now." She grasped both my hands in hers. "Promise me you won't make any hasty decisions, Gus. Don't sacrifice your birthright for a stupid fling."

"I won't; I promise." My decision would be one I gave a great deal of consideration, but I didn't rule out the idea altogether.

"And if you stay out late again, make sure you call me. I've been worried sick."

That I could agree to. "Deal."

The next morning found me yawning as I climbed the stairs to the third floor of the main house, clutching a pair of opera glasses. Would Beau be raking the drive this morning? Or had he decided to do something a little less strenuous? I was so tired after last night that even putting one foot in front of the other felt like a chore.

The padded window seat with its decorative cushions looked so inviting I just wanted to curl up on it and sleep, but I forced myself to squint through the glass. A lone figure stood halfway to the front gate, hunched over as he smoothed the gravel, a pointless task if ever there was one. Someone would drive over it within the hour.

Come on, look up.

A minute later, my wish was granted. Beau glanced to the sky, and even though I'd expected it, I still gasped at the sight of his hairless chin.

Beau was Mr. Midnight, no doubt about it. And now I had the hardest decision of my life to make.

As I watched him at work, a white van drove past and stopped outside the front door. There—not even an hour. Now he'd have to do that bit again.

My thoughts were interrupted by Dorothy calling me from downstairs, a hint of excitement in her voice.

"Miss Augusta? Ma'am?"

Mother always taught me not to yell, so I hurried down the stairs and found Dorothy in the hallway, holding a huge bunch of lilies. Yellow mixed with pink. Pollen dropped onto the carpet with every step Dorothy took.

"They came for you, ma'am."

I plucked the card from between the blooms, fingers shaking as I opened the tiny envelope.

My dearest Augusta,

I hope you enjoyed last night as much as I did.

Gregory.

I confess my heart sank, and I realised with a start that I'd hoped the bouquet had been sent by Midnight. But why would he? We only had sex—that was our unwritten agreement. It seemed Gregory was the hearts and flowers guy.

"Aren't they lovely?" Dorothy said. "I'll find a vase and bring them to the annex."

"Thank you."

Meanwhile, I needed to compose a suitable

response to Gregory. I considered phoning, but if he was at work, I didn't want to disturb him. A text message would have to do for now.

Me: Thank you so much for the flowers. They're beautiful.

With no desire to see Mother this morning for another lecture about wearing jeans, I headed back to the annex, thinking only of bed. But before I could crawl back under the duvet, my phone buzzed.

Gregory: Not as beautiful as you. Would you do me the honour of accompanying me to lunch tomorrow?

Angie's words echoed in my mind as I tapped out a reply.

Me: I'd love to. What time? And where shall we meet?

Gregory: I'll pick you up at twelve thirty.

CHAPTER 11

GREGORY BROUGHT HIS town car again, only this time he opened the door for me himself rather than letting the chauffeur do it. Once inside, he smiled at me across the middle seat.

"Thank you for coming today."

"It's my pleasure."

"Still…" He took a deep breath, and I sensed he wanted to get something off his chest. "After the way I acted on our first two encounters, I'm surprised you agreed. I behaved like a dolt. I confess, I only agreed to see you because Mother insisted, and I had no idea quite how lovely you'd turn out to be."

My heart fluttered at his words. "It's okay."

"No, it's not, and I intend to do everything in my power to make it up to you. I've grown really rather fond of you, Augusta."

Oh, hell. I should have been over the moon at Gregory's declaration, but the thrill was tempered by thoughts of Midnight. The driver glanced at us in the rear-view mirror, the nosy git, as Gregory reached across and twined his fingers in mine. A warmth flowed through me, a happiness at being wanted by a man I'd considered out of my league, but far from the inferno that consumed me during Midnight's illicit liaisons. Gregory and I rode on in companionable silence until the car pulled up outside Trattoria Luigi, a small Italian place that got rave reviews from every critic.

Gregory turned to me with a smile. "Pizza, right?"

I'd been thinking more of Pizza Express, but I couldn't deny he'd put the effort in. "It's perfect, thank you."

Gregory's hand rested on the small of my back as he steered me towards the best table in the house, then he waved the waiter away so he could pull out my chair himself.

"I've never been here before," he said. "Have you?"

"A couple of times with my sister."

"Ah yes, how is Angelica?"

"She's fine."

"Busy with her next book?"

"As always."

The waiter stopped by with menus, but I'd already decided what I wanted: Pepperoni pizza with extra cheese. Gregory ordered lasagne. Conversation flowed over two courses, easy talk about people we both knew from the old days and the new.

"Do you still fence?" I asked.

"Goodness, no. Its origins were in violence, and I'm a pacifist now. One thing my wife—ex-wife—taught me was that war is never the answer."

Ah yes, his ex-wife. What was the story there? Curiosity burned inside, but I didn't dare to ask. Was Phillipa's tale true? I decided to save that question for Angie later. After all, she knew every bit of gossip in a three-county radius.

"But what if the enemy doesn't hold the same beliefs about fighting? If they're bombing us, we're supposed to sit back and take it?"

He smiled, fork halfway to his mouth. "That's where dialogue comes in."

I wasn't sure I entirely agreed with him over that, but did it matter? Could two people have a relationship without agreeing on every little thing? Rupert had tended to share my views, to the extent that he often changed his to match, and sometimes his lack of backbone had annoyed me. I covered my eyes with one hand as I thought back to my brief marriage. That had been a match chosen by Mother, and where had it got me?

"Are you okay, darling?" Gregory asked.

"Great. Couldn't be better. This pizza tastes wonderful."

I'd been looking forward to homemade gelato for dessert, but Gregory assumed I didn't want any and called for the bill. Perhaps it was for the best—after all, three courses was hardly conducive to fitting into my dress for Mother's masquerade ball in two weeks' time. My deadline. I needed to make a decision by then—either to see where things went with the man sitting before me or throw myself at Beau's feet and my mother's mercy.

In the car on the way, Gregory held my hand across the middle seat once more, and every so often he glanced over and smiled. Oh, how I wished I could read minds. I wanted to know how he truly felt about me beneath his charming facade.

As it happened, he helped me out with that as the car pulled to a halt in front of my home.

"I had a marvellous time today," he said. "Thank you for accompanying me. Who knew Italian food could taste so good?"

"The company was lovely too."

He beamed, showing off the benefits of his LA dental work. "I second that. Augusta, I'd very much like to see you again, to see where this takes us. I haven't been able to get you out of my mind for the last week."

What was the old saying about buses? First there aren't any, and then two come along at once? Well, men were like buses, it seemed, not that I'd had any firsthand experience of public transport.

And the clock was ticking.

"I'd like that too. How about dinner later this week?"

"Splendid. Do you want to choose the cuisine again?"

"No, you pick. Surprise me."

Although even as the words left my mouth, I doubted anything would ever top Midnight and his chocolate-covered strawberries.

Angie was sitting in the study when I got back, posting messages to Sapphire's legion of Facebook fans.

"Good date?"

"Better than I thought it would be. Everything going okay with work?"

Speaking of work, I really needed to do some.

"I got a bit behind. The caretaker came in to measure for some shelves you asked about, and it was difficult to concentrate with him here."

"Why? Was he noisy?"

"No, hot."

My eyes widened, and Angie laughed.

"Don't worry, I'm not planning to slum it with the staff. But a girl can look, right? He's certainly an improvement on old Gerald, although that's not difficult seeing as Gerald had two chins and more wrinkles than a Shar-Pei. But enough with trivialities—I want to hear about Gregory. Has he kissed you yet?"

"Nope."

"Wonder what he's waiting for?"

"Perhaps because he's a gentleman? But you need to help me—what happened with his ex-wife? He mentioned her once, and I'm curious about why they got divorced."

"I'm not sure, but let me call Mathilda. If anybody knows, it'll be her."

I sat down and opened my laptop, but the words wouldn't come, and I ended up staring at a blank screen. Even peaceful music and a cup of coffee didn't help with my writer's block. I'd barely got two sentences typed by the time Angie sat on the desk in front of me half an hour later, blocking my view of the depressingly short paragraph.

"Apparently Gregory's ex cited irreconcilable differences in the divorce papers, but word is she complained to friends that he didn't look after her properly. Said he didn't pay her enough attention. Although Mathilda reckons he bought her a new Mercedes convertible a month before they split, so I don't know what she was moaning about."

So, Philippa's story was indeed true, it seemed. "Money doesn't buy happiness."

"But it does buy Louboutins and Chanel handbags, and that's the same thing."

"I'm not sure about that."

"Look at our parents—Father's away for work half the time, and you don't see Mother getting upset over it."

"But what about love?"

My parents' relationship was more akin to a business transaction, and after my talk with Angie in the early hours of Sunday morning, I thought I'd detected a softening of her heart.

"Love doesn't always win."

"Sometimes you need to fight for it."

"And sometimes you need to accept defeat graciously and make the best of what you have."

"You think I should choose Gregory, don't you?"

"I wish you didn't have to, but I think it would be best for everyone. Nobody wants to face Mother's wrath, least of all you and your stranger. Consider how difficult she'd make his life."

Another problem I hadn't thought of. Mother's ire wouldn't only affect me. Could I bear to line Midnight up in her sights and wait for her to blast both barrels?

Maybe Angie was right, and a relationship with Gregory would be the kindest thing for everyone.

Another day, and another posh restaurant, this time quintessentially British. Dishes included a traditional roast dinner and macaroni and cheese—my go-to comfort food.

"Two portions of the game pie," Gregory told the waiter. I opened my mouth to protest, but he held up a hand. "Trust me—it's delicious."

I'd never been the biggest fan of game, but Mother

was always telling me to expand my horizons. "I'm sure it will be."

"So, have you had a busy week? What is it you do for your sister exactly? I understand you're her personal assistant?"

"I help with book marketing, advertising on social media, organising events, sending out promotional copies, that sort of thing." Everything Angie did for me. "It's been quite a busy time, what with the book launch coming up next week."

"What's involved in that?"

"Angie will be doing signings at three local stores and four in London, a few interviews, plus we've got the masquerade ball at the end of it."

"Ah, yes. I'm very much looking forward to attending."

"Do you have your costume organised?"

"Our butler assures me it's all in hand. How about you?"

Back when the idea of the masquerade ball first came up almost four months ago, and before Midnight made an appearance, I'd sketched out my dress based on the picture of Lady Anne in my head. Dorothy had spent weeks sewing the outfit for me, although the idea of wearing it anywhere near Mr. M now gave me the jitters.

"My dress is almost finished."

"I'm sure you'll look wonderful."

Dinner arrived, and despite my reservations, I had to concede Gregory was right—the game pie did taste good. Rich and flavoursome with crisp pastry, I'd certainly order it again.

"I hate to say I told you so..." he said.

"But you did. Thank you."

"A friend of mine co-owns this place. The pheasants come from his estate."

"Please pass on my appreciation."

"I'll be sure to do that. Can I tempt you with apple crumble for dessert?"

"Does he grow the apples as well?"

Gregory roared with laughter, even though my question had been serious. "Not much fun in hunting apples, but I believe they buy in fresh produce every day."

Dessert tasted every bit as good as the main course, the tartness of the apples offset by creamy vanilla ice cream. The intimate setting, discreet staff, and good company all made for the perfect second proper date. I didn't count the business dinner Gregory had taken me to when he was behaving like a prick.

On the way home in his town car, Gregory shuffled as close as the seatbelt would allow, holding my hand again. He had a surgeon's hands, with long, slender fingers, soft skin, and buffed nails. I tried to imagine them roaming over my body, but no matter how much I willed it, I didn't feel the same shiver of excitement I got every time I thought about Midnight. Would Gregory ever be capable of that sort of passion?

When he climbed out of the car behind me back at home, I wondered if I'd find out.

"I'll walk you to the door," he said, settling one hand lightly around my waist.

"Thank you." My voice came out croaky.

We walked in silence, and my nerves built. Would he invite himself in for coffee, or more?

He stopped outside the annex, but when I reached

for the keypad, he gently grasped my hand. "I had a wonderful time tonight, darling."

"Me too."

His head dipped towards mine, and in the glow from the hall window, his lips parted slightly. Holy hell, he was going to kiss me! I felt a momentary panic—only two other men's lips had ever touched mine. What if I messed it up?

I closed my eyes as he pressed against me, his kiss soft at first, then deeper as I yielded. One touch of his tongue and he pulled back, smiling wide.

"You're a very special girl, Augusta."

"Er, thanks?"

"I'll see you at the ball."

He disappeared into the darkness, Midnight-fashion, leaving me to process what just happened. He'd kissed me. And it was nice. Not earth-shattering, toe-curling, spine-tingling, or any of those things. Just...nice.

Could I settle for nice? Could I go through the rest of my life without experiencing the fire Midnight lit inside me? At that moment, I wasn't sure.

I shuffled inside and found Angie waiting in the lounge.

"So?"

"So what?"

"I'd half expected you to bring Gregory back with you."

"He kissed me and left."

Angie clapped her hands and grinned. "He kissed you? That's something, at least."

"Yeah, it was something."

I wandered through to the study. I did my best

thinking in there, surrounded by my books, my old desk, all my familiar treasures. And...what was that?

"Where did these come from?"

I ran a hand along the polished wooden shelves, fitted perfectly into the alcove next to the printer. A stupid question, because I already knew the answer.

"The caretaker came by and put them up. I thought you'd arranged it with him?"

"Sort of."

My heart clenched as I realised what that meant—Beau knew I'd gone out with Gregory, because twice he'd come around while I was on dates. How did that make Beau feel? Upset? Angry? The last thing I wanted to do was hurt him.

"Did a nice job and fast too. He's good with his hands."

If only you knew, Angie. If only you knew.

"And not just his hands," she continued. "Did you hear about the drama the night before last?"

"What drama?"

"The caretaker caught two burglars trying to break into the shed behind the garage. You know, the one with the lawn mowers? He knocked one out, then chased the other through the woods and held him down until the police arrived. Men in uniform, Gus, and we slept right through it." She rolled her eyes. "Nobody ever tells us anything."

Wow. Beau was kind of a hero, but two against one? What if he'd got hurt? "That's crazy. Why did he go after them himself?"

"Dorothy said he heard voices and went to investigate. They reckon the crooks had cased the place in advance too. Beau heard noises in the woods last week, but he didn't see anyone then."

My heart seized at the thought of Beau tackling thieves alone. Maybe I should have a word with him, tell him not to be so stupid in future. But perhaps he'd find my concern strange?

Angie certainly would, so I changed the subject.

"I must remember to thank him for the shelves. They're perfect."

"Enough about the shelves—I want to hear all the juicy bits on Gregory. I take it you're going out with him again?"

"I'll see him at the masquerade ball."

"Do you want me to make myself scarce in the evening?"

"I'm not sure yet."

Her eyes narrowed. "Tell me you're not still thinking about that other man?"

I was, and far more than I should have been. "Just keeping my options open."

CHAPTER 12

"MAY I HAVE this dance?" Gregory asked.

He looked especially dashing in white breeches and a silver-edged mask.

"Of course."

I could barely breathe, and it wasn't all due to my overly tight corset. It was well after eleven o'clock—why hadn't Midnight messaged me yet?

Please be here. Please be here. Please be here. I repeated the mantra over and over in my head.

Gregory offered me his hand, and I tucked my phone into my faux-fur muff while my insides churned like a washing machine on crack. I'd spent all day psyching myself up for the big talk with Midnight, and if he didn't show, my nerves would snap like a frayed elastic band.

Gregory held me close for a foxtrot, and I prayed he wouldn't feel my heart pounding in my chest, and also that I wouldn't suffer a cardiac arrest in front of two hundred slightly inebriated partygoers. The foxtrot turned into a waltz, and I was saved from the tango when he spotted a familiar face across the ballroom and waved.

"Would you excuse me a moment, Augusta? That's Dr. Langston, and I need to speak with him about a referral. We've been playing voicemail tennis for days."

"Of course."

Out in the hallway, I checked my phone again. Whatever happened, this was the last night I'd be waiting on tenterhooks for a message from Midnight, so I had to take a small comfort from that at least.

Breath whooshed from me as I read the words lit up on the screen.

Mr. M: Meet me at midnight. Your desk, the pool house. Bring your filthy mind.

On second thoughts, I was glad he hadn't sent that message earlier. If I'd had two hours rather than one to think about what he wanted to do to me, I'd have needed to change my knickers for sure. Pale pink lace this time, bought specially for tonight's endeavours.

Thank goodness Angie had disappeared too. As she was on Team Gregory, I didn't want to feel her disapproval if she saw me sneak out.

Gregory met me with a glass of wine when I walked back into the ballroom, and boy did I need it. I necked half of it back before I realised what I was doing, much to his consternation.

"Is everything okay?"

"Uh..." I dropped my voice to a whisper. "I think my time of the month is coming, and the wine helps." When in doubt, blame it on a little pre-menstrual tension.

"Speaking as a doctor, I'm not sure that's entirely correct. You'd be better off lying down with a hot water bottle."

I seized upon his words. "Good idea. Best I do exactly that."

I'd got three steps before he grabbed my hand. "At least let me walk you home."

"Honestly, there's no need. I'll be fine."

"Please, I insist."

Eager to get things over with, I let him loop my arm through his and walked obediently beside him to my door.

"Do you mind if I kiss you?" he asked.

Rather than answer, I stood on tiptoe and pressed my lips to his. His arms wrapped around me, holding me against his chest as his tongue slid into my mouth, exploring. But there was still no damn spark. Nothing. Not a flicker.

"I'll call you tomorrow," I said, pulling back. And I would—I just wasn't sure I'd be able to give him the news he wanted.

"I hope you feel better."

The instant the door clicked behind me, I ran through to my bedroom to change into something that didn't restrict my ability to inhale. The conversation I needed to have with Midnight promised to be difficult enough already. A simpler dress would do.

Five minutes later, I checked out of the window for any sign of Gregory, but he'd disappeared, and thankfully Angie hadn't come back either. Presumably, she was still with her "date," the masked stud with the expensive watch and the sly smile, and I screwed my eyes shut at the thought of what they might be doing. Even Sapphire would be horrified by some of Angie's antics.

But I was alone, and a good thing too, because the last thing I needed was somebody I knew seeing me sneak off to the pool house. I say pool house, but as we rarely used the pool, it hardly ever served its intended purpose. Two stories high, Father had claimed the upstairs as his den—somewhere to smoke the cigars Mother didn't realise he indulged in and hide out when her urge to nag got too much—and downstairs was split in half. The left-hand side housed the changing area, shower, and cloakroom, while the wet bar and sofas on the right-hand side gave Angie somewhere to entertain away from the main house. And me somewhere to write. My desk facing the rose garden allowed me to escape for some peace and quiet when Dorothy began vacuuming.

As I slipped on a pair of flats and snuck along the path, I planned out how this needed to happen—talk first, don't let Midnight distract me.

Only it didn't quite work out that way.

Hands grabbed me the instant I walked in the door, and I would have screamed if Midnight's mouth hadn't come down hard on mine. The hard plastic of his mask scraped my nose, and I tore it off as he lifted me up and carried me to my desk. This wasn't like our previous trysts—even when he'd been fast, he'd still moved with a grace that belied his size, but today his movements were hurried, frantic even.

"What's wrong?"

I didn't get the chance to find out before he lifted my skirt, and I opened my legs wider to give him access. Gone was his gentle reverence. His kisses grew ever more intense, and he barely had time to roll a condom on before he shoved my knickers to the side and plunged into me.

"Please, I need you," he whispered.

All I could do was wrap my arms around his neck and my legs around his waist as he thrust. He needed me. Not wanted me, needed me. I didn't know why, but

I'd give him everything I had to offer, and in return he gave me the heady power of being desired in such a primal way.

My hands worked their way under his shirt, and as my orgasm built, I clawed at his back with a lust I'd never experienced before. We'd both turned into bloody animals. When I exploded, stars danced across my vision, and I went limp in his arms. He followed suit, leaning his forehead against mine as sweat ran down our faces.

"What the hell was all that about?" I asked, gasping for breath.

"Fuck. That was me being a selfish bastard. I'm so sorry, *trésor*."

As he slid out of me, I was left with a feeling of emptiness. "I don't get it?"

"I just wanted you one last time."

I stiffened in his arms as a chill swept through me. "The last time? You're telling me this...we're over?"

"Isn't that what you came here to tell me?"

"No! Heaven help me, but no."

"But what about Gregory? You danced with him tonight. You kissed him."

Oh, shit. Midnight saw all that? I belatedly realised he was wearing a bow tie and tuxedo—he must have crashed the party. "Yes, and it only confirmed my thoughts. I can't be with a man who doesn't make me feel the way you do. Gregory isn't the man for me."

"Wait a minute... Are you saying...?"

I reached a hand up and cupped his smooth face. "Beau, I know who you are."

Muscles at the top of his cheek twitched as his eyes widened, but he didn't deny it. "Shit."

"I know who you are and I still want you, but if we do this, it won't be easy for either of us. You'll get fired for sure when my family finds out, and Mother doesn't tolerate Angie and me dating people outside our social class, which means I'll most likely get cut off. We'll have to tread so, so carefully, or life will turn into a living hell for both of us."

He stayed silent.

Blood whooshed loud in my ears, and I gave a nervous laugh. "Now I'm waiting for you to tell me that was our last time."

"I don't care what happens to me, but I don't want you to lose everything." His voice hitched. "Not for a man like me."

"If I'm going to lose everything, I want it to be for a man exactly like you. A man who wants me. *Me*. Not my name or my money or my connections. Just me. And what's money if I can't use it to buy happiness?"

"But your family..."

"Angie will come around, my father's rarely here, and Mother's a toxic presence I can live without." I'd thought this through over and over, and when I looked at the hard facts, I could see that everything she'd done for my sister and me over the last few years was for her benefit rather than ours. "I can create another pen name and write anywhere."

"I don't know what to say."

Fingers trembling, I reached out and clicked the desk lamp on, bathing both of us in a soft yellow glow. Beau blinked back at me, startlingly handsome.

"Say yes," I whispered.

He pressed soft lips to mine. "I can't say anything but."

His earlier frenzy was replaced with a series of slow, liquid kisses that warmed me from head to toe, but rather than close my eyes and lose myself to him, I took advantage of the light and watched his every move. He did the same, creating another connection between us.

And I got to see the delights of his body for the first time too when I unbuttoned his shirt—his solid pecs and tightly defined abs. Idly, I traced the infinity loop tattooed over his heart.

"What's this for?"

"I got it for a girl."

"Oh."

I didn't want the details. The past didn't matter, just the present. My fingers fumbled with his hand-tied bowtie—no clip-on for him, which surprised me—then he helped by shrugging out of his shirt. I glimpsed the tattoo on his arm, and I couldn't help smiling—secretly I'd always had a thing for ink. Hey, maybe I'd even get my own, seeing as I was about to break every other one of Mother's rules.

Midnight—Beau—slid off the condom used in our earlier exploits, tied a knot in the end, and dropped it on the floor. We'd need to remember to pick it up before we left or it had the potential to lead to a very awkward conversation. Although Angie would take the heat if I begged—another reason I loved my sister.

"Care to do the honours?" He held out a fresh foil packet, grinning.

"With pleasure."

While Rupert had barely touched the sides, now I got a good look at Beau, I gulped. How in hell had that fitted?

As if reading my thoughts, he gently grasped my

chin and tilted it upwards. "Augusta, you were made to fit me." He kept his gaze locked on mine as he angled into me, pulling me forward until I settled snugly around him. "See?"

I glanced down. I could indeed see now. And I loved the way he disappeared inside me, right to the hilt.

"Make me come, Mr. Midnight," I whispered.

"With pleasure."

This time he gave me slow and sweet, and it was me who lost control as waves of bliss washed through me. Shit, I'd left a bloody bite mark on his neck. I tried to rub it away with my thumb, and he laughed.

"Leave it. It'll make me smile every time I look in the mirror."

"But what if someone sees? What if someone realises we're together?" I realised how bad that sounded, like I wanted to keep him a sordid little secret. "Not that I don't want to show you off to the world, but I just need a few weeks to make some arrangements."

He hugged me tighter. "Don't fret, *mon cœur*. I get it. Are you still sure about this?"

Ever the gentleman, he was still giving me the chance to back out, but no way would I take it. When I made my final decision, a dark cloud had lifted from my mind, and while the future scared me, I'd have the man I was crazy about by my side, holding my hand through the tough times. That much I knew.

"Yes, I'm sure. But I need to transfer the money I have access to and move anything I care about for safekeeping. Plus I need to make arrangements for Sapphire. Angie's my best friend as well as my sister, and I can't drop her in it. I expect I'll need to write more books for her in the future to keep up the pretence."

"I'll wait as long as it takes, and I promise I'll do whatever I can to help."

I'd finally found him. I'd found my soulmate. "Will you answer me one thing?"

"Of course."

"Why did you send me that message in the first place? I still don't understand. How did you know I wrote the books?"

He smiled, but it flickered at the edges, belying his nervousness. Why?

"Because you were always the creative one, Gus. Always."

"Huh?"

"And you once told me your stories were the dreams you wished would come true."

My emotions, already shaken from this evening's events, exploded like a firecracker and I burst into tears. I'd only ever told one person that, a boy, not a man.

Holy. Shit.

Chapter 13

I FLEW BACK in time sixteen years, to the day after my eleventh birthday. Mother had thrown me a huge party with circus performers, pony rides, and even a bloody ice sculpture—anything she could use to claim one-upmanship over all the other tennis club mums. It had turned into a bit of a contest that year, with one renting out an entire cinema and another hiring a TV chef to prepare the jelly and ice cream. Or rather, the vanilla panna cotta and sorbet.

Of course, as Mother had also been in charge of the guest list, she hadn't worried about inviting my actual friends, just the children of people she wanted to make an impression on. And that meant my best friend, Ben, got left out. As a scholarship student at the ridiculously expensive prep school Angie and I attended, Ben's parents didn't fit into my mother's plan to climb to the pinnacle of the social ladder.

Not that he was bitter about it. "Have a great time, Gus," he told me as we walked out of school together the Friday before. "I hope you get everything you want."

What I wanted was his company, but my pleas to Mother had fallen on deaf ears. "I just want it to be over."

He smiled shyly and drew a lumpy parcel from his

pocket. "I brought you a present. Sorry about all the sellotape."

"Thanks, I love it."

He giggled. "You don't even know what it is yet."

"Doesn't matter."

A group of other boys ran by, pausing long enough to flick Ben's cap to the ground. "Hey, four-eyes. Found your way back to the gutter yet?"

"Leave him alone!" I yelled.

They only laughed, and I went to run after them, but Ben stopped me. "It doesn't matter."

"It does. I hate that they're so mean to you."

"As long as you're my friend, I don't care."

"I'll always be your friend, Ben."

When I unwrapped the gift he'd given me, having survived my party by hiding in the bathroom for most of the time, I found a red fountain pen. I spent the rest of the weekend filling a notepad with stories where the forlorn princess triumphed over the evil queen, found her Prince Charming, and lived happily ever after. I was still writing away when Ben found me in the playground before school on Monday morning.

"Why do you write so much?" he asked.

And that's when I told him. "Because stories are the dreams I wish will come true."

"Am I in any of them?"

"You're in all of them."

My dreams turned into a nightmare two weeks later, when Ben came to school looking terrified. He'd gone chalk-white, and when I squeezed his hand, it shook.

"What's wrong?"

"Mum says we're leaving. Dad's got a new job, and

we're moving to Manchester."

"Where's Manchester?"

"I don't know, but she said it's far away."

I burst into tears, and I could tell he wanted to cry too. His chocolate brown eyes glistened behind his thick glasses. "But what will I do without you?"

"You'll be okay, Gus. You'll make new friends."

"But I'll miss you."

"I'll come back and find you. As soon as I'm old enough, I'll come back. I promise."

But he hadn't. From the twentieth of June, his eighteenth birthday, I waited on edge for a year in case our next visitor was the boy I'd never forgotten. Rupert was on the scene by then, as my suitor elect, and despite Mother's constant badgering I'd put off accepting his proposal for fifteen months in the hopes that Ben might return. But he hadn't.

Until now.

"Ben?" I whispered.

He nodded, biting his lip.

Before I could stop myself, I thumped him in the chest. "You're late! Nine bloody years late."

His worried look turned to confusion. "What do you mean?"

"You said you'd come back when you were old enough. I figured that meant eighteen, not twenty-flipping-seven. I refused to marry Rupert until I was twenty in case you turned up to get me out of there."

"But I did come back when I was eighteen. Your mother said you were engaged and didn't want to see me."

"She said *what?*" I could hardly get the words out, my teeth were clenched so hard.

"She left me standing at the door while she went to talk to you, then came back all apologetic and said you didn't think it was a good idea to rake over the past. That you'd just got engaged."

That... That bitch! "She didn't tell me you were there, I swear. *I swear.*"

"I'm beginning to get that."

"And I wasn't engaged when I was eighteen. Mother acted like it was a done deal, but I didn't say yes until I turned nineteen." I screwed my eyes shut for a second. "I can't believe she did that."

Midnight—Beau—Ben laid his forehead against mine once more. "Fuck. And I can't believe we wasted all this time. I should have tried harder to see you. But when you didn't reply to any of my letters, I figured you'd forgotten about me."

"Letters? What letters? I sent you letters, but I never got one back."

"I didn't get any letters. Not a single one."

The heat in my veins turned to anger. "Did you see your mum post your letters to me?"

"No, I always posted them myself. The post box was only a few yards away from the house. My mum just checked I'd stuck the stamp on properly."

"I always gave mine to Mother to post." And now I realised she hadn't. How could I have been so stupid? "She must have hidden yours from me too."

"Fucking hell. We've lost years over this. Years."

"Why couldn't my mother have been more like yours?"

His face darkened. "You'd have been welcome to her."

I thought back to the cheery woman I'd once

known, but that picture didn't fit with his tone. "What do you mean? She was always kind."

"Yeah, until I found out she'd been lying to me my entire life. She did something I'll never forgive her for."

"What? What did she do?"

"Not tonight, Gus. I'll tell you one day, but I don't want to put more of a downer on things this evening."

I forced a smile, then kissed him on the lips—chastely—just to let him know I understood. "So, why did you come back again after all these years?"

"Because I've never, ever been able to get you out of my mind." He touched his chest in an unconscious gesture as he said it, and my gaze landed on the infinity symbol.

I traced it with a finger. "Was that for me?"

He nodded, and the lump in my throat thickened.

"A year ago I was wandering along the high street in a tiny village in northern France when I stopped outside an antique shop. There was this pen in the window, and I had to buy it for you." He reached down to where his trousers hung around his knees and pulled a lumpy package from his pocket. "Here."

"Your wrapping hasn't got any better."

He traced a finger up my side. "I'm better at the unwrapping."

I tore at the sellotape with my teeth until I got to the box. It may have been a little time-worn, but the red-enamelled pen inside was pristine. And beautiful.

"Thank you." That deserved a kiss, and I was only too happy to oblige. "I'll keep it with the other pen you gave me."

"You still have that?"

"I use it most days."

He pulled me into a hug, nothing sexual, just two old friends reconnecting after too many years apart. Because that was what we were. Friends. Now lovers too, but friends above all else.

"Do you not think this was an elaborate plan to give me a pen? I mean, getting a job here and everything?"

"The job was kind of an accident. I only intended to drop the pen off with a note, but when your mother answered the door, she just assumed I was there to apply for the caretaker's position. Luckily, she didn't recognise me."

"I didn't either." That odd familiarity I felt when I first saw Beau? I'd assumed it was because he'd been Midnight, but I'd got it totally wrong. "What happened to your glasses? Are you wearing contacts?"

"No, laser surgery. And I learned to use the gym."

"Yes, I can see that."

"I only planned to stay long enough to check you were okay, but when I realised you were single again, and not particularly happy, I decided to stick around."

"How did you know I wasn't happy? Even I didn't realise that."

"Because you rarely smiled, or went out, or spoke to anybody but your sister. You'd turned into a recluse, not the girl I remembered." He traced my lips with his thumbs and pushed the corners up. "I want to see you smile again."

"I will now you're back." We stared at each other for a few seconds, and my smile grew wider. "So, what now? Want to take advantage of me again?"

"Much as I've enjoyed fucking you in strange places, I'd rather make love to you in my bed. What do you say?"

"Sounds perfect to me, Mr. Durham."

He helped me to stand on shaky legs, and I smoothed my dress down as he picked up the discarded condoms and did his trousers up. Without a doubt, this was the best night of my life, and it was only just beginning.

"Hang on, I need to call Angie. She was worried sick when I got home late the last night we spent together. What time is it?"

"Always the good sister." He pressed the button that made his watch light up and held it for me to look at. One thirty.

I'd dropped my small shoulder bag over by the door, and I fished my phone out while Ben slid an arm around my waist and pulled me tight against his side. Possessive, and I loved it.

The phone rang, and as it did so, I didn't just hear the tone in my ear but the faint sound of Sister Sledge's "We are Family" from somewhere nearby.

"Can you hear that?" I asked Ben.

"The music?"

"It's Angie's phone."

"Sounds like it's coming from upstairs."

"She must have dropped it there. I should fetch it for her."

"What was she doing in your father's den?"

"She was with some guy earlier, so probably what I was just doing down here with you."

Ben kept hold of my hand as I climbed the narrow staircase into the darkness above. *Honestly, Angie, you could have picked somewhere else.* Screwing on Father's furniture was just...icky.

At the top of the stairs, I flicked the light on and

looked around. The desk, the golf trophies, the photos of my father clay pigeon shooting. The cigar humidor, the decanter of scotch, Angie's broken body lying on the leather sofa.

Somebody started screaming, and it must have been me, but my mind disconnected itself from the scene. That couldn't be my sister with blood dripping down her pale green dress, eyes glazed as she stared at nothing.

It couldn't be.

Hands pushed me into a chair, and Ben rushed forwards, fingers on Angie's neck as he felt for a pulse. But it was pointless. She'd been here the whole time we were downstairs, while we screwed each other silly and poured our hearts out. The thought of that brought up everything I'd eaten earlier.

"Fuck!" Ben bit out, clutching at his hair. "Fuck, fuck, fuck."

I stumbled forward and grabbed at his arm to hold myself up. "She's dead. Angie's dead."

"Gus, it's worse."

How? My sister was lying dead in front of me. How could it possibly be worse? "What the hell are you talking about?"

"That's my knife in her side."

"You did this? You killed my sister?"

Now somebody was shrieking. Me. I was shrieking.

"Of course I didn't, but somebody wanted to make it look that way."

He stepped forward again and picked up the limp wrist nearest to us, and as he uncurled Angie's fingers, a bunch of keys dropped onto the floor.

"Don't tell me, those are yours too?"

"I lost them a couple of months back, but Dorothy lent me her spare set so I wouldn't get into trouble."

Nothing made sense in my head. Thoughts jumbled around and I snatched at one, grasped onto it. "Someone's trying to frame you?"

"Yes. Fuck, Gus, I never should have come here and brought this shit into your life. I thought it was safe, I swear. I'd never have come otherwise."

"What do you mean? What shit?"

The tears came now, thick and fast, making Angie's limp form go all blurry. How I wished I could erase that vision of her from my mind, because now it would cloud every good memory I had of her.

"We need to call the police. I'll stay until they come, but then I have to leave. This isn't going to be good, *trésor*. Nothing about this is going to turn out good. But I need you to remember two things: Whatever evidence the police find, it's bullshit, and also that I love you. I always have, and I always will."

I didn't know much, but I knew he spoke the truth. Ben wouldn't have done this to Angie, and more importantly, he wouldn't have done this to me.

"I'll remember. But why are you talking like you're leaving?"

"I have to."

"Why can't you stay and fight? I'll fight for you. I have some money we can use, and—"

He silenced me with a finger over my lips. "Because I can't fight from inside a jail cell, and that's where I'll end up. I'm going to find the man behind this and make him pay."

"You know who did it?"

"I'm ninety percent sure I do."

"Then you need to tell the police."

"I already tried that once, and this is the result."

I caught sight of Angie again and retched. Ben held my hair back as I puked bile over the carpet once more. "Please, don't leave," I spluttered. "We only just found each other."

"If there was any other way, I'd take it. If I stay, you'll be a target too, but if I leave, he'll assume you're disposable, just like all the women in *his* life."

"Are you coming back?"

"I wish I could, but I can't. After this, I'll always be running. Even if I can remove him from the picture, he's got friends in all the wrong places."

I heaved again, but nothing more came up. Instead, grief poured from me at the loss of the two people I loved most in one night. I needed Ben. Without him and Angie, I was nothing. "Please," I tried one more time. "Please."

"Just know I'll always watch you from a distance, and if I ever see a chance to help, I'll take it. But we can't be together."

I couldn't believe we were having this conversation. "But I love you."

"I love you too."

Ben lifted me over to the chair again and held my hand as he called the emergency services. Police and ambulance, although we both knew the latter was pointless.

"You should wait downstairs," he said, but I clutched the seat as he tried to help me up.

"I'm not leaving her."

"I'm so sorry, *trésor*."

"I don't understand. Why did this happen?"

"A while ago, I helped to put a man away for a crime, and he swore in the courtroom that he'd make me feel the same pain." Ben closed his eyes and lost another shade of colour. "He wasn't supposed to be released, but he's behind it. There's nobody else it would be. Shit, I don't know what to do. What to say when the police get here."

"I'll tell them I found her, and when I screamed, you came to see what the matter was."

"I hate the thought of you lying for me."

"And I hate the thought of you going to prison." Another thought struck me. "Do you think he's still out there? On the estate, I mean."

"I don't know. If he took my keys two months ago, he's been lurking for a while, and I didn't fucking realise. Once or twice, I had a feeling someone was out there, but then I caught those damn burglars, and I thought that was it. This was my fault."

"It wasn't!"

"I let my guard down. Look, until I tell you it's safe, don't go anywhere by yourself. Stay with your parents, or one of the staff, or Gregory."

"But I don't want Gregory. I want you."

"I know, *mon cœur*, and I'm so sorry."

His eyes shone with tears too.

Sirens sounded minutes later, and I tried to pull myself together as footsteps stormed up the stairs. I'd been wearing a mask my whole life, and I couldn't let it slip now, not when Ben's freedom depended on it.

He remained a respectful distance as the police arrived. Mother's wails came from downstairs as Father tried to placate her. Then silence.

A cop peered out the door. "Lady's fainted."

"It's probably for the best," one of his colleagues said. "Now, who can tell me what happened here?"

Ben looked him in the eye. "Miss Fordham here found her sister like that a few minutes ago."

"You were with her?"

"No, I was on the way back to my cottage when I heard her screaming."

"On your way back from where?"

"The party at the main house." He waved at his attire. "I... Well, I gatecrashed for the free booze."

The policeman raised an eyebrow. "And you are?"

"Beau Davies. The caretaker here."

"I see." The policeman knelt in front of me, and I didn't miss the look of disgust as he avoided the pool of vomit. "Can you talk me through what happened, ma'am?"

"Y-y-yes." I wiped my eyes, took a deep breath, and lied my head off.

When I got to the part about me coming to the pool house to hunt for the diamond earring I'd lost at some point during the day, I saw Ben slip out of the room.

And I cried inside.

CHAPTER 14

IN THE END, the ambulance crew took me to the hospital instead of Angie. Once Ben left, grief overcame me, and I cried until I was sick again, then cried some more. I woke the next morning, drained from nightmares starring Angie's lifeless eyes and groggy from the pills the doctors had given me, with Mother sedated in the next room and a policeman sitting on a plastic chair in the corner of mine.

I closed my eyes again, but it was too late.

"Miss Fordham? Are you awake?"

Busted. "Yes." It came out as a croak, and he walked over to the bed.

"Water?"

I sipped on the straw he offered me. "Thank you."

"Do you feel up to answering a few more questions?"

Was *no* an acceptable answer? "If it'll help find the person who killed my sister."

"We've had a bit of a breakthrough on that. How well do you know Beau Davies?"

"Beau the caretaker?" I wasn't sure whether I should admit to knowing his surname.

"That's right."

"Not well at all. Why?"

"He's disappeared. Last night, in fact."

"Perhaps he just went out?"

"It looks as if he left in a hurry, and his motorcycle is missing."

"I didn't even know he had a motorcycle."

That part was true.

Another, older, policeman walked in with two cups of coffee and gave me a kindly smile. "Ah, Miss Fordham. You're awake."

Ten out of ten for observation, but I bit back the sarcasm. "Yes, I am."

"I was just asking Miss Fordham about Mr. Davies," the first policeman said, taking a sip of coffee and then trying to style it out as it scalded his tongue.

"Do you mind if we record this conversation?" cop number two asked, taking over.

Yes, and I didn't want to be having it in the first place. "Not at all."

He fussed around setting up a digital recorder on the tray table as well as getting out a notepad and pen. A sliver of worry stabbed at me. "Where are my clothes?" They'd put me in a nasty paper nightgown, and the pen from Ben had been in the pocket of my dress.

"Right over there on the chair, ma'am."

I could hardly ask about the pen, could I? They'd want to know why it was so important to me, and I didn't have a plausible answer other than the truth. Instead, I muttered, "Good," and left it at that.

"Now, about Mr. Davies. How much has Geoff here told you?"

"Almost nothing."

"In that case, let's start at the beginning." He fiddled around with the recorder and a green light clicked on. "This is Detective Stuart Robinson and Detective Geoffrey Bell interviewing Miss Augusta Fordham." He gave me an encouraging smile. "You're here because you witnessed events surrounding the murder of Miss Angelica Fordham on the second of June. Do you understand this?"

I nodded.

"If you could keep all answers verbal for the tape, please."

"Yes."

"During this interview, we'll talk to you about events at the party that took place at Shotley Manor on the night of the murder and the subsequent discovery of the body."

Every time he mentioned the word murder, I wanted to be sick again, but there was nothing left inside me. Not even my heart. That had shattered last night.

"We'll also ask you about anything else which may become relevant during the interview in order to properly establish the facts and issues."

The man talked like a robot. He may have been a competent detective, but he most certainly failed the courses in sympathy and compassion.

"Could you walk us through the events of last night?"

I did so, basically saying the same things as I had in the pool house. The less I told them, the less I could trip over later.

"How long would you say there was between you finding your sister's body and Mr. Davies arriving?"

"I'm not sure. It seemed like hours, but it couldn't have been. Maybe a few minutes?"

"We've got reason to believe Beau Davies may have had something to do with your sister's murder."

"What reason?"

"Well, mainly the fact that he's disappeared. And a number of guests at the party last night saw her leave with a man fitting his description."

"I saw her with that man too, but it wasn't Beau."

Robinson fixed me with a hard stare. "How do you know that? He had one of those masks on, and Mr. Davies admitted he crashed the party."

Shit. I'd dropped myself right in it there. "I didn't know him that well, but my sister would never have gone anywhere with him."

"Why not?"

"Because he didn't have enough money." Hell, that made her sound like a materialistic cow.

"Perhaps she made an exception?"

"I don't think so. Not when there were so many other men for her to choose from." No, that painted her as a slut, which didn't help either. "Beau fitted some shelves in our apartment earlier in the week, and Angie was there while he did it. She said at the time that she admired his physique, but she'd never act on the attraction because he was a member of staff."

"So, Mr. Davies spent time alone with your sister recently?"

Dammit, couldn't I say anything right? "Yes, but she spent time with plenty of other men too. Maybe you should look into them as well?"

"We will. And where were you while these shelves were being installed?"

"Out with Gregory Fitzgerald."

"He's your boyfriend?"

"He's a friend."

"Your father seemed to think it was more serious than that."

"With the greatest respect, my father has no idea what goes on in my life or my sister's." I realised I'd used the present tense, and a tear leaked out through a crack in my mask. Detective Bell held out a box of tissues, and I grabbed a handful. "I want to go home."

No, actually I didn't. Because home would be full of Angie's things—her rainbow of post-it notes in our shared study, the shoes she left all over the hallway, her bottles of vitamins on the kitchen counter. The cracks grew into chasms as the tears became a waterfall, and the two men looked at each other.

"Are you okay?" Robinson asked me, which was possibly the most stupid question in all eternity.

"Just leave me alone."

The door to my room opened, and I recognised the newcomer in the suit as Sidney, my father's lawyer.

"What the devil do you think you're doing?" he snapped.

"Relax, we're only asking Miss Fordham a few questions," Robinson said. "She's a witness, not a suspect."

"And look at the state you've left her in. You don't say another word to her without me being present."

As the two chagrined detectives shuffled from the room, Sidney perched on the visitor's chair next to the bed. "Shall I get the nurse, child?"

"No, I just want to be on my own."

He patted my hand in a grandfatherly way and leaned back. "I'll sit here for a bit in case those two donkeys decide to come back. They know full well they shouldn't have pushed you into answering questions like that, not so soon after the tragedy."

I concentrated on slowing my breathing, and my pulse gradually slackened. Had I said anything that could hurt Ben? I sure hoped not. Nothing would bring my sister back, but if the man I loved ended up losing his life over this as well, I'd never forgive myself. Where was he? Did he have enough money? Somewhere to stay? I realised how little I knew about him. Did he have friends he could turn to?

"Will you be okay on your own for a while?" Sidney asked. "I need to deal with your mother."

I thought I detected a slight eye roll, and I couldn't blame him. Mother on a good day was bad enough, but after this?

Please, say they'd pumped her full of the good stuff.

Eight hours later, I sat at the dining table, my father at the end to my left and my mother opposite. Always one to seize on a retail opportunity, I'd heard her on the phone with her personal shopper earlier requesting a whole new wardrobe in black, and tonight she was channelling Morticia Addams.

"You should eat something, Augusta," Father said. "It's no good you starving."

"It won't hurt her to go without food for a few days," Mother said. "She's got reserves."

"Carolyn..." he warned.

My mother dropped her eyes and spread fois gras onto a piece of toast, swaying slightly. She dropped it and her eyes went out of focus, probably as a result of whatever cocktail of drugs she'd washed down with half a bottle of Tanqueray when she got in.

"Fine. You heard your father. Eat your dinner."

They say grief affects people in different ways. I'd been left hollow, while my father seemed somehow more human. My mother? Her humanity had evaporated completely, leaving only her inner bitch. She'd been sniping at both of us all afternoon.

"I'm not hungry." I shoved my chair back, ignoring her instructions to come back as I stomped down the corridor. But where to? Not the annex, and I couldn't go outside. I'd promised Ben.

The house I grew up in felt like a portal to hell as I walked the corridors, wanting to leave but at the same time, trapped. I ended up in my old bedroom, where a photo of Angie and me pinned to my corkboard sent me into a flood of tears again. Why? Why her? Ben said it was retaliation against him, but there was nobody to blame but the man who'd wielded the knife.

And I hoped Ben would make him pay.

CHAPTER 15

"MISS, ARE YOU all right?"

Dorothy's voice cut through my sniffles, and I looked up from my tear-soaked pillow.

"I hate this place," I mumbled.

"Now, now, ma'am, I know you've had a shock."

"It's not just that. My mother's like Satan in a dress."

"Maybe a nice cup of tea would help?"

I noticed she didn't disagree with me. "I'm not sure tea will be enough this time."

"Why don't you try?"

She held out a hand, a little uncertain, but I reached out and took it. Goodness knows, I could use a friend in this mess, and without Angie or Ben, the only people in the house apart from my parents were the staff.

"Shall I serve you some supper in the annex?" Dorothy asked.

"I can't go back there. Not right now, with all Angie's stuff there. Can I...? Can I come with you? To wherever you eat?"

"I'm not sure Mrs. Fordham—"

"Forget my mother." I was certainly trying to. "I'm not going to tell her."

Mary, the cook, and Bernie, the gardener, both did a double take when I walked in, and Mary shook her head. "You shouldn't be here, ma'am."

"I told her it was okay," Dorothy said. "Mrs. F's being impossible today. Did you order more gin?"

"Waitrose is delivering tomorrow at ten." Mary got up and opened her arms. "You look like you need a hug."

I began blubbing for the hundredth time that day all over her ample bosom, even more so when she stroked my hair like the grandma I'd never had. Father's mother died before I was born, and my mother fell out with Grandma Margaret while I was still in nappies, according to local gossip—not that my parents ever confirmed the rumours of the argument.

"Why don't you sit down and have some soup?" Mary asked. "You need to keep your strength up."

I didn't have much choice. After all, where else could I go?

There was one empty space left at the table, and my heart lurched when I realised who normally sat there. Beau. And these people had spent more time with him than me recently.

"Did the police ask you questions?"

They all looked at each other. Bernie shifted uncomfortably in his chair, and Mary broke the silence by placing a bowl of Scotch broth in front of me.

"It's not a good idea to talk about that."

"But I want to know what's going on, and nobody else will speak to me."

"The police didn't ask me much," Bernie said. "But I was out visiting my sister last night and missed the whole thing. They just wanted to know how well I knew Beau."

"And what did you tell them?"

"The truth. That he kept himself to himself."

"I don't think any of us really knew him," Dorothy said. "He ate with us some days, and he always lent a hand if we were short, but he lived out in that little cottage, and that's where he spent most of his time."

"Although I'll admit it surprised us when we heard what he'd done," Mary put in. "Never saw him as the violent type, but I'm not the best judge of character—that's why I've got two ex-husbands."

I took a spoonful of soup, which tasted of nothing. "I only spoke to him a few times, but he was always pleasant."

"You never can tell," Dorothy said. "At least your Mr. Fitzgerald is a true gentleman."

Gregory may have been a gentleman, but I was a bitch, because when he phoned me the next morning, I diverted him to voicemail, stuck my frilly, little-girl pillow over my head, and tried to go to sleep.

I failed.

Every time I closed my eyes, the events of Saturday night played over and over, a porn film followed by a snuff movie. A dream turned into a nightmare, and when finally I could take no more, an overwhelming feeling of loneliness swept through me as I got dressed in yesterday's clothes.

Of course, Mother noticed. Not my aching sadness, but my outfit.

"Didn't you wear that Donna Karan dress yesterday?"

"Yes." And the day before.

The pen from Ben still lay in the pocket, and I clasped it as if it could ward off evil spirits.

"Well, you need to change before you eat lunch.

What if we have visitors?"

"They wouldn't have seen me wearing it yesterday."

"That's not the point."

"Leave the girl alone, Carolyn," my father told her.

"We've got enough scandal in this house already without Augusta dressing like a bag lady."

Father's eyes met mine. "Just leave, sweetheart. Carolyn, give me the glass. You've drunk quite enough today."

I slipped from the room, but I couldn't help listening from the other side of the door. My parents rarely argued, mainly because my father always left for the office at the slightest sign of conflict, and I wanted to hear how he handled it.

Because sooner or later, it would be me left to deal with her tantrums all day.

"I'm not drunk," she snapped.

Father must have tried to take matters into his own hands, and the sound of glass smashing all over the marble floor of the dining room made me jump.

"Now look what you've done," Mother snapped. "Dorothy! I need another drink."

"No, she doesn't," Father called. Then his voice dropped, but I could still hear when I pressed my ear to the door. "You can't take your anger out on our daughter. It's not fair on her."

"She's never behaved like a child of ours. We've offered her the world, and she's got no ambition to do anything other than run marketing campaigns." Mother dissolved into sobs, and I feared her medication had worn off. "At least Angelica had talent."

Although I'd known how she felt for years, it still hurt to hear her say the words. I'd tried so hard to please her, but nothing I did was ever good enough. And now I was trapped.

The following morning, I accompanied Sidney to the police station for a formal interview. I didn't want to go, but at the same time, I desperately wanted to see the person who killed Angie behind bars. What had they found out about the man she was with at the ball?

"Don't say anything unless I give the okay," Sidney instructed. "They'll ask irrelevant questions, and you don't need to answer them."

With hindsight, having time to prepare for the interview was actually worse. At least in the hospital, being caught unawares had meant the pit of dread didn't build up in my stomach like Sauron's advancing army. It was the same two detectives again, Robinson and Bell, only this time Robinson chewed nicotine gum like a man on the edge.

After they'd gone through all the rubbish at the beginning for the tape, they started off with the same questions. How well did I know Beau? What happened on the night of Angie's death?

"I've already told you all this."

"If we could just go through it again," Robinson said.

"Do I have to?" I asked Sidney.

"Try some new questions, gentlemen."

The two detectives glanced at each other, and I knew they weren't happy with me. Robinson spoke up again. "Did Mr. Davies ever mention any friends to you, or relatives maybe?"

"No."

"Any trips he made outside of work?"

"No."

"Did you overhear him receive any phone calls?"

"No."

"Miss Fordham, you're not being very helpful here. Anyone would think you didn't want us to catch the man who raped your sister."

All the air left my lungs, and I felt like I'd been punched in the gut. Robinson kept his face perfectly neutral after landing that bombshell, the bastard.

"Angie was r-r-raped?"

"That's what the evidence shows, and right now, there's a man out there free to do it again."

"But what if it wasn't Beau? What about the other man Angie was with that evening?"

"Miss Fordham, you're the only person we've spoken to who believes that wasn't Mr. Davies. We're still working our way through the guest list, but I can tell you most of the men have been eliminated already."

"People often bring friends, acquaintances, people whose names don't appear on the list."

"We're questioning everybody. But Mr. Davies also sent a text message asking your sister to meet him in the pool house at eleven o'clock, and his fingerprints are all over the murder weapon."

A text? No, he couldn't have. He'd have told me. Right?

"We also found blonde hair like your sister's in Mr. Davies' bed, and while we haven't received the DNA results back yet, I'm confident we'll get a match."

Another nail in Ben's coffin, and also in my heart. Angie said she'd never sleep with Ben, but she'd been in his damn bed? Wait a minute. Hold on. The real killer had stolen Ben's keys, hadn't he? What if he'd planted Angie's hair? But how would he have got it? Either from her body that night or...or...or he'd been in our apartment too.

"I'm going to be sick."

I shoved the chair back and ran out of the room, looking both ways in a desperate attempt to find a bathroom until Bell steered me in the right direction. Once inside a stall, I retched up that morning's coffee and half a croissant. At this rate, I'd be developing an eating disorder too.

I sat on the closed toilet lid for ten minutes until a female police constable came in to check I was okay. When I realised she wasn't going to leave, I wiped my mouth and stood up, dreading the thought of more questioning.

As Robinson clicked the tape recorder on again and started speaking, he seemed convinced of Ben's guilt. And as they took me through that night in every painful detail once more, I had to confess a modicum of doubt crept into my mind too.

On the way back to Shotley Manor with Sidney driving, Gregory tried calling me twice, but I sent him to voicemail both times. With Ben having abandoned me, where did that leave my future? Should I try to salvage something with Gregory? Right then, I didn't know, nor did I have the energy to think about it.

As I walked into the kitchen, Mary pulled a big pan of macaroni and cheese out of the Aga, the cheese golden and bubbling on top.

"Thought you might need this, ma'am."

What I needed was a time machine and a loaded gun. "Thank you. That's very kind."

Dorothy bustled in as I was halfway through a bowlful, trying hard to resist the urge to wash it down with a bottle of red and an economy-sized packet of paracetamol.

"Did you hear the news in the village?"

"That Rebecca Larkin's having another baby?" Mary asked.

"No, about Beau."

Mary's eyes cut sideways to me, and she gave her head a small shake.

"Please tell me," I begged. "The only thing worse than knowing everything is knowing nothing at all."

Dorothy took a seat opposite me, the wooden chair scraping across the old stone floor. "Young Jade Bosley says he forced himself on her."

I dropped the fork I was holding. "He what?"

"That's what she told Dana Sherringham, and Dana convinced her to make a statement to the police."

"How? When?"

"A month ago, she says. They met in the pub. One night, things got a bit frisky, and he went back to her house while her parents were out. Wouldn't take no for an answer, apparently."

"And she's sure it was Beau?"

"Well, he gave a different name, but he fits the description. I expect the police will do one of those line-ups when they catch him."

He wouldn't. No, no, no. Not Ben. I thought back to our first time together, my nervousness, and later the way he'd wanted to take me back home when he found out how inexperienced I was. And all the other times? He'd been intense but never forceful. I didn't believe it.

Or was it just that I didn't *want* to believe it?

Could a monster have lurked within him? Had he lied to give himself time to make a clean getaway? What if I'd unwittingly played right into his hands? All the certainty I'd felt after we found Angie was slowly leaking away, and I no longer knew the lies from the truth.

But a little voice within me still whispered, "You understand what it's like to be accused of a murder you didn't commit."

CHAPTER 16

A GOOD NIGHT of sleep always worked miracles, and while I felt groggy from the temazepam I'd pinched from the bottle in Mother's bathroom, I also felt vaguely human for the first time in days.

And I knew what I needed to do. If Ben lied to me that night, he did so with such conviction I'd believed every word, no hesitation. And it stood to reason he might have lied about more than his relationship with my sister. That meant I needed to speak with my mother.

I found her in the garden room, drinking a glass of orange juice. She looked at me through dead eyes.

"May I join you?" I asked.

She shrugged, and I took that as a yes, leaning forward to pour a glass of juice for myself. Anything to delay the conversation.

"People keep talking about Beau," I said.

"I wish I'd never laid eyes on that bastard."

"How did he come to work here?"

"Stop blaming me! Everyone's fucking blaming me."

I'd never heard my mother curse like that before, and it shocked me into silence. I took a sip of juice, then spluttered as the vodka burned down my throat. Freaking heck, she was already on the sauce, and it wasn't even lunchtime. And worse, she was drinking it from a bloody pitcher.

"Nobody's blaming you. I'm just curious; that's all."

Her eyes wobbled as she tried to focus on me. "He came to the door one day, said he'd been down in the village and thought he'd stop by. I figured he'd seen the card in the supermarket window. Or the post office. Anyway, he spoke English, and he knew how to use tools. All those problems we'd been having with the flush on the downstairs toilet? He fixed them right then."

"So you hired him straight away?"

"Look, we'd only had three other applicants. One spoke Polish, the second didn't know which end of a screwdriver to hold, and the third didn't show up for the interview."

A yes, then. So, it did happen like Ben said. He'd just knocked on the door one day and been offered the job.

But what about the rest?

"Has Gregory said anything about me recently?"

Mother managed a half smile. "Mrs. Fitzgerald says he adores you."

"I'm not sure what to do about that. I mean, I like him, but he doesn't make me feel... I don't know... He doesn't make my heart race."

Confusion crossed her face. "Why does that matter? For goodness' sake, Augusta, do something right for once in your life and marry Gregory."

Marriage? We'd only flipping kissed twice. "I'm not ready for that, not again. Not so soon."

"It's been seven years since you managed to kill Rupert. Get over it."

I knew it was the vodka talking, but she nearly ended up wearing the whole bloody jug of it. "I did *not* kill Rupert. What happened was an accident."

She shrugged again. "So they say."

How could my own mother say something so hurtful? On any other day, I'd have run from the room, but right now I couldn't lose sight of my goal.

Half of the story Ben told me may have been true, but what about the most important part? Did he really come back for me before? I took a deep breath before I lit Mother's fuse. "Mother, you know Rupert was always my second choice, anyway. I always liked Ben Durham better."

"Who?"

"Ben Durham. We went to primary school together."

"Oh, Ben with the glasses? That snot-nosed child was no good at all. His father was an insurance clerk for goodness' sake, and his mother worked in a supermarket. Hardly worthy of the Fordham name."

"I just wish you hadn't sent him away when I was eighteen."

My nails dug into the leather seat as I waited for her to answer. She'd never give me the truth if I asked outright, but if I pretended I already knew? Would the alcohol have loosened her tongue enough for her to bite?

"It was for your own good, darling. He turned up in a cheap little hatchback and a pair of jeans."

That bitch. That nasty, nasty bitch. "How *did* you get him to leave?"

"So easily—I simply told him you were engaged. It was going to happen sooner or later. The stupid boy actually thought he had a hope of changing your mind until I told him you didn't want to see him."

That knife in my heart? She'd just twisted it, and I couldn't hold my anger in any longer. "How could you? How could you interfere in my life like that? You knew I was waiting for Ben to come back the way he promised, and you let me think he'd forgotten."

"Don't get your knickers in a twist, darling." She began to giggle, and I wanted to slap the smile off her face. "It all worked out in the end."

"I hate you." The emotion had gone from my voice —after the devastation of the last few days, she'd tipped me over the edge. The only way I could cope was not to think about it at all. "I hate what you did."

She tried to top up her drink and knocked the pitcher over, shrieking as the sticky juice ran all over her black wool dress.

"Dorothy! I need another drink."

When Dorothy found me curled up in the corner of the library, she fetched Bernie, and he carried me up to my old bedroom.

"Please, don't make me stay here," I begged.

"Do you want to go back to the annex?"

"Not there either."

After some deliberation, they tucked me into the single bed in the box room next to Dorothy's, a plain but functional space reserved for the occasional guest the staff invited to stay over. Dorothy fetched me some clothes and my laptop, and for the next two weeks, I refused to come out. Father came to see me every day, but Mother was conspicuous only by her absence.

"She's not doing well," he said. "Worse than usual."

"I don't care."

"You can't stay up here for the rest of your life."

"Want to bet?"

He stroked my knuckles the way he used to when I was a little girl. "I'm worried about you, Gussie." A nickname he hadn't used in years. "And I need to go away on business for a few days."

"Do you have to?"

"Afraid so. We've been working on this deal for the last year, and it's worth millions."

Money. It was always money. "Fine."

"And I hate to say it, but you'll have to talk to the police again at some point. Sidney's been keeping them at bay, but they're getting impatient."

"There's no point. They just keep asking the same questions, and they don't listen to anything I have to say."

"Could you try? For me?"

"Have they got anywhere at all?"

"Not yet, it seems. That Beau fellow has vanished from the face of the earth. Detective Sergeant Robinson assures me the DNA results should come back sometime this week, though."

About bloody time. Because I couldn't believe Ben had done that to my sister, which meant the DNA would give a lead to the killer. If I could just hold out until then, maybe the police would stop pestering me and search for the real culprit.

"Good, but I still have no faith in Robinson and Bell."

Father sank onto the edge of the bed. "In all

honesty, neither do I, Gussie. I've hired a private firm to investigate. The Earl of Northbury's son works for them."

"Will they be any better?"

"I don't know, but what do we have to lose?" He gave a long sigh, and pain leached from his eyes. "It's only money."

I watched the chauffeur put Father's suitcase in the boot of the Bentley the next morning, and five minutes later, the car purred off along the driveway, leaving Dorothy and me to deal with Mother, who'd taken to self-medicating the moment she woke up. The family doctor stopped by every afternoon to caution her about the dangers of liver damage and bring more sleeping pills.

"Sidney's here," Dorothy informed me at ten o'clock, right after *The Jeremy Kyle Show* finished. Usually, watching it cheered me up, but right now my life was in even more shit than his guests, so it was actually kind of depressing. Oh, for my biggest problem to be a wayward boyfriend who'd pawned my video games console.

"What does he want?"

"I'm not sure." Her voice dropped. "But I don't think it's good news."

"Show him up, and keep him away from Mother for crying out loud."

A few minutes later Sidney knocked on my door, and I could tell from his sombre expression that Dorothy was right.

"Do I need a drink first?"

I tried a joke to lighten the atmosphere, but it fell flat.

"Best if you don't. It's bad enough having one, er, inebriated lady to look after."

"Drunk. Don't water it down for my benefit." Because Mother certainly hadn't. "She's a drunk."

"I'm sure it will pass. Everybody's having a tough time at the moment."

"Why are you here, Sidney?"

"The DNA results have come in. I thought you should hear it from me rather than anybody else—the semen in Angelica matched Beau, and the hair on his pillow matched Angelica. The police are insisting on speaking to you again."

I sagged back against the wall, my legs jellied. It couldn't be. Anything but that. "I don't want to talk to them."

"You can refuse, but they can still force you to court based on your original statement. And your refusal will only raise more questions. I must admit, I don't understand it either. Why won't you help to catch your sister's killer?"

Because it was looking more and more like Ben might have been responsible, and if I changed my story now, I'd implicate myself as well. And Jade Bosley? What if Ben was a rapist too? Why, oh why, did this have to turn into such a big bloody mess?

"I just hate the way they talk to me."

"How about I ask for someone different to interview you? Maybe a woman?"

"I guess that might help."

He squeezed my shoulder. "Then I'll get it set up.

Hang in there, Augusta."

No sooner had he disappeared than Dorothy appeared with more bad news. "Gregory called again. What should I tell him?"

"The same. That I can't deal with anybody outside of family right now."

"Yes, ma'am, I'll tell him, but I don't think he's going to like it."

Tough. "Is there anything else?"

Dammit, I sounded so imperious, and I hated myself for it.

"That private detective your father hired is waiting downstairs."

"And he wants to speak to me?"

"I imagine he needs to start somewhere, ma'am. And we know even less than you do."

"Fine, send him up."

The sooner I spoke to him, the sooner I could get him to leave, and then I could get back to sorting out this mess in my head. How could Ben have slept with my sister, killed her, then done those crazy things with me within two hours and acted the way he did? Until we found the body, he hadn't given off any weird vibes at all.

Footsteps on the stairs announced the detective's arrival, and seconds later, a large figure darkened my doorway. I recognised him from Mother's parties.

"You're... You're..."

"Nye Holmes."

He held out a hand for me to shake, and inwardly, I cursed my sweaty palms.

"Augusta Fordham."

Of course, he already knew that, but manners had

been drilled into me from an early age.

"I understand your father told you I'd be coming?"

"He mentioned it."

Nye looked me up and down, obviously taking in my four-day-old pyjamas and the greasy hair plastered to the sides of my head as I perched on the edge of the bed, and I closed my eyes so I wouldn't see his disgust. Even wearing jeans and a day's worth of dark stubble, he still looked worthy of a modelling contract.

"Do you have time for some questions?"

Well, I had a few minutes between my meeting with NASA and my high-end fashion shoot, so I could hardly say no.

"Yes, I have time."

"How much do you know about—"

"Beau Davies? I've already answered that question a hundred times. Can't you read the police report?"

"I was going to ask how much you knew about jewellery, but we can start with Beau if you like."

"Jewellery?"

"I need to buy a gift for my fiancée, and I'm not sure whether she'd prefer earrings or a necklace. The guys at work weren't much help. They suggested a box of chocolates instead."

This was what my father was paying him for? Still, it helped me. "Uh, I'd go with earrings."

"Modern or classic?"

"Classic."

"Flashy or plain?"

"Plain. They go with everything."

"A girl can never go wrong with a pair of diamond studs, right?"

"Right."

"Is that why you tried so hard to find your missing earring?"

"Huh?"

"Your missing earring. The one you lost on the night Angie died."

"Oh, yes."

"Did you ever find it?"

"No, I didn't."

His face softened into a sympathetic smile. "I'm so sorry that happened to your family. Angie was a great girl. Between you and me, I can't understand how she got into that position with the caretaker, but your father only hired us to find him, not look into the whys and wherefores."

My ears pricked. Was it possible Nye shared some of my initial doubts?

"What do you mean?"

"Angie vetted her guys and knocked them back if they didn't have enough zeroes on their bank balance. No exceptions. I overheard her talking to a friend once about how she turned down a guy because he wore a Timex. It became a standing joke among the guys—you want to impress Angie, you'd better borrow a good watch. I'm wondering what kind of watch a caretaker would have been able to afford."

I screwed my eyes shut, remembering the way Ben's digital watch lit up in the dark when he pressed that button on the side. "Beau's watch wasn't expensive. I think it was a Casio."

"Interesting. So, she wouldn't have gone with him voluntarily, yet nobody saw her being forced out of the house and all the way across the grounds."

"She was with somebody else. I kept telling the

police that, but they wouldn't listen." I closed my eyes again, trying to remember what the man looked like. Most of his face had been obscured, but the wrist resting on her left shoulder sure hadn't been graced with a Casio. "Patek Phillipe. The man at the party was wearing a Patek Phillipe."

"Are you sure?"

"My father has one."

"Curious. Of course, it could have been a fake. But you know what else is curious?"

"What?"

"Until he came to work here, Beau Davies didn't exist."

CHAPTER 17

I TUCKED MY hands between my legs so Nye wouldn't see them trembling. "What do you mean, Beau didn't exist?"

"The police can't find any record of him having a passport, a driver's licence, a bank account, anything in fact. Your mother paid him in cash. Not sure the taxman would like that."

"Why don't you call and tell him?" A little snark crept into my voice.

"Report your mother?"

I slumped back against the pillow. "We haven't been seeing eye to eye lately. Okay, ever."

"Not my place to comment on that."

No, it wasn't, and I had other things I wanted to discuss. "What do you think about the man with Angie at the party? Have the police found him?"

"They're not looking. According to the reports I've read, Beau crashed the party, and that's who she was with."

"They're wrong."

"Why are you so sure? I know we spoke about the watch, but you can pick up a reasonable imitation for a few dollars on any London backstreet. And the man was wearing a mask."

Because my nipples didn't stand to attention when I

got near him? Because he reeked of expensive cologne rather than Ben's musk mixed with lime? "Because my sister may have been tipsy, but as you pointed out, she'd never have gone with a man like Beau. They say she was in his bed in the cottage, and even if he hid his face, she'd have realised who he was if he took her there, don't you think?"

"I get that you believe that, but the DNA says otherwise."

"I know." And it still hadn't sunk in how wrong I'd been about Ben. "Could they have made a mistake with the DNA? I mean, how did they match it if...B-Beau isn't here?"

Shit, I'd almost called him Ben. Thank goodness he'd chosen another name that began with the same letter.

"A sample from his toothbrush, another from his hairbrush, and a third from skin cells on a shirt in his laundry basket."

Shit. "So that's it? You just look for him, and if you find him, he's going straight to jail?"

"When I find him. Not if. When. He'll have a trial first, but I doubt he'll get bail. He's already proven he's a flight risk."

Nye sounded so confident that the last bit of hope I had for Ben leached away. "I can't help you anymore."

"Can't? Or won't?"

"I don't know anything."

He shook his head, and his next words sent a chill down my spine. "I'm not so sure about that." His eyes didn't leave mine as he stood up. "Right, I'm going to search the cottage and then have a chat with your mother. Wish me luck."

What was that saying about keeping your friends close but your enemies closer? If there was something in the cottage, I wanted to see.

"Can I come? Not to talk to Mother, but to the cottage?"

"I thought you weren't interested in helping?"

"It's better than sitting here."

He thought for a few seconds, then sighed. "Okay, as long as you don't touch anything. Are you getting dressed first?"

I looked down at myself, still wearing flannel pyjamas decorated with children's cartoon characters. "I should probably take a shower."

"In that case, I'll speak to Carolyn first and get it over with."

"Nye?"

He paused halfway to the door. "What?"

"Good luck."

"Are you sure we're allowed in here?" I asked Nye.

"The police have released the scene now."

"You have a key?"

"Your father left it for me. Remember, don't touch anything." He snapped on a pair of latex gloves and then opened the door.

I'd never been inside the caretaker's cottage, not even when Gerald lived there, and it seemed nobody had redecorated since the seventies. I inhaled deeply, hoping to smell some trace of Ben, but all I got was the mustiness of old carpet and faded wallpaper. If not for his belongings still scattered around, I'd have wondered whether he ever existed.

The front door opened straight into the tiny lounge, and Nye stood in the centre for five long minutes, thinking, as his eyes took in the details. Black fingerprint powder covered every surface, and the tattered remains of blue and white crime scene tape hung from the door frame.

Nye wandered through to the kitchen, where clean dishes were stacked up in the drainer next to the sink, before heading up the narrow staircase. I should have been here on Saturday night following a very different man to the first floor, and I wanted to scream at the injustice of it. What cruel quirk made fate snatch our happiness away from us?

"Looks as if Beau left in a hurry," Nye said. "Doesn't seem like he took much."

Nye was right. Toiletries still sat on the bathroom vanity unit, and when he opened the wardrobe, clothes filled the shelves. The place sat frozen in time, waiting for an owner who would never return.

"What did my mother say?" I asked Nye as he pulled open the top drawer in the battered wooden chest opposite the bed. Underpants were folded neatly on one side, socks on the other.

"Nothing useful. A handful of expletives, some rambling about Angelica's many talents, and then she started crying. I don't think Dorothy likes me now either."

"Why?"

"She glared at me like the tears were my fault."

"They weren't. Mother's always been a drama queen."

"I still remember her throwing a fit at one of my

grandma's parties because a waiter served her warm champagne."

I couldn't help giggling. "A heinous crime."

"My grandmother's fault entirely—she hires the staff based on their looks rather than their knowledge of wine."

"Like those men serving the canapés at her Wimbledon party last year?"

The more time I spent with Nye, the more snippets from the past I recalled. His grandmother, Ivy, was adorable but a little bonkers.

"And the shirtless waiters at her summer barbecue," Nye muttered.

We stopped talking as he got to work, emptying out the contents of the drawers and wardrobe, tipping up the mattress, and searching through the bathroom cupboard. When we got downstairs again, he repeated the process in the kitchen and the lounge, although the latter only contained a battered sofa and a television.

"Nothing," I said. "There's nothing useful here, is there?"

"I'm more interested in what isn't here."

"What do you mean?"

He beckoned me forward and climbed the stairs again, stopping in front of the wardrobe. After searching it, he'd re-folded all the clothes and put them back. Who knew how long they'd sit there? I couldn't see Mother organising Ben's replacement in the near future, and Father never got involved with the household staff.

"What do you see here?" Nye asked.

"Uh, shirts? Trousers?"

He pointed to the bottom shelf. "How about there?"

"Nothing."

"Precisely. When the rest of the stuff is crammed in so tightly, why did he leave that shelf empty?"

"I've got no idea. Maybe it was all in the wash?"

"His laundry basket held one pair of trousers, two t-shirts, and a couple of pairs of socks. No underpants. Either he got lax on his hygiene, or he went commando."

I could confirm it was the latter, but I wasn't about to tell Nye that. "Do you think he took something with him?"

"Yeah, I do."

"What?"

"An interesting question. If you were leaving home in a hurry, what would you pack?"

"Uh..."

I wouldn't know where to start. Angie and I had holidayed in our villa in Barbados twice a year, and Dorothy had always packed for me.

"Come on, hurry up. Time's ticking, and you're about to have the police hunting for you. What do you take?"

"My toiletries. Clothes, shoes, a jacket. My MacBook and my favourite stationery."

"Seriously? Life or death and you'd pick pens?"

At the mention of the word 'death,' I choked out a sob, and Nye's expression softened.

"Sorry."

"It's okay. I just can't stop getting upset every time I think about it."

"Do you want to go back to the house?"

I shook my head and pasted on a shaky smile. "No, I don't."

He stepped in close and turned my chin to face him. "You're braver than you think, Augusta."

Why did he have to be nice? It got me all confused. I wanted to hate Nye for what he planned to do to Ben, but at the same time, I liked him.

"I don't know about that. Okay, I'll leave the stationery behind."

"Look around—Davies left *everything* behind. The only thing missing was in this space, and if I was a betting man, I'd guess he'd prepared a go-bag."

"A what?"

"A bag with all the essentials he needed if he had to leave in a hurry. The man was prepared to run. But why?"

Nausea spread through my belly. Ben had planned to leave? I was as clueless as Nye.

"I really don't know."

"This time, Augusta, I believe you."

"Now what?" I asked as we walked back to the house.

Nye had locked the door on the cottage, shutting away the remains of Ben's life in Sandlebury.

"I need to get back to London. I've got a meeting at one."

"About Beau?"

"No, about one of my other cases. I'm only working this one personally as a favour to your father—usually, I'd assign a missing person's case like this to a member of my team."

"Will you be coming back?"

"At some point. I need to speak to my police

contacts and see if we can work together on this, plus run a wider electronic search on our mysterious Mr. Davies. I don't suppose you've got a photo of him?"

Only an out-of-focus snap from his tenth birthday party, and Nye wasn't having that. "No, I'm afraid not."

"And your father told me there's no CCTV on the estate?"

I shook my head. "Mother always hated the idea of having cameras everywhere, and so did Angie."

"Because she used to sneak out?"

"Sometimes."

A low vibration interrupted us, and Nye pulled a sleek black phone from his pocket and glanced at the screen.

"Hey, Jannie."

He listened, eyebrows knitting together. "Sorry, for a moment there, I thought you said you'd cleared my entire schedule for the next month."

And he really didn't sound happy about it.

"But it's just a missing suspect. Why is he so important?"

My ears pricked up as Nye took a few steps away from me. I knew I shouldn't have been listening in to his conversation, but I couldn't help myself. Anyone would have done it, right?

"Why not? Hang on, they're both coming?"

Both who?

"That's all the information she gave? Too damn right I'm coming back to the office."

He hung up, and for a second, I thought he was going to throw his phone. His face went through confusion and anger before he gritted his teeth and took a deep breath.

"What's wrong?" I ventured.

"Does your father know a guy called Charles Black?"

"I'm not sure, but the name doesn't sound familiar. Why? Who is he?"

"The owner of the company I work for. And for some unfathomable reason, he's taken a personal interest in this case. As of now, I'm on it full-time for, and I quote, as long as it takes."

"And you think my father might have influenced that?"

"I can't understand why else it would have happened."

"Do you want me to ask him?"

"Would you mind?"

Five minutes and a phone call later, we'd ascertained that Father was as surprised as us, although he did offer to buy Mr. Black a box of cigars in appreciation of him taking the whole affair so seriously.

And Nye was even more confused. "Thing is, it's not like he's just told me to put more people on it. Black's flying in personally with a team."

"Is that unusual?"

"I've worked at Blackwood for nine years, and it's never happened before."

"So, what happens now?"

"I'm heading to the office to find out what the hell's going on, and you can put your pyjamas on again and go back to bed."

No way. He wasn't leaving me out of this. "I want to come with you."

"I've got enough shit to deal with, thanks."

Did he just liken me to excrement? "How dare you

be so bloody rude?"

He pinched the bridge of his nose and sighed. "Sorry, that came out wrong."

"I'll accept your apology if you take me with you. And if you don't, I'll phone my father and get him to call more people because you're not leaving me in the dark."

I'd already been there once, and look where it got me.

"Fine, you can come. But I'm going to keep asking all those questions you don't want to answer." He leaned in close. "And so will Charles Black. You may be able to fob me off with bullshit, but I'd like to see you try it with him."

I gulped, and the rational part of my brain wondered whether going to meet Nye's boss was a good idea.

But that didn't stop me from getting into Nye's BMW ten minutes later, and in no time, we were whizzing down the M40 to find out why Ben had suddenly become so important.

CHAPTER 18

I STUCK CLOSE to Nye as he exited the car in a basement car park and strode to a lift in the corner. When we got inside, he pressed the button for the fourth floor and we rose quickly upwards.

"Will it be busy?" I asked.

The idea of dealing with a room full of people made me feel quite ill.

"One o'clock on a Thursday? Half the people will have gone out for lunch."

Thank goodness. The lift doors opened into a large, open-plan room filled with rows of desks and the occasional coffee table with chairs clustered around it. Only a quarter of the seats were occupied, and I garnered a few curious glances as I followed Nye to a glass-fronted office in the corner. Before we could go inside, a small black lady sitting at a desk next to it waved him down.

"They're setting up on the fifth floor."

"What the hell? How does this warrant being a fifth-floor job?"

She shrugged. "Above my clearance grade. Is this Augusta Fordham?"

Nye nodded and introduced us. "Janelle, this is Augusta. Augusta, meet Janelle, my assistant. If you need anything, just ask her."

"I'm so sorry about your sister," she said, reaching out to grasp my hands.

"Me too."

"Would you both like some lunch?"

The butterflies in my stomach turned their noses up at the thought of food, but I'd skipped breakfast in favour of mid-morning television, so I needed to eat something. "Maybe a small snack?"

"Can you bring some sandwiches up?" Nye asked. "Who else is there?"

"Luke just arrived, and Dev too."

Nye led me back to the lift. "Who are Luke and Dev?" I whispered as he passed a fob over a panel at the side and pressed the button for the fifth floor.

"Luke's a computer guy. He doesn't officially work for Blackwood, but we often use him as a consultant. Dev... Dev works on some of our more challenging jobs."

"What did you mean about it being a fifth-floor job?"

"They run the more unusual projects from there. I'm just not sure how this falls under their remit. We've worked hundreds of similar cases without the directors doing more than signing off on my monthly report."

As we alighted from the lift, an older lady sitting behind a sleek grey desk pointed at a conference room in the corner. She looked like a receptionist but behaved like a sentry.

The door was closed and remained that way until Nye pressed his thumb on a pad to the right of it, below an electronic plaque designating it as the home of Project Carbon. I'd barely had time to puzzle over that when the door slid to the side with a soft whoosh.

Inside, a man with dirty blonde hair sat behind a laptop, a steaming mug of coffee resting beside him on a coaster. Luke? I put him in his early thirties, but with an air of authority I could never hope to possess.

A second man lounged on a padded black leather chair, his boot-clad feet resting on the polished table. Like Luke, he wouldn't have looked out of place in a magazine shoot, with light brown skin so smooth he looked airbrushed. He must be Dev.

Luke glanced up at us, then carried on typing, but Dev raised an eyebrow.

"New assistant?"

"This is Augusta. Her father's our client on the Davies case."

"You know what's going on with it?"

"Not a clue. I take it from that question that you don't either?"

"Nope. But it's important enough that Black's running the project personally, and he's called Emmy in to help him. She's due to fly back from Morocco at one thirty. Plus Logan and Xavier are coming too."

"Bloody hell. What's this guy done?"

"Your guess is as good as mine, but I wouldn't want to be on the run with that team after me."

A shiver rippled through me as Nye turned to Luke. "Have you heard anything?"

"Mack said if I lent a hand, she'd dress up in kinky underwear."

"Mack is his wife," Nye explained. "She works for the company too."

A soft knock signalled Janelle's arrival with food, and although the sandwich platter and fresh fruit were perfectly acceptable fare, I couldn't stomach a bite. The men demolished the lot while I sat on the furthest chair, worrying more with every passing second.

What the hell had Ben done to attract this sort of attention?

Once Nye had eaten, he left, leaving me to mull over my thoughts alone. When he returned half an hour later, he was followed by a huge man who filled the room with his presence. One look into his bottomless eyes and I realised that being caught by the police might be the better option for Ben. Five minutes alone with that giant, and I'd be begging for a jail cell myself.

Three others came in after them—two men, one with a beard, one without—and a dark-haired girl whose face was devoid of all expression.

"Emmy's in a cab from Heathrow," the giant said.

Was this the man Nye called Black? It had to be, surely. His attire certainly suggested so.

I shrank back as he fixed me with his gaze, but rather than speaking to me, he turned to Nye and raised an eyebrow.

"Angelica Fordham's sister."

"I know who she is; I'm more curious as to why she's here."

"Because she knows a thing or two about our target, and I'm hoping at some point she'll share."

Thanks, Nye.

I expected more questions, but the man merely nodded and pressed an intercom button near the door. "Simone, could you make sure Emmy's got coffee waiting when she arrives."

The dark-haired woman took a seat at the opposite end of the table, and I caught her staring at me. Rather than looking away, she studied me with an intensity bordering on painful. At that moment, I wished I'd stayed at home. Even afternoon drinkies with my mother would have been more pleasant than the pressure cooker I'd trapped myself in. I stared out longingly through the solitary window on the far wall, seeing nothing but a grey sky.

Well done, Augusta.

Five minutes later, a blonde lady strode through the door, holding a frothy mug of coffee in one hand and a donut in the other. The big man took the donut from her and scored a perfect bull's-eye in the rubbish bin sitting in the corner of the room.

The look on her face said he was lucky not to get the coffee dumped over him, but she slammed it on the table, marched out, and came back thirty seconds later with a chocolate éclair. Middle finger raised towards him, she sauntered to the end of the table furthest from the door and took a seat beside me.

"Emmy," she said, grinning.

Finally, a friendly face. "Augusta."

"Yeah, I know. Sorry about your sister."

Had Nye told everyone in the entire company about what happened? It felt as if my life didn't belong to me anymore, but I had to stay polite.

"Thank you."

"Don't worry, we'll catch the bastard."

Would they? Or would they catch Ben instead?

Dev twisted a knob next to the intercom. As the lights dimmed, the glass looking out onto the open-plan office frosted over, and the wall opposite lit up with a shield logo that was replicated on the table in front of Black. The room fell silent, and all heads turned in his direction as we waited for him to speak.

"I'm sure you're all wondering why we're here today. Beau Davies isn't the type of case the Special Projects department would usually get involved in, but it seems our unfortunate suspect now has two of our clients interested in finding him."

Two? Who the heck was the other one?

"Client number two wants Mr. Davies brought in by us rather than the police, which means we don't share our information with the Met. Use anything we can get from them, but the flow goes one way only."

"Why our custody and not the cops?" Dev asked.

"Personal reasons."

"Who's the client?"

Black appeared to mull that over for a few seconds. "I'll keep that to myself for now."

"W-w-what did Beau do?" I asked. I hated to draw attention to myself, but at the same time, I needed to know.

"Nothing you need to worry about."

A non-answer that only made me worry more.

"So, what's the plan, boss?" Emmy asked.

"At the moment, Davies holds all the cards. We don't have a photo of him, and we don't know anything about his background, only that he took off on a cherry-red motorcycle, which might be a Kawasaki or a Honda."

"Or a Suzuki," Nye put in.

"Or a Suzuki. But this case has been all over the TV, so he's got limited places to hide."

I'd carefully avoided all media coverage. Dorothy had told me the literary world was devastated by the loss of Sapphire Duvall, so much that they'd even opened an online book of condolence that had collected over thirty thousand names. And Father kept mentioning the news, even when I asked him not to. Apparently, the police were asking anyone with suspicions about a recently arrived stranger to call a special hotline.

"Even without his face being broadcast, there's a good description, and any man travelling alone is going to raise suspicions," Black continued. "In a way, the cops have been victims of their own success—over fifteen thousand people have called their tip line, and they don't have the manpower to follow up all the leads properly."

"Have we got access to their results?" the stranger without the beard asked. His accent was odd, and I couldn't place it.

Luke spoke from behind his laptop. "Right here. They're up to fifteen and a half thousand now, and it's increasing by a hundred every hour."

"We need to think smarter," Nye said. "If you were on the run, where would you head?"

"From the UK? Egypt," Emmy said, at the same time as the dark-haired girl piped up with, "Venezuela."

"I'm already cross-referencing flight manifests from the UK to all non-extradition countries," Luke announced.

"And if you stayed in the UK? City or country?" Nye asked.

"The city," Emmy said.

"Why? When you *were* on the run, didn't you pick the countryside?"

My ears pricked up. Emmy had been on the run?

"Yes, because I had agencies from the CIA to Interpol hunting for me, and I knew they'd tap into the

CCTV networks. Facial recognition software is both a blessing and a curse. But Davies doesn't have that problem because we don't have a picture of him, and village communities are too close-knit. If he turned up alone, four hundred little old ladies would be gossiping within the hour. Trust me on that."

Luke chuckled. "Yeah, I still remember the rumours circulating in Lower Foxford about you running over your ex's new girlfriend."

"Oh, you're one to talk. Didn't they reckon you got a swimwear model pregnant?"

Black glowered at both of them. "Do you think we could avoid a rehash of your past dalliances?"

"Whatever." Emmy rolled her eyes at him, but he'd turned to the screen where a large-scale map of the British Isles had appeared.

"What about Davies's friends?" Dev asked.

Nye shook his head. "The staff at Shotley Manor said he never had visitors and rarely left the estate."

"How about that girl in the village?" Dev glanced at his notes. "Jade Bosley claims he assaulted her."

"I spoke to her earlier, but she changed her story ten times in half an hour. The only consistent part was where a brown-eyed stranger showed up and they had sex. First he had blonde hair, then brown hair, and the location changed from the lounge to the bedroom to the back of his car. When I questioned that, she admitted they might have done it more than once in the course of the night. Gut feeling? She's a troubled young woman who's attention seeking."

"Okay, so we'll leave that one to the police," Black decided. "It doesn't sound like it impacts our investigation, and from what we've found, Beau Davies doesn't have a car."

"His phone records don't show a lot either," Luke said. "He called the pizza place every Friday, Mrs. Fordham on occasion, a DIY store in the next town, the local garage—"

"The garage?" Nye and Black said at the same time, as Luke put the list up on the screen.

"Yes, Sandlebury Motors."

Nye smiled, and it made me nervous. "Reckon he took his bike in for repair?"

"Let's hope so," Dev said, tapping away on a tablet in front of him. "I'll get someone to take a trip out there."

"I'll go," Emmy offered.

"You?"

"Why not?"

Meanwhile, Black had been staring at the phone records. "You know what's missing from there?"

"Calls to his family?" Luke suggested.

"The police report said Davies texted Angelica to meet him in the pool house at eleven. Where's that message?"

All heads swivelled to the screen. Sure enough, it was conspicuous by its absence. And what's more, his texts to me weren't on there either, which meant Beau had a second phone.

"Did it get sent from that number?" the man with the beard asked, nodding at the screen.

"Hang on…" Luke began flicking through documents on the screen until an image of a phone display appeared. One message, no preamble, no reply. *If you want a good time, meet me in the pool house at eleven. Beau.* "Yes, same number."

"But Davies didn't send it?"

Silence fell for a few seconds before Luke spoke up again. "Somebody could have spoofed it."

"How convincing is that?"

Luke typed away, and the phone on the table next to bearded guy buzzed. He picked it up, read the message, and burst into laughter.

"Sorry, Xav, you're not my type," he said to the man sitting next to him.

Xav held his hand out for the phone, then chuckled too. "Is that even possible? You'd have to be a contortionist."

Luke cut in. "Logan, if you received that message, what would you have thought?"

"That Xav needed therapy."

"I meant about its origins."

"Well, yeah, it's from Xav, isn't it?"

Black looked thoughtful. "So, we've established that it's straightforward to spoof a message, and if all the other clues are screaming that a man's guilty, the police aren't going to look for evidence to the contrary."

The dark-haired girl spoke for only the second time. "You think there's a chance he might not be guilty?"

"I think not everything about this case is as it seems. But our primary objective remains the same: find Beau Davies."

CHAPTER 19

THE TEAM FILTERED out of the room until only Nye, Emmy, and I were left.

"Do you need a lift home?" he asked. "Or do you have friends in London to stay with?"

I didn't have friends at all, not proper ones. "I can call a taxi."

"Don't be silly," Emmy said. "I'm going to Sandlebury anyway, so you can catch a ride with me."

"Are you sure?"

"Of course. It'll be nice to have somebody to keep me awake. I didn't get much sleep last night."

"Are you sure you're safe to drive?"

"I'm fine. Just let me grab another coffee. You want one?"

"Maybe a cup of tea?"

We put little plastic lids on our cups so we could take them with us, and I followed Emmy back down to the parking garage.

"Nice Aston Martin," I remarked, spotting one in the corner.

They'd always been my favourite car, but the idea of actually getting behind the wheel of one scared me a little.

"Isn't it? Afraid my car isn't that posh, though."

She bleeped open the doors of a black Volkswagen

Golf a few spaces up.

"I've got a Polo. VWs are ever so reliable, aren't they?"

"Not too bad on fuel either."

"Do you think we'll make it back to Sandlebury in time? The garage shuts at five thirty prompt, and Ned Blakely never works overtime. He's always in the pub by six."

"As long as we don't hit traffic, we should be okay."

She fiddled around with the SatNav, and sure enough, it said we'd arrive with twenty minutes to spare.

Emmy knew the short cuts through London's back streets, and by the time we got onto the A40, we'd only lost five minutes. With quiet classical music playing from the speakers, I almost managed to relax as we chugged up the motorway towards home. Then I thought of Mother waiting for me and tension seeped into my muscles again.

"Why were you at the meeting today?" Emmy asked, snapping me out of my misery. "I understand you have a personal connection, but clients don't usually get so involved."

"Because I want to know what's going on. People always leave me in the dark, and I hate it."

Ben included.

"Still, I'm surprised Nye agreed."

"Uh, he accidentally called me a rude word, and I told him I'd only accept his apology if he let me come along."

She chuckled softly. "He's normally charming."

"I know. I've met him at some of my mother's parties, and when he got engaged, two of Angelica's friends ended up on antidepressants."

"There are more men out there."

And the ones I'd met at Blackwood certainly seemed...eligible. Except for Black. He scared me. The thought of him leading the hunt for Beau made me more nervous with every passing second.

"What happens now? With looking for Beau, I mean?"

"If we find details of the bike, we can start looking for it on the ANPR system."

"What's that?"

"Automatic Number Plate Recognition. Basically, a network of thousands of cameras that feed data on every vehicle that passes them into a central database."

"Oh."

"You don't sound super enthusiastic. I figured you'd be keen to catch the man who killed your sister?"

"I am. Yes, I am." Even to my own ears, I didn't sound convincing. "Do you really think somebody could have...?" What did Luke call it? "Spoofed that text message?"

"We already proved it could be done."

"I thought at first somebody might have framed Beau."

"But now you're not so sure?"

"DNA doesn't lie."

There, I'd done it. I'd voiced my biggest fear. The secrets had been eating away at me, and if I tried to hold them all in, I'd have crumbled from the inside out.

"It doesn't lie, but you sure can use it to bend the truth."

"What do you mean?"

"We've all been conditioned to accept it as gospel.

That because DNA is at a crime scene, its owner must have been too. But it's also easy to manipulate."

"What do you think about the case?"

"Truthfully? There's too much evidence. A man who's covered his tracks as carefully as Beau did doesn't kill a girl and then leave DNA all over her body, a message on her phone, and a knife with his freaking initials etched into the handle sticking out of her side. But then again, he's gone on the run, which doesn't exactly make him look innocent."

"Back in the meeting, Nye said you went on the run once?"

"Yeah, I did."

"W-w-what did you do?" She didn't reply, and I feared I'd overstepped the mark. "You don't have to answer. I'm sorry if—"

"I got accused of killing my husband."

Her husband died? "I'm so sorry."

"Shit happens." She stared straight ahead, eyes fixed on the tarmac zipping past under the wheels.

"It happened to me too," I said softly. "Only I got put in prison."

Emmy glanced over at me, and my fingers gripped onto the edges of the seat, nails digging into the leather.

"That's awful. But it was a mistake, right?"

"Of course it was a mistake!"

"Sorry. Just had to check."

"It happened on our honeymoon. We were in Thailand, and he'd spent weeks planning our itinerary. The first day, we...well, we stayed in the hotel." My only sexual experience before Midnight. "We spent the second day on the beach, and on the third day, we travelled inland to visit some temples. There was this one up on top of a hill, and Rupert wanted to get a photo of me next to it, so he backed up a bit, and I told him to stop, but he fell right off the edge of the terrace."

A tear rolled down my cheek as the memories of that terrible afternoon flooded through my mind. The way he'd told me to smile as I rushed forwards to grab him, how I'd clutched at empty air as he lost his footing.

"Then some bloody goat herder standing about half a mile away told the police I pushed him."

She reached over and squeezed my hand. "I'm sorry you went through that. It must have been doubly devastating."

"It got worse when they locked me up in a hell-hole for six weeks. I was stuck in a cell with a whole bunch of drug traffickers and one woman who really did kill a man, and she scared the crap out of me. Not that there was anywhere to crap. We didn't have a proper toilet and the cell smelled like a sewer."

"Bloody hell. What happened then?"

"Father brought in an army of lawyers and the British ambassador, and eventually the goat herder admitted he may have been mistaken." I shuddered at the memory of eating slop from a bowl. "I'm never going back to that awful country again."

"I can understand that. The Thai authorities do have their own unique brand of justice, although in some cases it's well-deserved. That's why you're giving Beau the benefit of the doubt, isn't it?"

"What if the British police make an awful mistake too?"

"The UK legal system is a lot more transparent. And

I get that you want to think the best of people, but you've only spoken to Beau three times, according to your statement, and I hate to say it, but that might not have been enough to form a solid opinion of him, especially as we know he's been hiding things like his true identity. Whether or not he killed your sister, he sure looks guilty of something."

I chewed at the inside of my cheek, the words "I knew him better than that" balanced on the tip of my tongue. But as Emmy wound through the lanes that led to Sandlebury, I kept my mouth closed. I still didn't know enough about Blackwood's intentions to believe they'd do the right thing for Ben.

Instead, I turned the tables back on Emmy. "What were *you* doing in the meeting today?"

"I've had luck with finding people in the past, so Black asked me to lend a hand."

"I heard you flew in from Morocco?"

"Yeah."

"What's it like there? I always wanted to travel. Thailand was supposed to be the start of the adventure, but look how that turned out."

"Well, Morocco's hot. That's about all I can tell you. I went to sit on the beach for a week, and he called me back after two nights."

"Sorry."

"It's hardly your fault. Didn't you go on holiday when you were a kid?"

"Mother always insisted we go to our villa in Barbados." I let out a long breath. "Listen to me—I sound like a spoiled brat. Of course, I loved going to Barbados, but I just wished I could see a bit more of the world. But not Magaluf. One of Angie's friends got married last year and they went there for the hen party. She hated everything about the place."

And she came back with terrible food poisoning. I'd held her hair back while she puked for three days.

"Okay, not Magaluf. Where would you like to go?"

"What's the point in thinking about it? I don't have anybody to go with anymore, and I'd never travel alone."

"Why not?"

"What if I got lost? Or somebody stole my wallet? Or I got ill?"

"You'd manage. That's part of the fun."

I shook my head. "I don't think I ever will."

The sign for Sandlebury Village flashed past on the right-hand side, flanked by two stone pillars and a neatly mown grass verge. We'd won the Best Kept Village competition two years running, and the Parish Council took the whole affair very seriously.

"I know SatNav says turn left, but it doesn't mention how that road is only single width and leads to the local riding school. Ten to one you'll get stuck behind a horse. It's best to go straight on and then take the next junction."

"Thanks."

We made it to the garage with five minutes to spare, and Ned was just flipping the open sign to closed.

"Oh, no you don't," Emmy muttered, leaping from the car almost before it came to a stop. "You're not closing early."

I hurried along behind her as she strode over, wearing a smile that transformed her from beautiful to stunning. Any man approached by a girl with her looks couldn't help but take notice, and Ned was no exception despite being in his early sixties.

"Hi," she said, holding out a hand.

He shook it and smoothed down a few wayward clumps of hair with his fingers.

"You got a problem with your car?"

"The car could do with its oil checking, but we actually came to ask you a couple of questions."

His open demeanour turned a little frosty. "You with the police?"

"No, a private investigations firm. We've got a client looking for Beau Davies, and we understand you might have spoken to him."

"And I'll tell you the same thing I told the police—I never saw him or his motorcycle."

"What did you talk about on the phone? We see from his phone records that he called you."

"He wanted to borrow a spanner."

"And?"

"And what?"

"Did you lend it to him?"

"Uh...no."

"But he called you again? Several times?"

Ned took a step back and folded his arms. "Okay, so I did lend him a spanner. But that was it. I don't know nothing about anything else."

So Ned *had* seen Ben.

Emmy glanced through the open door of the workshop. A single car sat on a hoist, missing its two front wheels, but that wasn't what caught her eye.

"I see you use Snap-On tools. They're the best, right?"

"That they are. My old dad taught me that you buy once, and you buy quality."

"A good lesson. These cheap imports don't last, do they? What does a Snap-On spanner cost? Twenty pounds? Thirty?"

"Something like that."

"And you lent yours out to a stranger, no questions asked?"

Ned realised he'd been trapped and took another step backwards, but Emmy simply smiled and matched him.

"I'm a nice guy, okay? Helping the neighbours and all that."

"I wish I believed you, Ned, but I just don't. One of those calls lasted almost ten minutes."

"Look, I got nothing more to say to you people. Beau Davies was a good man, and all those rumours coming out of the gossip mill that is the Women's Institute are a load of shite. Those ladies have got nothing better to do than crow over other people's misfortune."

At least it wasn't only me who hated that. "It was my sister who got killed, and I don't believe he did it either," I added quietly.

Ned turned his glower on me, then his expression softened. "I'm sorry about your sister, but why are you helping them?"

"Because they've already found one anomaly in the evidence, and I'm hoping they find more. If they can't track down Beau, the other option is him running forever, and I'd hate for him to have to do that."

"What are your intentions if you do find him?" Ned asked Emmy.

"We'll evaluate the evidence. If we don't believe he killed Miss Fordham, we'll do our utmost to get him cleared."

Was she telling Ned what he wanted to hear or speaking the truth? Either way, Ned seemed happy with her answer.

"You'd better do right by that boy. He did come to borrow a spanner, but like you said, I wasn't letting him take my tools away with him. He brought the bike with him. And when he'd finished, he helped me to put the gearbox back in a Ford Mondeo. Damn near saved my back."

"And the other times you spoke?"

"The same. Wanted to borrow a tool or two, but he always gave me a hand in return. You don't get many men like him nowadays."

"Can you tell us more about his bike?"

"It's a Triumph. Modern bike, but he customised it so it looks like a classic."

"I don't suppose you know the registration number?"

"I've got a photo of it on my notice board. Nice bike, it is."

CHAPTER 20

NED POINTED OUT the photo, and Emmy snapped a picture of it on her phone. He was right—it was a nice bike. If things had been different, I could have been riding around on the back with my arms wrapped tightly around Ben's waist. A tear escaped at the thought, and I wiped it away before Emmy noticed.

"Can I offer you a coffee?" I asked as we pulled into the driveway at home.

"I wouldn't say no. My caffeine levels are already dropping."

Just when I thought the day couldn't get any more awkward, it did. "Oh, sh...sugar."

"What?"

I pointed at the Jaguar parked on the drive, the same model as my father drove but green instead of maroon. "Gregory's here."

"Who's Gregory?"

I shouldn't have sighed in resignation the way I did —after all, Gregory was a perfectly nice man—but I couldn't help it. "The man my mother wants me to marry."

"And I take it you don't share her enthusiasm?"

"On paper, he's perfect. He's got a good job, a wealthy family, and he's handsome. But there's something missing. There's no spark between us, at least for me. Does that sound crazy?"

"No, it doesn't. The right man's out there for everyone. You just need to find him. Don't sell yourself short and settle for less, because in the long run, you'll only end up miserable."

I already did find him. Another tear trickled down my cheek, and this time I couldn't hide it, or the others that followed.

"Hey, it's okay," Emmy said, pulling me into a slightly awkward hug with the gear knob poking in my side. "What's wrong?"

"I don't know how to tell Gregory. I keep thinking maybe I should simply abide by with Mother's wishes, but then I'd hate myself for it. I've put off speaking to him since Angie died, but it's not fair on him to carry on."

"No, it isn't."

"But what should I say?"

"Tell him what you told me—that he's a nice guy but not the one for you."

"But what if he hates me? I haven't got many friends, and I can't afford to lose another one."

"If he hates you, he's not as good a friend as you thought he was."

"I'm so scared of being alone," I whispered.

"You won't be. Look, do you want me to wait while you speak to him?"

"Would you?"

"Yeah, I will."

Maybe, just maybe, I'd made another friend. Emmy and I snuck in the back door, and I set Mary to work in the kitchen with a cafetière before walking to my doom in the garden room. Gregory's face lit up, but Mother's dark aura eclipsed him.

"Augusta, where on earth have you been?" she asked.

"I was helping the investigators Father hired."

"He's paying them good money, and you most certainly shouldn't be doing their dirty work."

"It wasn't like that."

"Augusta, listen to your mother," Gregory said. "You shouldn't be involved in anything to do with that piece of scum who killed Angelica. Leave it to the professionals."

"Gregory's come by to cheer you up. He's booked a table for the two of you at La Rive. Isn't that kind of him?"

"Yes, but—"

Gregory checked his watch. I was paying more attention to wrist wear now, and his Rolex cost more than my car.

"The table's booked for seven, so you'll need to change quickly."

"I thought we'd spoken about your penchant for denim, Augusta. It's not suitable attire for a young lady."

"Enough!" They both stared at me. "Gregory, I'm not going to La Rive. The last thing I want to do is go out and enjoy myself so soon after Angie's death, and...and...I don't think we should see each other anymore. Not romantically."

His jaw dropped. "What do you mean? We're perfect together."

Mother cut in before I could reply. "The trauma's getting to her. She doesn't mean that at all."

"Yes, I do. There's no...no fire between us. Sure, we

get on okay, but that's not a basis for a relationship."

"Of course it is," Mother snapped. "Relationships have been built on far less."

"Not for me."

She leaned back in the armchair and took a swig of whatever was in her glass. Something clear with a ragged slice of lemon floating in it. Water? Vodka? Gin?

"I see what's happened. You've been reading Angelica's books. She got all those silly notions in her head once, and look where it got her. She rejected every suitable man in favour of partying, and it killed her."

"Her lifestyle didn't kill her. Some sick bastard with a knife killed her."

"Language, Augusta. She wouldn't have been in that position if she'd settled down with a man like Gregory. And where has that left this family? You're out of a job, to start with, and I can't see you walking into another. Not when Angie had all the talent."

Even Gregory looked shocked at that last part. And me? I saw red in every hue. "Angie had the talent? I wrote those damn books. Every last one of them."

"Don't you dare tarnish Angelica's memory."

"It's true."

"Augusta, your mother's right. It's not kind to lie about your sister's writing ability."

"I'm not lying. We had an agreement because Angie liked doing all the publicity, and I hated it."

Mother waved her glass at me, and liquid sloshed onto the Persian rug. "Sometimes, I don't know what to do with you. I raised you better than this."

"You barely raised me at all! My schoolteachers and the household staff raised me."

Gregory sidled a little closer to my mother and

dropped his voice, but not enough so I couldn't hear. "I've got an excellent colleague in the psychiatry department. I could get him to squeeze in an appointment on an emergency basis if that would help?"

"I don't need a bloody psychiatrist."

"You're in denial," Mother said, slurring slightly. "This is precisely why you need a psychic...psycho...psychiatrist."

"I've had enough of this. I'm leaving."

I didn't know where I was going to go, but one thing was certain—I couldn't be around my mother or puppet-boy a moment longer. Furious, I stormed towards the door. Mother took a few wobbly steps in my direction, but the reflection in the mirror on the wall showed Gregory putting a hand on her arm.

"Best to leave her today. I'll give Mervyn a call in the morning."

Sod that. I wouldn't be sticking around to get sectioned or whatever else they had planned for me. If they thought for one second that their ridiculous idea would get me to bend to their wishes, they had another think coming.

"Didn't go well, I take it?" Emmy said as I stomped into the kitchen.

"You were right about one thing—Gregory isn't the friend I thought he was."

"Shoot, I'm sorry. You've had a tough time of it lately."

"Yes, well, it doesn't look like things will be improving any time soon. Dorothy, could you help me pack?"

"You're going somewhere, ma'am?"

"Somewhere. Anywhere. As long as I'm not stuck in this house with Satan's Stepford wife I don't really care."

I'd charge a hotel room to my credit card, and Father could fight over it with his accountant later.

Emmy followed as I led the way upstairs. "If it helps, I've got a spare room you're welcome to borrow."

Gosh, how kind, but I'd feel terrible about imposing. "I don't want to be any trouble."

"Honestly, it's no trouble. It might be a bit dusty—I can't remember the last time anybody stayed in there."

"Only if you're sure?"

"I'm sure. I won't be around all the time, though." She made a face. "Work."

"In that case, thank you. I'll just grab a few things."

Half an hour later, Emmy programmed her number into my phone, then helped me to lift two of my suitcases into the boot of my car and a third into the backseat. Dorothy didn't understand the concept of packing light, and I couldn't bring myself to go into the annex and direct her. The evening's events had left me drained, and all I wanted to do was curl up under a duvet with a good book. Not a romance. My heart hurt enough without reading about someone else's happiness. Travel books were out too. Non-fiction, possibly.

"Got everything?"

"I think so."

"I'll drive slowly so you can keep up. If you get lost, flash your lights or call me."

An hour and a quarter later, the adrenalin had worn off, and I gulped back tears as I turned right into the undercroft car park of a smart-looking apartment building in Camden. Emmy reversed neatly into a space near the entrance and pointed at the one next to it. Parking had never been my strong suit, but I managed to get between the lines on only my third attempt. Then I realised I couldn't get the door open wide enough to get my suitcase out of the backseat and burst into tears.

Emmy knocked on the window. "Don't worry; I'll sort it."

I stumbled out, wishing like crazy that I had her poise and fortitude. Instead, it was all I could do not to trip over my own feet as I wheeled a suitcase behind her into the building.

"We're on the third floor."

The hallway was clean and tidy if not a little spartan, and Emmy's apartment wasn't all that different. The only personal touch was a small group of framed photos on a side table, and I couldn't help taking a closer look.

"Is that the girl from the meeting?"

"Sofia?"

"Is that her name?"

"Yeah, and yes, it is. I've known her a long time now."

"She didn't say very much this morning."

"She's been under some stress lately. We all have." Emmy crossed the lounge and opened a door on the far side. "Well, this is it. Sorry it's kind of small."

"It's perfect."

Reminiscent of the box room I'd been sleeping in for the last few weeks, in fact, and at the sight of the bed in front of me, complete with a maroon velvet bedspread and a pile of fluffy pillows, my mouth yawned all of its own accord.

"Tired?" Emmy asked.

Exhausted. "Would you mind if I just went to bed?"

"Of course not. You don't want any dinner?"

"I'm really not hungry."

"If you change your mind, feel free to raid the fridge. Otherwise, I'll see you in the morning."

CHAPTER 21

WHEN I WOKE the next day, still air told me the apartment was empty, but that didn't stop me from peering around the door jamb just in case there was anyone home to see how atrocious I looked in the morning. Nope, nobody.

In the tiny kitchen, I found the cupboards stocked with the basics and a note from Emmy propped against a jar of Nescafé instant on the fold-out table.

Gone to work, call if you need anything. E.

Things I needed... My sister back, Ben back, and a new mother, but I could hardly request those.

Even the little things made me ache inside, like the jar of coffee. Angie had made me my first cupful every morning, and the thought of boiling the kettle for myself made me gulp back tears.

A chirp from my phone sent me rummaging through my handbag in the foolish hope the message might be from Ben, but no such luck. It was only Dorothy.

Dorothy: Your mother asked me to remind you it's your sister's funeral tomorrow, and the cars will be leaving the house at ten sharp.

Oh, for goodness' sake, how did they think I would forget? I'd been trying to block it from my mind, but it lurked in the background and popped up unbidden every time I let my guard down.

The phone chirped again.

Dorothy: I'm sorry about what happened with your mother yesterday, and we all hope you're okay.

Well, now I felt guilty for leaving the staff behind to face Mother alone.

Me: I'm okay. Please tell Mother I'll make my own way to the funeral.

She wouldn't be happy about that, but I'd grown sick of trying to please her. Nothing I did would ever be good enough. I knew that now.

I'd intended to read a book, but instead, I ended up staring out the window at the passing traffic. Pedestrians and cars going about their business as if all was right with the world while I crumbled inside.

"You okay?"

Emmy's voice made me jump so violently I nearly fell off the seat. "I didn't even hear you come back."

"Sorry. Sneaking up on people is a bad habit."

"It's all right. I'm just really nervy at the moment. H-h-has anything more happened with the case?"

"We know Beau came to London. Luke's got a picture of his motorbike driving down the A40. The question is, did he stay here?"

I shrugged and kept quiet as Emmy headed towards the kitchen. If only I *did* have a clue where Ben had gone, I could try to find him.

"I stopped by for some lunch," Emmy said, rummaging in the fridge. "Only there's a flaw in my plan in that I forgot to go grocery shopping. Do you want to head out and grab a sandwich?"

"I'm not exactly dressed for going out."

Unless, of course, we were going to Wal-Mart. I'd

probably fit in quite well there.

"Don't worry—I'll catch up on emails while you change."

Tempting though it was to make an excuse, I didn't much fancy staying by myself in the apartment either, so I took a shower and got dressed. At least Emmy didn't bat an eyelid when I wore jeans.

"Lunch by the canal?" she suggested. "There's a nice pub not too far away."

"Do you have time for that?"

"Blackwood's flexible, and considering I was out working until three this morning, I think I can take an hour to eat."

"Three? What were you doing?"

"Talking to people."

"What sort of people are awake at that time in the morning?"

"The kind of people you wouldn't have come across living on your nice estate in rural Oxfordshire. Well, for the most part."

"You think Beau might be mixed up with them?"

"He's on the run. He can't simply check into a hotel or rent a car from Avis."

"I guess. Did you find anything?"

"Not yet, but if he's in London, we will."

That was what worried me.

At the Fox and Pheasant, we settled down opposite each other at an outside table, and for once the sun peeped out. Most of this June had been grey and overcast, or maybe that was just my soul.

"What would you like, ladies?" a waiter asked, tapping a pencil on his order pad.

"The burgers are good here," Emmy said, then

smiled up at him. "Give me a cheeseburger with everything and a side order of fries."

I couldn't possibly stomach that much food. "A Caesar salad, please."

"You want chicken or bacon with it?"

"Just plain."

"Still no appetite?" Emmy asked as he walked away.

"Not much of one. Everything's getting too much— first Angie, then the row with Mother and Gregory, and I've got to go to the funeral tomorrow."

"Do you want to catch a lift with one of us?"

"What, to the funeral? You're going? But you didn't even know Angie."

"Statistics say there's a good chance a killer will show up at his victim's funeral, so we'll be sending a team. The police too."

Great, even Angie's last send-off was going to turn into a bloody circus. One last indignity in her life. "Is that necessary? I'm quite sure Beau won't show up there."

"Who said anything about Beau?"

"But the police..."

"The police are looking for Beau, but like you said, he's not that stupid. Blackwood's keeping an open mind, and that means seeing who else is hanging around."

A tiny bud of hope formed in my chest. "Really?"

"Client number two is leading the charge on that one."

"What about my father? Won't he be angry?"

"I believe his exact words were 'bring in the man who killed my daughter.' And we will, whether that was Beau Davies or somebody else. But at this moment, we've got little to go on, and finding Beau represents our best chance at unravelling this whole mess."

Her words made it sound as if they were coming around to the idea of a second culprit, but a part of me still worried about Ben ending up in jail. Like Emmy said, the police weren't quite so open to new suggestions. When I'd suggested the possibility to the family liaison officer the week before last, she'd all but laughed in my face.

"I hope you find the other man."

"But not Beau?"

"I'm worried about him."

Emmy's phone trilled on the table beside her, and she put it to her ear. I strained my ears to hear the other end of the conversation, but it wasn't loud enough. All I got was Emmy's side.

"Really? Interesting... Any idea who she was? ... And they left on a bike? ... Well, ask Luke to get the CCTV footage. I'll be back in an hour."

At the mention of a bike, I froze inside, trying desperately to maintain a calm exterior. Were they talking about Ben?

"Looks like you were right to be worried," Emmy said to me.

Oh, hell. "Why? What's happened?"

"A man fitting Beau's description went into A&E at King's College the night before last, but he wasn't alone. The doctors reckoned he and the girl with him had both been in a fight."

"He had a girl with him? What girl?"

"We don't know. She had a knife wound to her thigh that nicked her femoral artery, plus a head wound. They wanted to keep her in, but when the nurse asked for her details, she legged it. The pair of them took off on a motorbike that sounds like Beau's."

"Was he hurt badly?"

"Not sure. He refused treatment and just asked staff to look after the girl."

I stood up, even though I wasn't sure what to do or where to go. And who was the girl? Why was he with another woman? I tamped down the jealousy that welled up inside me.

"We have to help."

"We don't even know for sure it was him yet, not until we get hold of the CCTV footage. Would you mind coming to the office later to take a look at it?"

I nodded. "Can't we go now?"

"There's no point. We might as well eat lunch seeing as it's ordered."

How could I contemplate eating after that revelation? The remains of the juice I'd drunk for breakfast rose in my throat, and I swallowed it back down again, fighting the urge to run for the bathroom.

"I'm not hungry anymore."

"I'll eat mine quickly."

Emmy wolfed down her burger as soon as it arrived, then attacked the fries as I picked at a couple of croutons.

"Do you want any of these?" she offered.

I shook my head. What I wanted was to get in a cab, go to Blackwood's headquarters, and find out what the hell was going on. When Emmy finally dropped two twenty pound notes on the table and stood up, it was all I could do to stop myself from running out of the restaurant.

And the cab took forever. It was after three when

we drew up outside the huge building with its fancy glass atrium, something I'd missed seeing on my first visit there.

"We'll go straight up to the fifth floor," Emmy said, her trainers squeaking on the polished floor as she strode past the receptionist with a quick wave.

"Do you think there'll be any news?"

"Let's hope so."

The same people were in the conference room as on my first visit—Black, Nye, Luke, Xav, and the woman I now knew as Sofia—except the bearded guy and Dev were missing. Nobody said why. Nye smiled, while Black drilled me with a gaze that left me squirming in my calfskin boots.

"Anything?" Emmy asked.

Luke glanced up from his screen. "We've got them walking into the hospital. I'm just going through the exterior footage to see if there's a decent picture of the bike. The camera closest to the entrance wasn't working that night."

"Bloody cutbacks," Nye muttered.

"Can you play what we've got?" Emmy asked.

Seconds later, the stark waiting room of a hospital flickered onto the screen. A lady sat next to a small boy who appeared to have glued a model of the Starship Enterprise to his hand, and a few seats away, a middle-aged man in football kit held his wrist. Then the sliding doors opened, and a man rushed in with a woman in his arms. Even with the towel wrapped around her thigh, it was obvious she was bleeding badly, and her face was a mess too. But my gaze only lingered on her for a second.

"Is that Beau?" Emmy asked.

I nodded. Despite the untidy beard and the blood running from his nose, I couldn't mistake him for anybody else. "What happened?"

"Davies and his friend weren't particularly forthcoming with the details," Nye said. "He just told them to help the girl." Nye waved at the screen, and sure enough, Beau could be seen shaking his head at a nurse and pointing. "And she told the doctor it was a mugging gone wrong."

"And the doctor's thoughts?" Black asked.

"She didn't look like the kind of girl who'd have anything worth stealing, and she seemed nervous as hell."

"Of who? Davies? The staff?"

"Not any of them. When she left, she stole a bunch of medical supplies from the nursing station, and Davies was in the car park waiting for her."

"Got the footage now," Luke announced. "Same bike."

On screen, the girl stumbled out of the exit and looked both ways before spotting Beau to the left. A different camera showed them under a light in the parking lot. A few words, and she hopped on the back of the bike, wrapped an arm around Beau, then they took off.

"Thoughts?" Black asked.

"Dev and Logan are still at the hospital talking to people," Nye told us. "The woman gave her name as Irena and spoke English with an Eastern European accent."

"She wasn't scared of Davies, and he didn't treat her like a stranger," Xav said. "But however the evening started out, he didn't plan on her riding pillion. He cared enough to get her medical treatment and risk being spotted by waiting for her afterwards, but he didn't care enough to put a helmet on her? Doesn't stack up."

Emmy reached for the jug of coffee in the centre of the table. "In those clothes, she looks like a hooker, and he looks like he's been sleeping rough. Maybe they met on the streets?"

"Or he was using her services?" Black suggested.

"Don't be ridiculous," Sofia snapped.

Black fixed her with his gaze. "Why do you say that?" The question wasn't argumentative, merely curious.

"Because a man on the run's going to have other priorities."

"Not if he's fucked in the head." He held up a hand before she could argue. "I agree with you, but your reasoning's off. You need to keep your head and think objectively."

"Fine. You do the reasoning."

I felt nauseous at the thought of Ben consorting with a prostitute, and Black's cold demeanour didn't help matters.

"Where's Angelica Fordham's autopsy report?" He turned to me. "Augusta, do you want to wait outside?"

Yes. "Will there be photos?"

He looked at the table for a second, then at Luke. "Send them directly to my tablet."

Bile rose in my throat as he studied the broken body that would forever be fixed in my mind, his face impassive. Would he remain so calm if it was *his* sister in the pictures? Was he even capable of emotion? The man appeared to have all the compassion of a toaster.

"Yes, it's as I remembered. Angelica had seventeen stab wounds with sixteen to her torso, but the pathologist reckoned the first, and the one that did the damage, was to her femoral artery. Sound familiar?"

Nye nodded. "You think our second guy stabbed the girl from the hospital and Beau found her."

"I'd say he did more than that, judging by the damage to his face. Looks like Mr. Davies is doing the same thing we are: hunting for Angelica's killer."

"Playing devil's advocate here, what about all the evidence against him?"

Sofia let out a huff and waved her hand in a dismissive gesture. "That could have been faked."

"The police are going to want proof of that, and indeed the courts if it gets that far," Nye said. "So, how? Let's start from the beginning, shall we? How did Angelica and her killer meet?"

"That's obvious—at the party."

"We've cleared everyone on the guest list."

"He could have crashed. Nobody would have noticed. It was a masked ball, after all. He picked the perfect night."

"Augusta, would it have been possible for a stranger to attend?"

Finally, a question I could answer. "Mother always put a person on the door to collect the invitations and hang up coats, but only for the first hour, then he got reassigned to drinks duty. And he'd be from an agency, so he wouldn't know the faces that went with the names. Oh, and the side door was always open for the smokers to go in and out."

"That's a yes, then. And how would he have convinced your sister to go to the pool house with him?"

Much as I hated to tarnish her memory, I had to be honest. "Without much difficulty. A fancy watch, nice clothes, a posh accent. She tended to go for the superficial."

"No particular type?"

"Rich."

He nodded. "I see. Right, we've also got the forensics, and some of that's fairly damning at first glance. We've already discussed the message on Angelica's phone, so...initials and clear fingerprints on the knife?"

"The initials mean nothing," Xav said. "Anybody could have engraved them, but the fingerprints... I'd have stolen the knife in advance, killed her with an identical blade, then inserted Davies's knife into the final stab wound."

Boy, he'd really got into this role-playing game, hadn't he? The way he spoke, I could almost imagine he *had* killed someone before.

"Angelica's hair on Beau's pillow?"

"The unknown subject could have taken it from her head and then planted it before he left for the night. Where did he steal the knife from? If it was in the cottage, our unsub would have had practice at picking the lock before the night of Angelica's death."

"He had a key," I blurted, and everyone turned to stare at me. Oh, shit.

If I'd thought Black was scary before, the way he looked at me now meant I wanted to wither and die.

"How exactly do you know that?"

CHAPTER 22

I TRIED TO answer Black, but no sound came out. After a hasty swallow, I managed a broken whisper. "Angie had Beau's keys in her hand when we found her."

"When we found her? I thought you found her alone?" Black asked.

A tear rolled down my cheek and plopped onto the shiny wooden table. "Beau was with me. We found her together."

"And why was he with you?"

"We were downstairs in the pool house, uh, talking."

"The kind of talking that doesn't require many clothes?"

Now I couldn't speak at all, so I just nodded.

"For fuck's sake. Why the hell didn't you tell us this before?"

"I was scared, okay? I don't want Beau going to prison, because I'm sure he didn't kill Angie. He was as shocked as me when we found her."

Black spoke through clenched teeth, anger rolling off him. "Start again from the beginning, with the truth this time."

"I met Beau in the pool house just before midnight, and we...we had sex." Oh, heck, could this be any more embarrassing? "Twice. Then I decided to sneak back to his cottage and spend the night with him, only I needed to phone Angie first because the last time I arrived back late, she got worried. But when I called her, the phone rang upstairs, and we went up and found her."

"And when you got home late the last time, were you with Beau again?"

I nodded again.

"In the pool house?"

"The garage. We fell asleep on the backseat of Father's vintage Cadillac."

"So this was a regular thing?"

"Sort of. Only after Mother's parties. For the last five, we met up afterwards."

"And who instigated this?"

"He did."

"How?"

"He sent me a text message asking me to meet him."

"And even though he was the janitor, you agreed?"

"I didn't know who he was at first. It was sort of a surprise?"

Black rolled his eyes. "So essentially, you went to meet a stranger for sex?"

His attitude got my back right up. "Haven't you ever done anything impulsive when you've had a few drinks?"

"Like getting married in Vegas?"

"Yeah, exactly like that."

He held up his left hand to reveal a ring I hadn't noticed before. "Thirteen years and counting."

Oh. What kind of woman managed to put up with him for thirteen years? I'd struggle for thirteen minutes.

"I guess that counts."

"Can we get back onto the subject now? Beau? Your sister?"

"We found her, and he recognised his knife, then when he checked for a pulse, his keys fell out of her hand. He said he'd lost them a couple of months back and Dorothy lent him her spare set so he wouldn't get into trouble."

"Check that with Dorothy," Black instructed Nye. "Then what?"

"Beau said that if the man had his keys, he must have been lurking for two months but he hadn't noticed. Beau was devastated. I told him not to blame himself, but he did."

"Anything else? A clue as to why the man went to all this trouble to frame him?"

"Beau said he put the man in prison, and he swore that he'd get revenge by doing the same, except he wasn't due to be released for...for... I don't know how long, but it wasn't soon."

"Did he say what the man went to prison for?"

I racked my brains, but nothing came to me except the horrible sight of Angie lying on Father's leather sofa. "I don't think so. Everything from that night's really hazy."

"What about your previous encounters? What did he say during those?"

"Not a lot. I mean, we didn't talk a lot, just...just..."

"Fucked?"

My cheeks burned as colour rose up them. "You don't need to be so crude."

"Maybe if you hadn't held up this search for weeks,

I'd show a little more understanding."

The tears came. I couldn't help it. I didn't want to tell them about Ben's past in case it hindered him, and Black behaving like such an asshole only made me more determined to hold on to the secrets I still had left. Instead, I shoved my chair back and stumbled towards the door.

"Now look what you've done." Emmy glared at him and followed, wrapping an arm around my shoulders as she helped me to the nearest ladies' room.

She fetched me a wedge of toilet paper as I leaned on the edge of the vanity unit, staring at my blurry self in the mirror. How had everything fallen apart like this?

"I won't ask if you're okay, because that's a stupid question, but is there anything I can do to help?"

"I just want to go home. Well, not home, but back to your apartment. Can I?"

"Of course. I'll drive you."

"What about Black? Will he be angry?"

"Don't worry about him."

Once I'd dried my eyes as best I could, Emmy led me out through the open-plan office, where curious men and women pretended not to look at me from behind their computer monitors. Emmy shielded me from the worst of the stares, then we were in the lift whizzing down to the basement.

"How will we get back home if you don't have your car?"

"We have pool vehicles."

A lockbox on the wall yielded row upon row of keys, and Emmy grinned as she selected a bunch. "Let's take this one." She aimed the fob into the cavernous garage, and a nearby Porsche 911 flashed its lights. My eyes widened.

"This is a pool car?"

"Nope. It's Black's. Figured it's the least he can do after the way he upset you."

I smothered a giggle. "You're stealing his car?"

"I prefer the term borrow."

She climbed behind the wheel while I hopped into the passenger side.

"Bloody Nora—look how far my feet are from the pedals."

She slid the seat forward while I settled my handbag into the footwell. Whoever usually sat in the passenger side was a more normal height.

"Buckle up," Emmy said. "Safety first."

I half expected security guards to come running after us as she headed for the exit, but the metal shutter rolled up without any sirens going off, and then we were out in the street.

"You want to head straight back or go for a joyride first? Driving always helps me to relax."

Oh sod it, I might as well go full rebel. "Maybe a short drive?"

She grinned at me, and I couldn't help smiling back. "You got it."

Before too long, we were out of London, driving along the motorway to nowhere in particular, and my heart rate began to decrease. Events at the meeting had left me shaken, and although my trust in Ben had grown stronger, one thing still bothered me.

"You know how we were going through all the evidence?"

Emmy kept her eyes focused on the road. "Yes?"

"We never discussed the DNA i-i-inside my sister."

"It's been bothering you, hasn't it?"

"I can't believe Beau would have done that, not when..."

"Not when you were waiting for him so soon afterwards."

"Exactly." Somebody understood me.

"It could have been faked."

"How?"

"First there are the remote options—either our culprit could have paid off an employee at the forensics lab to doctor the results, or hacked into the system and changed them, but the first one's dodgy because if he approached the wrong person, they could have blown his plan, and Luke hasn't spotted any evidence of the second."

"Is there another way?"

"Two, but neither of them is palatable."

"I need to know."

She sighed. "Fine, but try not to throw up in the car, okay?"

I gripped the door handle, knuckles white. "Okay."

"So, our guy could have used a female accomplice to collect the sample for him."

"You mean she slept with him, just so he could be framed later?"

"Precisely."

Emmy was right—I did feel ill. Blood whooshed in my ears as I sat back and willed myself not to faint. "That's insane."

"But it happens. I can name three prominent figures who fell from grace after falling for the charms of the wrong woman."

"Are you serious?"

"Deadly."

"How do you know?"

"Because I know the woman."

"But that's insane! I mean, you should tell somebody. Those poor men, having their lives turned upside down like that."

"One was a prominent anti-gay campaigner responsible for inciting riots that led to the deaths of three people and the misery of thousands more. He disappeared from radar after a sex tape of him with a younger man emerged, and the clincher? DNA evidence on the sheets."

"Oh my goodness. You're talking about Ryland Hughes?"

The story had been all over the news the year before last, and Angie had shown me the grainy tape on some dodgy internet site. At the time, Hughes had denied ever sleeping with another man. The evidence had been planted?

"No names. But don't you think he deserved it?"

I recalled the arrogant, opinionated asswipe who'd dominated so many broadcasts with the hate he spewed. "I guess he did."

"So, it goes to show the method works."

"What's the second way?"

"Did you use condoms when you slept with Beau?"

"Yes."

"And what happened to them afterwards?"

"Surely you can't think that I had something—"

"Not you, but what happened to them?"

"I don't know. It's not something I thought about. Wait, the last night in the pool house, Beau tied a knot in the end of one and dropped it on the floor. I guess he must have taken it with him because I don't remember seeing it later, and the police didn't find it."

"If he threw them in the bin instead of flushing them, it's possible somebody took one. We already know the guy had a key to Beau's cottage."

"But how did the bastard know to look...?" It hit me then, like being slammed into a brick wall by a professional wrestler. "He was watching us? Those nights I was with Beau, that sick freak was watching us?"

I clawed at the door handle, so desperate to get out that the speed of the car didn't register.

"Hey! We're doing fifty."

"I'm going to throw up."

Emmy did an emergency stop, slewing to a halt just as I got the door open, leaned out, and puked. The seatbelt cut across my stomach. She released me, then climbed out and came to the passenger side, stepping around the remains of the croutons and a few lettuce leaves I'd managed to force down earlier.

"Here, have a tissue."

"Th-th-thanks." The idea I could have been an unwitting participant in framing Beau left me shaking, but not as much as the fear that somebody had watched our most intimate moments.

"I did warn you."

"I know, but I just didn't expect..."

"You really cared about him, didn't you?"

"I l-l-loved him. I still do. Whoever killed Angie didn't just steal my sister; he stole the man I wanted to spend the rest of my life with as well."

"Why all the secrecy?"

"Mother."

"Ah."

I didn't need to say any more. I could tell by Emmy's eyes that she understood.

"She'd have cut me off the instant she found out I chose Beau over Gregory, and I needed to buy some time for us to make plans."

"I get it; I really do, and Blackwood's goals are the same as yours. Every single one of us wants to see this bastard burn. Is there anything you can tell us, anything else at all that would help? Even if you don't think it's important, it might turn out to be."

At her kind words, the dam holding back my tears burst and I dissolved in her arms. No matter what I did, I couldn't stop crying.

"I don't know. I don't know what to do."

If I told her Ben's true identity, would Blackwood tell the police? They said they wouldn't, but so many people had lied, I didn't know who to believe anymore. I had visions of Ben being hunted with dogs through the streets of London, then thrown in a jail cell.

"Shhh, it's okay. There's more, isn't there?"

"Yes."

"Look, you've had enough upset today. Let's get the funeral over with tomorrow and then we can talk, okay? That'll give you time to consider things."

"Really?"

"I realise how important Beau is to you."

"I'll do anything to help the man I love."

"That's something I can understand."

CHAPTER 23

THE DAY OF the funeral dawned dark and grey, and the thought of Angie's last day being filled with drizzle rather than the sunshine she'd brought into my life made me cry again in the shower as I washed away yesterday's tears.

When I got into the living room wearing a black dress and ballet pumps, I found Emmy already dressed in a charcoal trouser suit, expensive from the cut of it, but her choice of footwear made me do a double take.

"They're in case I have to run," she explained when she caught me looking at the black trainers. "But I'm really hoping I don't have to do that."

"Has that ever happened before? At a funeral, I mean?"

"Only once."

"Oh my goodness. Who? Why?"

"A father showed up at his daughter's funeral, only he'd violated his bail bond. I ended up chasing him across the cemetery until he tripped and fell into a freshly dug grave."

"A grieving father? You arrested a grieving father?"

"It was him who murdered her. Boy, that was a really long time ago now." She put an arm around my shoulders and squeezed. "I promise I'll try not to hurdle any headstones today."

The thought made me giggle even as my heart ached. "Mother would have a fit."

We stared at each other for a few seconds, before she said, "Maybe I should," at the same time as I blurted, "Perhaps you should." Then we both started laughing.

"We mustn't laugh," I spluttered.

"It's better than crying."

True, and I'd be doing enough of that later. That thought sobered me up as I drank a quick cup of coffee, grabbed my handbag, and followed Emmy down to the car park.

"Are we taking the Porsche again?"

"It would be rude not to."

"Is Black going to the funeral?"

"No. With his height, he sticks out too much. Nye will go, probably Xav and Sofia. Logan and Dev have the wrong looks to fit in with your crowd."

When I was a little girl, I didn't care what people looked like or how they dressed, but as a teenager, I'd been conditioned to believe it mattered more than anything. That the colour of a person's skin trumped their heart, and the labels they wore were more important than their personality. Well, no longer. Ben had taught me many lessons in my life, and the most important one I needed to remember was to judge a person by what was on the inside.

And as Emmy squeezed my hand in a show of solidarity before she started the car engine, I believed she was a good person.

Mother was already seated in the front pew at St. James's chapel when we arrived. I'd been there many times for christenings and marriages but never for the funeral of somebody close to me. Today, I found little comfort in the old wooden carvings and stained glass windows I'd found so fascinating as a child.

I took my place next to Father while Emmy slipped into a seat a couple of rows back. I'd spotted Nye near the entrance with his fiancée, but Xav and Sofia remained out of sight.

Mother glanced over, dabbing her eyes with a lace handkerchief. "I'm surprised you showed up."

"Carolyn..." my father warned.

"She abandoned us in our time of need."

"I just needed some space," I whispered.

"Carolyn, we'll talk about this afterwards."

Thankfully, the vicar picked that moment to arrive, pausing to offer a few words of condolence before climbing into the pulpit. Father gripped my hand as the first bars of the funeral march played, and I somehow held it together while six pallbearers I didn't recognise carried Angie's oak coffin down the aisle and placed it gently on a wooden frame. Roses. White roses. She'd always loved them in life, and now they mourned her in death, a huge arrangement of them on the coffin lid interspersed with sprays of freesias and eucalyptus. I focused on the flowers as the vicar spoke, trying to block out the end with memories of happier times. The plays she'd been in at school, her first car, the time we'd snuck out to a pop concert and told Mother we were at the Tate Gallery, our giggles after her first kiss when she admitted the boy's lips felt more like a kipper. I needed to focus on the good we'd shared, or grief would have consumed me.

And then it was over, at least the service. Just the burial to deal with now.

We all trooped outside to the graveyard, and Emmy took my hand while my father comforted Mother, whose sobs drowned out the vicar's words as Angie's body was lowered into the ground.

"You holding up?" Emmy whispered.

I managed a nod, not daring to attempt anything more.

Then Angie was gone. Father stepped forward and sprinkled a handful of dirt into the grave, organ music played through hidden speakers, and mutterings began about the predicted variety of canapés at the wake. And, more importantly, would there be free booze?

Being the target of everyone's sympathy was the last thing I wanted. I tried to make a quick escape, but Father caught up with us at the entrance to the cemetery.

"Augusta, are you coming home tonight?"

"I wasn't planning to."

"Your mother needs you. She's concerned about all this acting out."

"Acting out? She thinks I'm acting out? She and Gregory wanted to send me to a psychiatrist."

"They're just worried. We all are."

"Try worrying about her. Have you seen how much she's been drinking lately? Vodka for breakfast, gin for lunch, a bottle of red with dinner."

He ran a hand through his hair that was now more silver than brown, leaving it a mess at odds with his perfectly pressed suit. "Dorothy made me aware of the problem. But this is a difficult time for your mother, and you need to allow her a little leeway."

"I'm allowing her plenty of leeway by moving out."

"Augusta..."

"Look, she needs help. She's impossible to live with, and you're never around."

"Things have been busy at work."

"And work comes before family; I know that."

"That's not how it is."

"It's exactly how it is. I'm sorry, but I just can't be at home right now."

A crowd had gathered around the gate, and I didn't have the composure to push past them at the moment. Father tried to follow as I walked back into the cemetery, but I waved him away.

"Not now, okay?"

Emmy trailed me back to Angie's grave, and damp from the grass seeped through the fabric of my dress as I sank to the ground beside both of them.

"This is all such a mess," I whispered.

"I'll help you fix it if you'll let me."

The black hole yawned beside us, and I didn't want to attend another funeral in the near future. Ben had already been hurt once. What if the man went after him again? Being dead was worse than being in jail, and neither of us could do this alone anymore.

"His name isn't Beau."

"We figured as much, but I'll admit we're struggling with his history. Do you know who he really is?"

"Ben. Ben Durham."

"He told you that?"

"Kind of. It turned out I already knew."

The whole story came spilling out, from the way I'd fallen in little-girl love with Ben as an eight-year-old to realising he and Beau were one and the same person.

At the end, Emmy shook her head incredulously. "I figured there was more, but never that much more. So, he wasn't running away when he arrived at Shotley Manor, he was running to someone. You."

"I guess."

"Shit, honey, this must be destroying you."

"Pretty much."

"We'll find him; I promise. Now we've got a name to go on, things should get easier. Are you ready to head back to London?"

"Right now, I want to curl into a ball and rock."

"Could you do it in bed? It looks like it's about to rain."

She scrambled up and offered a hand, pulling me to my feet just as two men wearing black suits and earpieces arrived in front of her.

"Nothing stirring," said the taller of the pair. "We're gonna head back now."

"Thanks, boys. We'll be right behind you."

Only before we could follow, my phone vibrated in my bag, and a sixth sense told me who the message was from. I scrambled through the contents, shoving away tissues, my notepad, and several tubes of lip balm in my haste to get to my mobile.

Emmy looked over my shoulder as I read the message.

Unknown: Mon cœur, any words I can offer will be inadequate today, but I want you to know I'm thinking of you, the way I have every second since I left. You're strong, trésor, stronger than you believe, and your soul is my light in a dark world. I love you, and I always will. B

I'd barely got to the end of the message when Emmy snatched the phone from me, dialled, and pressed it to my ear. "If he answers, speak to him."

Oh, hell, what was I supposed to say? My heart took off like an Olympic sprinter as the phone rang once, twice, three times. Then silence.

"Hello? Ben?"

"Gus, we shouldn't be speaking."

A sob escaped, and I blinked back tears. "I just wanted to hear your voice. Are you all right?"

A pause. "Yes, I'm all right. I wish I could be there for you today. Every day."

In the background, Emmy was muttering on her own phone, and I knew without a doubt she was trying to trace the call. I also knew that I had to let her. It was my only hope of actually having Ben there with me every day.

"I want that too, more than anything. Did you find the man you were looking for?"

"Once, but he got away. Fuck. He got released, and they didn't even tell me. If I'd known..."

"You didn't. And there's nothing we can do to change the past, but please don't let him take our future too."

"If only it was that simple. I have to go, *mon cœur*. It's not just the police after me now."

"I know. My father hired Blackwood Security."

"And word on the street says Emerson Black herself is looking for me, and that's worse than the cops. I love you."

"I love you too. Please—"

But there was a click, and he hung up.

Hang on. Emerson Black. Emmy Black?

"Are you Emerson Black?"

She rolled her eyes. "Busted."

"You're married to that...that...?"

"Bastard? Go on, you can say it. He's never been the easiest man to get along with."

"You said your husband died. I thought you understood what I was going through."

"Technically I said I got accused of killing him, which is true. I just left out the part about him not actually being dead."

Oh, that sneaky... "How could you let me think that?"

"Because Black recognised that you needed a friend, and he understood the type of person you needed that friend to be."

"So you caring about me, that was all a lie?"

Didn't she think I'd been hurt enough yet?

"No, I just bent the truth at some points."

"Like where?"

"Uh, I don't really drive a Volkswagen or live in a teeny apartment."

"You set all that up?"

"Black did, and I went along with it. Like you said, we'll do anything to help the men we love."

"You both manipulated me."

And so damn smoothly I'd never suspected a thing. These people lived in a whole different world, didn't they? One where truth was a rarity, a weakness, and nothing was as it appeared.

"Look on the bright side—we're on your team."

"I don't know whether to hug you or hate you."

"How about you reserve judgement until we find Ben Durham? What did he have to say?"

"Why should I tell you? All you've done is lie."

"Would you have told us the truth any other way?"

I thought about that for a minute, and I had to admit she was right. If they'd tried to force the information out of me, I'd never have given it. And at heart, I did believe they wanted to help.

"You can't keep lying."

"Okay, I promise." She held up both hands. "Look, I haven't got any fingers crossed."

I sighed, then made my decision. "Fine. I'll tell you."

CHAPTER 24

WE DIDN'T GO back to the little apartment in Camden. Instead of the bustle of the high street and market, intimidating yet somehow comfortable in their anonymity, huge homes zipped past on quiet streets. Even though I'd grown up with money, I couldn't help gawping at the houses hidden behind walls and hedges, too big even for my father to afford.

"Where are we?"

"Belgravia."

"Why?"

"It's where we're running the real investigation."

What did she mean the "real investigation?" She spoke like everything so far had been a game. A charade. "I don't understand."

"You will soon enough. I promised no more lies, yeah?"

Minutes later, she turned left into the short driveway of a huge white mansion, down a ramp, and into an underground parking garage reminiscent of the one at Blackwood's headquarters.

"This is another office?"

"It's our home. Your things have already been moved here from the apartment."

I wanted to protest that somebody had gone into a place I'd adopted as my sanctuary and handled my belongings, my personal items, without obtaining my consent or even bothering to ask for it. But what actually came out was, "What, all of them?"

She smirked a little. "Dev couldn't believe how much luggage you brought."

Dammit, I felt all off balance. I shook my head in an attempt to dislodge some of the rocks that had taken up residence in here. "What makes you think I want to stay at this place?"

"There's a man on the loose taking out girls connected with Ben. We'd prefer you didn't end up being his next victim."

When she put it so bluntly, I could hardly argue. "Thank you, I guess."

"We're not leaving you unprotected, and if you're here, it means we can free up the surveillance team that was watching you at the apartment to do more useful things. I'm assuming you can see the logic in that?"

"You've been watching me?"

"Too damn right we've been watching you."

She was out of the car before my half-formed words could escape from my mouth. Invasion of privacy. Peeping Tom. Big brother. They all got spluttered at empty air.

My muscles got ahead of my brain as I tried to exit with the seatbelt still on, and by the time I'd slammed the car door, hard, she was already halfway to the lift in the corner.

"You're welcome," she called back over her shoulder.

If the meeting room at Blackwood's headquarters was the corporate equivalent of a modern art gallery, with its white walls, chrome accents, and designer lighting, the conference room at Emmy's house was the equivalent of a school classroom. No, scratch that. It was the love child of a school classroom and a branch of Staples, one who'd been shagging a computer lab and possibly a library on the side. The only similarity was the tag on the door: Project Carbon. Only this one had been drawn in biro and attached with sellotape.

Inside, corkboards and post-it notes covered two of the walls, with a digital display taking up the whole of a third. A printer whirred in the corner, spewing out more paper to go with the sheets already littering every surface. I spotted Luke behind two laptops plus a third screen, and when the printer started beeping and flashing a red light, he gave it a dirty look.

"Nye, the damn thing's jammed again. Give it a thump, would you?"

"Nye's a bit old school," Emmy explained. "He likes paper. It drives Luke crazy."

Nye gave me a wave as he crossed the room to deal with the offending gadget, which I noticed was the same model as mine at home. Yes, I liked printing things too. Editing was so much easier with everything in front of me and a rainbow of pens at the ready.

Nye took Luke at his word and smacked the heel of his hand on the side of the printer, then narrowed his eyes when nothing happened.

"It didn't work."

Luke shrugged. "Try turning it off and on again."

I took pity on them both and stepped forwards. "I bet the paper's caught in the feeder. Here, let me fix it."

"Be my guest."

A little TLC got the rollers turning, and the printer was soon churning its way through a small forest again. "There you go."

With the crisis averted, I took a step back and surveyed the room. Besides Luke and Nye, I spotted Sofia sitting cross-legged on the huge table in the centre of the room and Xav behind his own laptop at the far end, his face devoid of all expression as usual.

"How are we getting on?" Emmy asked.

Luke took a sip of coffee before answering. "We've found Ben Durham on the register at St. Ethelbert's Prep School at the same time as Augusta attended, and like she said, he left aged eleven. He did one year at Sonham Middle School in Manchester, then attended Hadley Grange just down the road until he turned eighteen. Another scholarship, and it looks like he was a bright boy. Straight As all the way. Then he disappeared."

"He can't just have disappeared."

"Well, he did. He's never earned a penny under his national insurance number, and his passport expired when he turned twenty. He's got no criminal record, not even a parking ticket, and he isn't registered with a doctor. Still working on the bank records."

"What about the phone call he made to Augusta?"

Nye pointed at a red pin stuck in a map of London on the corkboard. "That came from a shopping centre in Brixton, and the phone's turned off now. We've sent a couple of teams to check for witnesses and cameras, but I'm not convinced we'll find much."

"Brixton's near the hospital."

"It is. Looks like he's sticking in that area."

"Anything on our escaped prisoner?"

Emmy had updated everyone from the car as we drove back to London, although how she managed to hold a conversation considering the speed she was going at, I had no idea. She'd driven so sedately in the Volkswagen, and even yesterday in the Porsche, but it seemed that had all been part of the act. When we got in the car after the funeral, she'd mashed the accelerator to the floor and didn't lift her foot until we reached the outskirts of London. My fingers hurt from gripping the edges of the seat so hard, and I suspected the leather had ten fingernail-shaped dents in it.

Nye waved his hand at a wedge of paper next to him. The results of his search for our missing convict?

"According to my contacts, the only high-profile escapee this year was that armed robber whose buddies held up the van taking him to court, and they caught him two weeks later. The other absconsions have all been minor—shoplifters leaving open prisons, that sort of thing, and we can't find Ben Durham mixed up in any of it."

"Try France," Emmy suggested. "Ben calls Augusta *mon cœur*, and there's the French connection from his other phone."

"What French connection?" I asked.

This whole lack-of-information thing was starting to wear really, really thin.

"Ben messaged you just before midnight on the day of Angelica's death, right?"

"Yes."

"And between the hours of eight and eleven on the dates of your mother's four previous parties?"

"You went through my phone records?" I asked,

even though I already knew the answer.

Of course they went through my phone records. They'd probably checked my diary and my internet shopping habits as well if Luke had anything to do with it. Oh, hell, did he know I'd bought the *Fifty Shades of Grey* extended version? Could he tell I'd streamed it at least ten times? Thank goodness I'd ventured into town to buy the lingerie I wore for Ben on our second meeting. Except, shit, he'd probably seen my credit card bill as well. Mental note: pay cash, and only buy DVDs in the future.

"Just part of our job. Anyway, Ben sent those texts from a second, unregistered phone rather than his regular one. The only other activity on that second phone was a series of incoming phone calls originating from a mobile in the south of France, also unregistered. Does the village of Mougins mean anything to you?"

A thread of a conversation came back to me. "No, but Ben said he spent some time in France. I think he worked there for a while."

Emmy's mouth flattened into a thin line, and she blew out a steady breath. "Are there any other little snippets you've forgotten to tell us?"

The events of that awful night still jumbled together in my head like that one drawer where you tucked everything special but never quite got around to tidying. "Everything's so confused."

She pointed to a seat. "I suggest you sit down and un-confuse things, otherwise you'd better get that outfit to the dry-cleaner sharpish because you'll be needing to wear it again soon."

This new Emmy understood how to hurt people. Her words sliced between my ribs at just the right angle to jab me in the heart. And the worst of it? I knew she was right.

Think, Gus, think.

"He gave me a pen as a gift. A proper old-fashioned fountain pen with red enamel. He said he bought it from an antique shop in northern France."

"Do you still have it?"

I'd carried it with me since the day Ben left, going so far as to choose outfits with pockets to accommodate it. Today it rested against my hip, ruining the line of my dress, something that Mother would have chastised me for on any other occasion. Now I palmed the cool barrel, turning it over in my hands before I handed it to Emmy.

"I want it back."

Her face softened. "We'll look after it. Is there anything else? What we really need is a good photo of him."

"I don't have a recent photo; I'm sure of that much."

And how I wished I'd taken one. Just one. Something to look at before I went to sleep at night and my increasingly blurry dreams took over.

"Any scars? Other distinguishing marks?"

Yes! "Tattoos. He had tattoos."

"What kind of tattoos? Where?"

"An infinity symbol over his heart that he got for me." The simplest but my favourite. "A Chinese symbol at the top of his back that he said happened while he was drunk, and, uh, this circle with flames coming out of it on his arm."

"Can you draw them?"

"I can try."

Nye passed me a sheet of plain white paper, and Emmy handed me my fountain pen. I drew the infinity symbol first. A thin black line, simple. Nothing to indicate the complexities locked into the heart that lay underneath it.

"I never saw the symbol on his back. Ben said he didn't know what it meant either."

"How about the third one?"

I started with the circle at the bottom, then added a thinner line inside it and closed my eyes as I tried to remember what the rest of it looked like. One tall central flame, I was sure of that part, and shorter ones either side. The outermost curved downwards like a Fleur de Lys. My lines went wobbly as I recalled the one and only time I'd seen the pattern gracing Ben's arm, and I itched to be able to reach out and touch it.

I'd barely got the outline done when Emmy began tapping away on her phone. She held up the screen for me to see.

"Did it look like that?"

Yes! "Exactly like that. Where did you find it?"

"I've seen it a few times before."

"Where? What does it mean?"

Could we finally have found a clue to Ben's hidden identity?

CHAPTER 25

EMMY TAPPED THE phone, and the symbol appeared on the big screen that dominated one wall of the room.

"*La grenade à sept flammes.* The seven-flame grenade. It's the emblem of the French Foreign Legion. And if Ben Durham cared enough to get it permanently inked on his body, I very much suspect he was a legionnaire."

"*Legio patria nostra*," Xav muttered.

"What?" I didn't understand any of that.

"Their motto. The legion is our fatherland."

"It would also explain why we can't find any trace of Durham after he turned eighteen. All recruits are required to join under an assumed name," Emmy said.

"Why? Isn't that dishonest?"

"Joining the legion represents a fresh start. Many of the recruits have, shall we say, troubled histories."

The thought of a young Ben running to France to get away from his old life was another ice crystal through my fragile heart. Was it a coincidence that he'd joined up so soon after my mother told him I'd moved on? I hoped so, but I suspected otherwise. Hang on, didn't he say he'd had problems with his own mother too?

At the other end of the table, Luke tapped away on his keyboard. "I think the legion uses a separate computer network, and I've never tried to access it. I'll call Mack, but it might take us a while to get that information. Also, my French is shit."

"I can translate," Emmy said. "Or Xav or Sofia. But I've got a better idea. This may be a case where human intelligence wins out."

She pushed back her chair and headed for the door.

"Where are you going?

"I need to make a few phone calls."

She swept from the room, and as soon as the door closed behind her, everybody began speaking at once.

"Bloody hell," Nye said. "We've gone from having no leads to all the leads in the space of a day. Wonder what made him join the legion?"

"He had some family problems when he was eighteen," I said. "An argument with his mother and one with mine."

"Did he say what about?"

My breath hitched as I spoke. "My mother told him I didn't want to be with him anymore. She lied."

"Cold. How about his own mother?"

Cold? Yes, that pretty much summed my darling mother up. "Ben said his mother lied to him too, but he didn't elaborate on what she lied about."

"What was her name?" Sofia asked.

"Uh... Lynn. Lynn Durham."

Sofia nodded but didn't say anything more.

Beside Nye, Logan flicked his eyes to the corkboard. "Ben Durham, Beau Davies, BD. He likes those initials, doesn't he? He's used them three times. What's the betting he'll go for a fourth?"

"Three times?" I asked.

An odd look crossed his face, almost like...panic? "I

meant twice."

"No, you said three times. What aren't you telling me?"

"You'll have to ask Black about that one."

Right. He only said that because he knew I wouldn't dare. What was it with these people? I'd told them everything, and still they kept secrets from me. And now I didn't have any bargaining chips left.

As everybody around me got busy, I shrunk back on my chair in the corner to think. Okay, to worry. *Ben, what did you get yourself into?*

It wasn't long before Emmy slipped back into the room, brow creased into a frown.

"Well?" Sofia asked.

"I've got good news and bad news."

"What's the good news?"

"Help's on its way, with a top-level security clearance and macarons from Pierre Hermé."

"And the bad news?"

"That's also the bad news."

Silence descended, and Sofia's eyes widened as she obviously realised what that meant. "Gideon?"

"I only wanted to ask him a few questions. I didn't realise he'd drop everything and jump on the bloody Eurostar."

Xav roared with laughter, surprising because I'd never even seen him smile before.

"I could have told you he'd do that."

"Why? I told him he didn't have to."

"Because Gideon still wants to fuck you, my dear."

"Who's Gideon?" I asked, not expecting anybody to answer.

Emmy sagged into the nearest chair and groaned.

"A Frenchman with excellent connections, a filthy mouth, and the ability to make women drop their knickers simply by clicking his fingers."

"It certainly worked with you," Xav said.

"That's because he knows what to do with those fingers. Fuck my life. What am I supposed to tell Black?"

Xav still wore a grin. "I don't know, but I suggest you do it sooner rather than later. What's the journey time from Paris? Two and a half hours?"

"Two and a quarter," Luke helpfully put in.

"Shit shit shit. I'm going to need some fancy underwear to get out of this one."

"For who?" Xav asked.

"Black, you asshole. If it was Gideon, I wouldn't be wearing any. Fuck!"

Sofia hopped down off the table. "I need to sort out my hair."

"You have a boyfriend now," Xav reminded her.

"Yes, but this is Gideon."

Xav's grin only got wider. "I need to get popcorn."

"Where's Emmy?" Black asked when he walked in three hours later.

Xav, Nye, and Luke all looked at each other. Their expressions were clear: *Do you want to tell him or should I?* Because clearly Emmy hadn't.

In the end, Xav shrugged. Obviously his balls were bigger than everybody else's, metaphorically speaking. Because I hadn't checked out his package at all. No, not once. Okay, maybe once. But with that face and body, any girl with a pulse would have, okay?

"St. Pancras."

"Why's she gone there? Have we had a break in the case?"

"Ben Durham used to be in the French Foreign Legion."

"So, what's she doing? Going to Paris?"

"Not exactly. Paris is coming here."

Black put it together quicker than the others had done. "Gideon Renard is on his way?"

"Apparently so."

"Why the hell didn't she call me? I could have picked him up myself."

"I think that's what she was afraid of. If the guy's eating through a straw, he won't be much help to us."

"I wouldn't have damaged him. Merely reminded him that we get on a lot better when he's in a different country than my wife."

"Sofia went with her," I offered.

"He warrants a fan club now?"

I didn't know how to answer that, so I slunk back to my corner again, staring at the display board where Luke cycled through text and images so fast my head hurt. I didn't spot any pictures of Ben, and that was the only thing I was watching for.

Half an hour later, I found out what all the fuss was about, and I had to admit the man following Emmy into the room did have a certain something. Dressed in a suit, with light brown slicked back hair, high cheekbones, and a strong jaw, he exuded pheromones. I noticed Sofia chose to walk behind him, and her eyes kept drifting downwards.

Then he spoke, and filthy or not, his words in that

French accent did funny things to my insides.

"*Bonjour, tout le monde.*"

He held out a pastry box, and Nye's eyes lit up while Black's glowered with the warmth of liquid nitrogen.

Muttered greetings came from everyone except Black, who pushed his chair back and shook Gideon's hand, all the time looking like he'd rather chop it off.

"It's been a while," he said.

"*Oui.* Several months. I trust you are well?"

Black wrapped an arm around Emmy's waist, and there was no mistaking his message: Keep your hands off. "Never better. So, Ben Durham—I assume you have some information to share if you've come all this way?"

"I do."

"Well, do tell, then you can go back home again."

Gideon simply smiled at Emmy, and I was surprised Black didn't rip his head off his shoulders.

"If Ben Durham is the man I think he is, there is a good reason for me being here." He looked over at Sofia, and she sighed. A quick glance sideways showed Emmy biting her lip. "As well as taking in the sights of London, of course. It's always been one of my favourite cities, and I 'ave vacation to use."

Black's jaw twitched at the news that Gideon might not be returning to France immediately, but his demeanour remained coldly professional. "Care to give us the details?"

"*Mais oui.*"

He pulled a laptop from his briefcase, but before he could open it, a grey-haired lady who reminded me of Dorothy bustled in and flung her arms wide. "Gideon! Nobody told me you were coming. It's been years."

"Always a pleasure, Ruth."

He hugged her, and I noticed she blushed.

"Are you still fond of a good steak for dinner?"

"If it's cooked by you, *cherie*."

"Then that's what you shall have. And I'll bring you coffee right away. Black, one sugar?"

He nodded and turned that smile on her full beam, holding his gaze as colour spread up her cheeks.

Yes, it seemed he certainly did warrant a fan club.

Gideon fiddled with his laptop, and I couldn't help watching his hands. Long, elegant fingers and the recollection of Emmy's earlier comment made me go the same colour as the housekeeper.

"What's your network password?" he asked Luke.

Five minutes later, the IT gremlins had been banished, and a photo appeared on the screen. My heart leapt as Ben looked back at me wearing some sort of dress uniform—a white cap with a black peak, a pale green shirt with fancy red-tasselled epaulettes, and a row of medals.

"Is this the man you're looking for?" Gideon asked.

I nodded, words stuck behind the lump blocking my throat.

He nodded back. "Benoit Durant. A most interesting man, and one I had the pleasure of meeting once or twice."

Benoit Durant? Ben's third-slash-fourth name?

"Under what circumstances?" Black asked.

"We were planning to offer him a job until the unfortunate incident at the beginning of last year. But I'm getting ahead of myself. I should start at the beginning."

We all gathered around while Gideon took the seat to the right of Black's and paused for a few seconds, fingers steepled as he thought through his words.

"Ben Durant joined the foreign legion at eighteen, and even during the selection process, it was evident he possessed skills most of his peers did not. Many who join the legion are followers, and the culture is to do as you're told without asking questions. But Ben did ask questions, and while it rankled some, it also meant he caught the attention of those in command, and that's how he initially got onto DGSE's radar a number of years ago."

"What's DGSE?" I whispered to Nye, who was sitting next to me.

"*Direction Générale de la Sécurité Extérieure.* France's external intelligence agency."

"Like MI6 or the CIA?"

"That's right."

Wow. That sounded serious, but how did it leave Ben on the run now?

Gideon continued, "We borrowed Ben for the occasional job over the years, after he became a French citizen at nineteen by the process known as *Français par le sang versé.*" He glanced at me. "It means French by spilled blood. He was shot while hunting illegal gold miners in French Guiana."

My hands flew to my mouth. "Shot? Where?"

"In his left leg. Not too serious, luckily."

"So, what went wrong last year?" Black asked.

"Ben was stationed in Chad, with the deuxième Régiment Étranger de Parachutistes. Their mission was to disrupt the extremist groups operating in the region —never easy, but relatively routine. Except one day, Ben walked in on his French commanding officer and a first class legionnaire raping a woman and her ten-year-old daughter. According to his testimony, they laughed and invited him to join in, but that didn't sit too well with his moral values. Unfortunately, in the ensuing fight the first class legionnaire, a Polish man by the name of Radek Bosko, died, and Durant damn near took out the officer as well."

Emmy moved to sit next to me at that latest revelation. "Are you okay?"

I shook my head. What was the point in lying? Ben had killed a man. That should have scared me, but under the circumstances, I felt pride rather than fear.

She caught Gideon's eye. "Go easy, Ren."

He gave a barely perceptible nod. "The mother died, but the little girl survived. Of course, it got hushed up. France didn't want the bad publicity, and the officer's father was and still is a prominent politician. The affair was a disaster all round. The child, Kali, gave a statement saying Ben only pushed Bosko and he hit his head, which fitted with the autopsy findings. But he laid into Guy Leroux and broke his nose and three ribs as well as damaging his kidneys."

"Good," I muttered.

"Ben got dishonourably discharged, and Leroux got sent to a secure hospital after several of the regiment testified with a promise of immunity to say it wasn't the first time he'd acted like that."

"Hospital?" Black asked. "Surely that deserved prison? Leroux senior's influence again?"

"*Oui.*"

"How did he get out? Escape?"

"Would you believe he got released when his latest psychological evaluation came back clear? It stinks like the *puitain de merde* his papa is. I didn't find out until

Emmy called me earlier—the corrupt assholes who made that decision have done a good job of keeping it quiet. Money, I suspect."

"And now Leroux junior's in London."

"It certainly seems that way."

Bile rose in my throat, and I fought to swallow it back down. That...that animal was after Ben, and judging by the camera footage from the hospital, he'd already hurt him once.

"What resources does he have? How well trained is he?" Black asked.

"Resources? Everything his papa has to offer. In terms of training, both he and Ben are well practised in both armed and unarmed combat. It could go either way."

Sofia leapt up and began pacing. "We need to bring Ben in. Now."

"Agreed," Black said.

But how?

CHAPTER 26

I FOUND OUT the plan early the next morning. Well, early for me. Nine thirty. I'd never been an early riser, but most of these people looked as if they got up with the larks and did a day's work before I stumbled downstairs for breakfast. At least I managed to find the kitchen in the maze of rooms that made Shotley Manor look like a council house.

Sofia was at the table, staring into a cup of coffee with rapt concentration, while Gideon sat opposite eating a pain au chocolat. Every so often, he glanced at the iPad by his side, but Ruth kept interrupting him with questions about lunch, which he answered with good grace. And that voice that was like molten caramel to the ears.

"Yes, tomato soup would be wonderful, but all your cooking tastes delicious."

"Would you prefer cheese croutons? Or fresh bread? Or a green salad?"

He turned that smile on me, and my knees went a little weak. "Augusta, which would you like best?"

"Huh?" I'd been too busy staring at the way his perfectly pressed shirt stretched across his back to concentrate.

"How do you like your soup?"

"Uh, in a bowl?"

Dammit. Was it possible to reverse time, just for a few seconds, so I could get my foot out of my mouth?

The corners of Gideon's lips twitched, and I knew he was trying not to laugh, but thankfully Emmy chose that moment to walk in and save me.

"Okay, we've got a plan." She took a croissant from the plate at Gideon's elbow and bit into it, then looked at me. "But I don't think you're going to like it."

From the glint in her eye and the way my gut churned, I did believe she might be right. "What plan?"

"We need to be proactive. Exploit Ben's weakness."

"Ben isn't weak," I said. "He only ran away because —"

She held up a hand, cutting me off. "That's not what I meant. Everybody's got a weakness. An Achilles' heel, if you like. Gideon here isn't fond of small spaces, for example. It's always entertaining taking the elevator with him. I have issues sleeping. With Ben, it's women."

"He's not a womaniser."

"No, that's Casanova here." She patted Gideon on the shoulder, then sidestepped as he pinched her bottom. "Ben needs to protect women. Look after them. Not only did he save Kali from Leroux in Chad, he also tried to adopt her afterwards. The courts wouldn't agree, seeing as he was a single guy with no fixed abode, but he fought bloody hard. I bet he left Shotley Manor as much to draw Leroux away from you as to save himself, and when we last saw him, he was taking a woman to the hospital."

"So, what are you going to do? H-h-hurt a woman to make him come out of hiding?"

Black materialised behind Emmy, snaking an arm

around her waist as he eyed Gideon. "I don't think we need to go that far. With the right girl, a little upset should do the trick."

"What girl? Kali?"

"Kali's vanished. She disappeared from the orphanage in Chad one night, and out there the police don't give a missing girl the same degree of priority as they do in the UK. No, we need you for that role."

"Me?"

"He cares about you. We know that from his last phone call."

"But I can't call him. Luke said his phone's been turned off since the funeral."

"We were thinking of something more dramatic."

His smile scared me more than his usual stern demeanour. Because it wasn't a cheery expression or even one of relief. It was pure cunning, and his eyes were two glittering obsidian spheres as they focused in on me.

"L-l-like what?"

"A press conference. If you sob your pretty little heart out on TV, Ben's going to call. I guarantee it."

TV? I couldn't even do my own book signings because I hated the idea of people staring at me. Judging me. And I bet he wasn't talking about some two-second soundbite on an obscure satellite station in the middle of the night either.

"I can't. Not with millions of people watching me. I'll have a heart attack."

He shrugged. "A touch drastic, but it would do the trick."

Was he serious? I looked for a clue that he was joking but got nothing.

"I can't. I just can't. There must be other options."

"Sure. We can keep tapping our networks and hope we get lucky or wait for Leroux's next victim to show up in the hospital."

That wasn't fair, trying to pile the blame on me, but he was unrepentant. And his gaze hurt. The way it drilled into me, I could still feel the pain even when I looked away.

Emmy left his side and wrapped an arm around my shoulders. "It wouldn't be that bad. It's not like there'd be loads of people in the studio, just the production crew."

"But I'd know people were watching it." My family, people I went to school with, Gregory, the villagers in Sandlebury. "I'd fall apart."

"And that's why we need you to do it."

"What about the motorbike? Can't you try to trace that again?"

Yes, I knew I was clutching at straws, but I reached out anyway.

"Not if he isn't riding it."

The image of Ben's bloody face on the hospital security camera played across my mind. What would happen next time? Would Leroux get out the knife he seemed so fond of? And if Ben did get badly hurt, I knew I'd look back and wish I'd tried everything to help him, even if it meant laying myself bare in front of a television audience.

And that also meant I had the bargaining chip I needed.

I clasped my hands together to stop them from shaking. "I'll do it on one condition."

"Name it."

"I want to know everything that's going on. Who the hell is this second client that everyone's so cagey about?"

"That isn't my decision to make."

Sofia slumped into her chair, staring at nothing. She looked rougher today than I'd ever seen her. "Tell her. Just fucking tell her."

Emmy shrugged, and I steeled myself for her words, unsure whether I'd want to hear them. But I needed to.

"Mack and Luke are experimenting with a program that keeps a watch for people on Blackwood's wanted list via our DNA database. Not just for exact matches. It also evaluates the samples for close matches—parents, children, siblings—in case they can lead us to our targets."

"And Ben's one of your targets?"

"Yes. Our system flagged him up right after Nye entered the DNA results from Angelica's autopsy."

"What did Ben do?" I whispered.

This was getting worse and worse.

"Nothing. He was on our list because his sister's looking for him."

A little of the load lifted from my shoulders. "There's been a mistake. Ben doesn't have a sister. I mean, I've known him since we were little, and he doesn't have any siblings at all."

"Correction: Ben doesn't know he has a sister."

"But—"

This time Sofia interrupted, and when I looked, she had tears streaming down her cheeks. "My mother left with him when I was four. Luke found a photo taken at your school sports day when Ben was nine, and my mother was in it, cheering him on in the egg and fucking spoon race. While my daddy molested me daily in our fucking perfect-from-the-outside house in fucking Ohio, and the neighbours all said what a great father he was for raising me alone, my mother was dealing with eggs and fucking spoons."

I was left speechless as she ran into the hallway with Emmy close behind. And I wasn't the only one lost for words. A stunned silence descended over the whole room.

Unsurprisingly, it was Black who regained his composure first.

"I'll get that press conference set up, shall I?"

Two days later, I sat nervously in front of the cameras at the BBC's London studio. They'd perched me on something the height of a barstool that wobbled every time I moved, with a tiny table between me and Susie Sawyer, a news anchor more famous for doing the splits on *Strictly Come Dancing* than her grasp of current affairs. The make-up lady had really trowelled it onto me, and under the hot lights, I felt like a melting bloody waxwork. I only hoped the mascara was waterproof because Black wanted tears. Lots of them.

Off to the side, my father smiled. Yes, my father. You didn't read that wrong, and believe me, I was more surprised than anybody when he phoned yesterday and said he'd be coming along.

"The police told me you'd be making an appeal, Gussie," he'd said.

"I thought I should try to help."

"I only hope the police catch that sick bastard. If I ever lay eyes on Beau Davies again, I'll strangle him with my bare hands. We took him into our home, paid him good wages, and this—"

"Daddy, please. That's not making me feel any better."

"Sorry. I know it can't be easy."

Oh, Daddy, you don't know the half of it. "I'll cope."

"I'll come tomorrow and give you some moral support."

"Really, you don't have to. I've got friends coming with me."

"Friends?"

He was right to sound suspicious seeing as I'd never had any. "Uh, sort of. People from Blackwood. They've been really kind to me."

"Good to hear we're getting our money's worth. They don't come cheap. Sorry, Gussie, I need to go. The other line's ringing."

I'd hoped a last-minute work meeting would stop him from showing up, the way it had for every parent-teacher evening, most of Sapphire's book launches, and my graduation. But no such luck. Why did he suddenly decide to start acting like a parent now?

"Are you ready?" Susie asked.

"No."

She laughed, fake all the way. "Relax. It'll be over before you know it."

In the end, it wasn't as difficult as I'd feared. She asked me two questions about Angie's life, I burst into tears, and they kept flowing like the champagne at one of Mother's parties. When Susie asked if I had any final words, only the fear of Ben getting hurt let me pull myself together enough to make the plea Black had scripted for me.

"Catch the man who killed my sister. If you know anything, please call the police. Next time it could be your sister or your daughter who gets hurt. Please, just call."

Father gave me a fierce hug as I stumbled off set, pursued by a spiky-haired girl intent on unhooking my microphone.

"I'm so proud of you, Gussie."

That was the first time he'd ever told me that, or even hinted at it, and I felt even worse for lying to him about the true reasons for the charade.

"Angie always said I just needed a push to get over my fear of public speaking."

The tears came again, and Father handed me his handkerchief.

"She'd have been proud today too." He put an arm around my shoulders and steered me towards the exit, Nye following along behind. "And I need to say I'm sorry."

"For what."

"For not having been around much lately. Now I've spent the last few days with your mother, I realise how difficult things must have been."

Did he expect me to brush it all off? Because I wasn't going to. "Yes, it's been hell."

"I'm sorry," he said again. "I'm trying to convince Carolyn to get the help she needs."

"Let me guess, she refuses to accept there's a problem?"

He dragged a hand through greying hair. "She drank an entire bottle of wine with lunch yesterday."

"Did she have vodka with her cornflakes again?

He looked at me sharply. "Are you being serious?"

"Unfortunately."

"I can't apologise enough for what a terrible father I've been. Let me take you out for lunch. I know it won't make up for this, but..."

Shit. My phone burned a hole in my pocket as I prayed for it to ring. The last thing I needed was lunch with my father to throw a spanner into the works.

"How about we meet up next week? I'm feeling really drained after the interview."

A look of desperation crept into his eyes. "Just a coffee, then? There's a café right across the road."

I glanced at Nye, who nodded but tapped his watch. I got it: be quick.

"Okay, I'd love a coffee."

Five minutes later, I blew across the froth of my cappuccino in an attempt to cool it down. My phone sat next to me, its screen black, but that could change at any moment.

Ring. Please, ring.

"How's London?" Father asked. "Busy?"

"I haven't been out much."

"No, of course not. Do you need more money? Clothes? A new car?"

"I'm fine, thank you." Every time he tried to buy me, I felt cheap. Like a trinket to be treasured before I went out of fashion. "I've got money in my bank account."

"Your mother said you made up a story about being Sapphire Duvall."

A statement, not a question, but I answered it anyway. "It wasn't a story."

"You wrote the books?"

I nodded.

"All of them?"

"Yes."

"How could I not have known that? My own daughter and I didn't realise how much talent you had."

I stayed silent. I could tell him exactly why he didn't realise. The same reason he had no clue how apathetic I was towards Rupert, and the same reason he thought every problem could be solved with cash. Because he looked but didn't *see*.

"It doesn't matter."

"Yes, it does, and I want to make things up to you. Will you come home tonight? We can have a proper family dinner."

Even if I hadn't been twitching inside as I waited for my damn phone to ring, I couldn't have thought of anything I'd rather do less. "I'm happy in London."

"But you've never been a town girl."

"Maybe I've changed. And until you prove you've changed, and Mother too, I'm not coming home."

My father no longer looked like a confident chief executive as he walked out of Starbucks. Instead, he was a sad father, a lonely husband, and a defeated man.

And I stood my ground.

"You did good," Nye said.

I twisted the edge of my jumper with my fingers, watching as my father flagged down a cab. "I hurt him."

"He's hurt you too, and your wounds go deeper. Be selfish for a change."

I didn't want to be selfish. I wanted to share my life with Ben. The question was, would I ever be able to?

CHAPTER 27

ALL LEAVE FOR Blackwood had been cancelled, and employees fanned out across London as we waited for Ben to call, with a particular emphasis on the area south of the river where he'd been spotted. The digital display on the dashboard of Black's Porsche Cayenne showed each of them as a green dot moving around a map and us as a larger black one. They sure did have a lot of people.

Beside me in the backseat, Sofia stared into space. Yesterday, when we'd sat in the Project Carbon meeting room and planned out the logistics, Black hadn't been keen on her coming at all, but she'd insisted. Privately, I agreed with him.

Since she'd blurted out her secret to the room, I'd rarely seen her with dry eyes, and today she chewed on her bottom lip as she wiped her face with her sleeve.

"You okay?" I whispered.

She shrugged.

Oh, hell, I couldn't leave her like that. I clicked my seatbelt undone and shuffled into the middle, wrapping her up in a hug. She stiffened for a second, then relaxed against me as I glimpsed Black's dark eyes watching us in the mirror.

"Are you sure you don't want me to send the plane for Leo?" Emmy asked.

"No," Sofia croaked. "I don't want him to see me like this."

Who was Leo? Her boyfriend?

"He won't judge you."

"I know, but he's been through enough shit recently as it is. And this... I've got a bad feeling."

"Enough with the thinking. It's not good for you." Outside, the golden arches of a McDonald's flashed past, catching Emmy's attention. "Hey, does anyone want a burger?"

An hour passed, then two, three, four, and I began to lose hope as well as regretting drinking two cups of coffee. It was all right for Black. We'd parked up, and he'd made a quick trip up a nearby alley half an hour before to relieve himself.

"Uh, is there a restroom anywhere near here?"

He pointed at the alley.

"Er, no. Just no."

"Can we go to McDonald's now?" Emmy asked.

Black shook his head. "No more junk food. You ate macarons and chocolate truffles for breakfast."

"How do you even know that?"

He shrugged and started the engine. "Can't give my secrets away, can I?"

We compromised by going to a café that served salad, then it was back to waiting again. Emmy slumped across the centre console, resting her head in Black's lap, and despite the way they bickered, I couldn't help feeling a twinge of jealousy at their closeness. What if I'd lost my only chance at that?

"Are you okay?" I asked Sofia again.

"I'm prepared."

That wasn't exactly my question, but I understood

why she didn't want to talk about it.

"I'm not. I'm still trembling inside from being on TV earlier. I went to the studio with Angie once, while she did an interview as Sapphire, and even that made me nervous."

"Thanks for doing it." Sofia managed a half smile. "I get that you don't like publicity."

"Crazy, huh? Angie loved it. I think that's why I enjoy writing so much—because I can spill my innermost thoughts onto paper, but nobody truly knows me."

"Most people I know wear masks. Few ever take them off."

"You included?" I asked, even though the answer was obvious.

"Me included."

We lapsed into silence, and Sofia settled into a zen-like state as darkness fell and another hour ticked by. Ben wasn't going to call, was he? Had he somehow missed the broadcasts? Black said a man on the run would keep up with the news, but what if he was wrong? Or what if Ben had run into Leroux again, or the—

It rang.

My phone rang.

"Unknown number," Black said. Luke had linked my mobile to Blackwood's computer system. "You planning to answer it?"

I unfroze and almost dropped the damn thing in my haste to snatch it up. Sofia gripped my other hand, nails digging into my palm.

Remember, deep breaths. Keep him talking.

"Gus?" Ben's voice came through on speaker, a little

quiet, a little tired, but unmistakably him.

"Ben? I've been so worried about you."

He laughed, but I could tell it was forced. "Isn't that my line? I saw you on the news today. What the hell was all that for?"

"The police made me do it. They said that if I cared about Angie then I'd do an appeal, and I could hardly refuse in case it made them suspicious. I'm so sorry."

My words made me feel ill. I didn't mind the occasional fib, but outright lying to the man I loved? What if he never forgave me?

In the front, Emmy and Black communicated with hand signals as a red dot appeared on Emmy's laptop screen. Black checked the mirror and pulled out smoothly into light traffic.

"Don't worry, *trésor*. I'm staying indoors in the daytime. How about you? Are you holding up okay?"

"Sort of. Mother became unbearable, so I'm staying with an old friend in London."

"Fuck. Gus, you shouldn't be in London. It's not safe."

"I remembered what you said, and I'm not going out alone."

Black swung left onto a side street, and I grasped the handle above the door so I didn't tip into Sofia's lap. Her expression had hardened into one of determination rather than the worry she'd been showing all day, while I fell apart inside.

"Are you in a car?" Ben asked. "I can hear traffic."

Think, Gus, think. "The flat I'm in is right next to the main road."

"Who knows you're there?"

"Just me and, uh, Sarah."

A pause. "Sarah?"

"We went to school together."

"Right. Well, you need to keep your location quiet. It's important."

"I will, but I'm worried about you. Do you have enough money? Food?"

"I'm okay at the moment." Another pause. "I can't talk for much longer. I just needed to hear your voice. To know you're okay."

"I miss you."

"And I miss you too, more than you could ever know."

"Please call me again. I need to hear you speak. I can't cope otherwise."

He didn't answer right away, and I thought he'd come up with an excuse, but he surprised me. "Okay, but it won't be for a few days. Love you, *mon cœur*. Stay strong."

"I love you too."

The line went dead, and I gulped in all the breaths I hadn't taken as the phone slipped out of my sweaty palm.

"Did we get him? Please say we got him."

Emmy motioned at me to stay quiet and cupped a hand over her earpiece. "We've got a visual. Team nine. They're following. Are you ready for this?"

No. "Yes."

One shot. I had one shot to convince him to come in. No easy task, because he'd realise as soon as I showed up that I'd betrayed him. He said he loved me, but would it be enough?

Black pulled into a parking space forty yards away from a junction. "Out of the car. In thirty seconds, he's going to walk around that corner."

I could barely stand as my feet hit the pavement, and I clutched at the door handle to stay upright. Emmy took her place behind me, and Sofia got out too. Ten. Nine. Eight...

Shit, there he was.

"Ben!"

He paused mid-stride, and I froze. Should I carry on walking, or would he run?

"Ben, it's me."

He looked behind him, then left and right, sizing up the situation. Oh, hell, this didn't look good.

"Ben, please just talk to me. We're trying to help."

His gaze zeroed in on Emmy, and he ran. Out of the corner of my eye, I saw her arm come up, and before I could properly register what was happening, she'd fired the gun in her hand.

"You shot him! You bitch! How could you—"

"Relax, it's only a tranquilliser. Get in the car."

Sofia dragged me into the backseat while Emmy sprinted off, and I glimpsed a smile on Black's face as he drove along behind, no doubt amused that his wife was doing all the hard work. Ben got about a hundred yards before his steps began to slow, and within seconds, Emmy had shoved him into a shop doorway.

Black leapt out of the car faster than I thought he'd be able to move, and almost before I could blink, he'd dumped a handcuffed and groggy Ben next to me in the backseat. Another click, and Ben's ankle was secured to a metal ring in the floor as well. Sofia climbed in on the other side of him, then we took off.

"Well, that went better than I thought," Emmy said.

"Better? You bloody shot him! How could that

possibly be a good thing?"

"No witnesses."

"I can't believe you!" I tried to hug Ben, but he kept flopping over, and he smelled pretty bad too. "I'm so sorry. I'm so, so sorry."

He groaned a little, but that was it until he keeled sideways. I tore off my cardigan, rolled it into a makeshift pillow, and tucked it into the crook of his neck, all the time giving Emmy death glares through the gap in the seats.

"Is this normal?" I asked.

"Reasonably so," Sofia said.

She'd gone back to looking worried.

"How can you stay so calm?"

"Would you rather we all panicked?" Black asked.

"Well, no..."

I trailed off as dark streets rushed past, the passers-by outside oblivious to the wanted man now unconscious in the backseat beside me.

As the adrenaline wore off, I came to the sickening realisation that the worst was yet to come. My focus on finding Ben had overshadowed the difficulties still facing us—proving his innocence, catching Leroux, and working out whether our fledgling relationship could survive the hell that bastard had unleashed on it.

But for now, I simply held Ben's hand. Sofia did the same on the other side, which I thought was sweet until I realised she'd done it to keep an eye on his pulse rather than out of compassion.

Did she care as much as I hoped she did? Because if I'd misjudged her, Ben's future was on the line.

CHAPTER 28

BACK IN THE underground garage, Ben was still breathing quietly as Black undid the ankle cuff, scooped him up, and carried him into the elevator. Ben wasn't a small man, but Black's muscles bulged as he lifted him like he weighed nothing.

"What happens now?" I asked, hurrying in behind them.

"We get him comfortable, and then we wake him up," Emmy replied.

"Comfortable" meant propping him up on an expensive-looking leather sofa and shackling his legs together. I hated to think what they'd consider uncomfortable.

"Is that really necessary?"

Gideon walked through the door, trailed by Xav. "For a man with Ben's skills, very much so, at least until we can explain what's going on. Otherwise, he may be tempted to fight first and ask questions later."

Could they blame him?

"Ready?" Emmy asked.

Sofia nodded, and I noticed her hand trembling as she reached out and injected a vial of clear liquid into Ben's forearm.

"What's that?"

"Just something to reverse the tranquilliser,"

Emmy told me. "A couple of minutes and he'll be wide awake."

He was. Wide awake and glaring at everyone with murder in his eyes. Except for me. No, when his eyes met mine, I got a sense of betrayal followed by sadness. I'd rather have had his anger.

Nobody spoke until Gideon stepped forward.

"Mr. Durant. It's been, what, two years?"

"Something like that." Ben spoke through gritted teeth, but he sounded more lucid than I thought he would.

"How are you feeling?"

"How the fuck do you think?"

Gideon merely nodded. "It's best if I explain a few things, but first I need to start with a question. Do you know where Guy Leroux is?"

Ben couldn't hide his surprise, but he quickly recovered and shook his head. "London somewhere. Always one step ahead of me."

"No matter. Now we don't have to look for you as well, we can concentrate our efforts on finding him."

"So what do you plan to do with me? Call the police?"

Gideon chuckled, and even managed to make that sound sexy. "*Non*. The police still...how do the English say it? Have their heads up their arses with regards to the Fordham case. Fixing that comes after dealing with Leroux in terms of priorities."

I couldn't keep my mouth shut any longer. "They know you didn't do it."

"Really? Then why did they snatch me off the street?"

"Because they're trying to help you. We all are."

"Funny way—"

Black waved him quiet. "You know who I am?"

Ben looked him up and down. "I can take a guess."

"Then you know that if I wanted you in jail, you'd be in jail. And if I wanted you dead, you'd be six fucking feet under. So let's stop with the 'he said, she said,' and concentrate on our primary objective, shall we? Where the hell is Leroux?"

The colour drained out of Ben's face. "Shit. What time is it? How long have I been out?"

"An hour, give or take."

Ben tried to get up, but the shackles meant he didn't get more than two steps before Black planted himself in the way.

"Sit."

I put my hands on my hips. "Don't speak to him that way."

But Ben had already sat, head in his hands. "I need to get back to Roxy."

The colour drained out of me too, and I sank down beside him. "Who the hell is Roxy?"

He managed half a smile, but it disappeared almost instantly. "Don't get upset. It's not like that. Leroux tried to kill her, and I've been doing my best to keep her safe. But I've fucking failed at that too because now I'm here and she's alone."

"Where is she?" Black asked.

Ben hesitated, and Black blew out a breath. Patience didn't seem to be his strong suit.

"If you don't tell us, we can't help her," Black said.

I watched Ben go through the same struggle as I did, only I'd agonised for weeks over whether to trust Blackwood and Ben didn't have that long. I reached for his hand, steeling myself for him to snatch it away and beyond relieved when he didn't.

"They're good people. Please let them help."

"She's in a bedsit in Peckham."

"Address?"

Ben mumbled it. "But I should go. She's been through hell, and she's scared of strangers. Especially men."

Black's voice lost a little of its hard edge. "We'll take it easy. Does she have a phone?"

Ben nodded.

"Then call her."

When Ben struggled to get his own phone out of his jacket pocket, I leaned in to help him, heart thumping as I got close. At least he didn't shuffle away from me.

Rather than try to hold the phone to his ear with two cuffed hands, he put it on speaker and laid it on the table as it rang.

"Ben?" Roxy's voice shook when she answered.

"Yes, it's me. I...er, I got delayed. But I bumped into some old friends, and they've offered to help us, okay? They're on their way to pick you up."

"Are you sure? I thought we were on our own."

"So did I. But someone's smiling down on us today." He met my eyes as he echoed my earlier words. "They're good people. We need to let them help."

He hung up and closed his eyes for a second as he took a shuddering breath. A tear ran down my cheek, and I quickly wiped it away before he saw.

"It'll be okay, Midnight," I whispered.

Ben opened his eyes again. "The key's in my pocket."

"Gus, find it. Emmy, take Gideon and Xav and get

over there."

Black left the room with his phone clamped to his ear, followed by his chosen team, leaving me alone with Ben and Sofia. An uncomfortable silence reigned, and I needed to say something, anything, to break it.

"I thought Black didn't like Gideon being near Emmy?"

"He doesn't," Sofia said. "But he'll always pick the best team for the job. Work comes before his personal feelings."

How strange it must be to be able to tuck your emotions away into a box like that. In the past few weeks, I'd been through agony, despair, and desperate sadness, but no matter how bad it got, the only thing worse than having those feelings would be to have none at all.

"I pity him for that."

She didn't reply before Black came back in and sat on the coffee table opposite Ben. "They're on their way. If I un-cuff you, are you going to try anything stupid?"

Ben shook his head, then stretched his limbs once Black had freed them. I didn't know whether Ben would want me to move away or not, but I did know I wanted to be close to him. So I stayed put.

Ruth brought in tea and snacks, and as Ben ate one sandwich then another, I realised how much weight he'd lost. The beard hid the gauntness of his face, but when he took his jacket off, there was no mistaking how thin he'd got. I longed to wrap my arms around him, but I forced myself to hold back.

"We need to go over the case," Black said. "We've put some information together, but we don't know all the history. Apparently, a certain French senator is rather proficient at burying it."

"That bastard. His son was supposed to be locked up indefinitely, did you know that?"

"Yes. We also know Leroux senior pulled strings to get him out. But we'll deal with him later. Guy Leroux is our current problem, not Bertrand. Now, can you start from the beginning?"

Ben talked us through the story, and between detective work and guesswork, it seemed we'd already unearthed most of it. Ben had walked in on the most heinous of acts, did the right thing by standing up for two women in trouble, then lost his job and got dragged through the courts afterwards. Black only interrupted once, to tell us Emmy's team was on their way back with Roxy, but afterwards, he did have one question.

"What happened to the girl? We understand she's missing."

"I don't know."

"Really? Because if I had to guess, I'd say she was somewhere near Mougins."

Ben stared at him for a second, then closed his eyes. "Fuck."

"What happened?"

"Is she safe?"

"We've got no reason to believe otherwise."

Ben sighed. "I couldn't leave her in Africa. After her mother died, she had nobody. When I couldn't get her to France through proper channels, I spent the last of my savings on smuggling her in."

"Where is she?"

"With an old friend of mine from the legion. He and his wife tried to have kids for years, but nothing worked. We timed Kali's arrival over the border with their move to Mougins. Everyone there believes she's their daughter, and she won't say otherwise. She's the brightest kid I've ever met."

The pride in his voice when he spoke about her was evident, and I fell in love with him just a little bit more. Before I could stop myself, I slipped an arm around his waist.

How would he respond?

I held my breath as he reciprocated and then leaned over to kiss my hair, and I knew at that moment we'd be okay. No matter what we had to face, we'd do it together.

And later. We'd do it later. Our tender moment was interrupted as the door burst open. Emmy came through first, followed by Gideon with the blonde woman from the hospital cradled in his arms. Ben leapt up and crouched at her side as Gideon lowered her to the sofa.

"Are you okay?"

She nodded, looking around the room, wide-eyed.

Black didn't come any closer, but left it to Ben and Gideon to offer some comfort. In the hospital, Roxy had been wearing a short skirt and bandeau top, but in the pair of baggy jogging bottoms and oversized sweatshirt she had on now, she looked even more vulnerable.

"Do we need a doctor?" Black asked.

Her eyes focused in on him, and she shook her head.

"Sure? I can get someone to come here, no questions asked."

Ben answered for her. "Roxy got through four years

of a medical degree. She's been keeping her wounds clean. Mine too."

Emmy raised an eyebrow, and I imagined my face showed surprise too. How did she end up here, in this state?

The door opened again, and Ruth walked in, wearing make-up I'd never seen her in before and an elegant black dress. Not her usual attire. Black had obviously called her back from somewhere.

He jerked his head towards Roxy, but Ruth already knew what to do.

"Oh, you poor love. Let's take you upstairs and get you cleaned up. You look like you could do with a good meal in you as well."

Gideon helped Roxy to stand, then Ruth took over, leading her from the room in the kindly manner my own mother had never managed to exhibit.

Then the room went quiet again. What now?

"Everybody sit," Black said. "And we'll continue our discussion."

CHAPTER 29

"WHAT HAPPENED TO Roxy? How did she get from studying medicine to that?" Black jerked his thumb towards the door she'd just walked out of.

"I only know the bare bones," Ben said. "Funnily enough, she doesn't enjoy talking about it. Her father owed money to some guy, and they couldn't afford to repay it. The guy told her she could earn enough to cover it by modelling in London over her summer break, only when she got here, another man took her passport and forced her into the sex trade."

"Who?" Gideon asked.

He looked different, and at first I found it difficult to put my finger on why. The only evidence of the evening's escapades was a smudge of dirt near the collar of his white shirt. Then I realised. It was his eyes. Earlier they'd twinkled with an easygoing charm, but now darkness radiated from their depths.

"I don't know who. We've been too concerned with surviving to trawl through our personal histories."

"No matter. We will find out."

The way he said the words sent a shiver down my spine. What did he plan to do?

Three sofas were arranged around the coffee table in a U shape, and Black settled onto the one opposite us. I expected Emmy to sit next to him, but she squashed next to Sofia instead and wrapped an arm around her shoulders. Gideon leaned against the wall, more interested in his phone.

"So," Black said to Ben. "Now your immediate survival isn't at stake, I'm curious about your history. What made you join the legion?"

"Why does that matter?"

"The lifestyle? The discipline? A burning desire to learn French? Or were you running from something?"

"That's none of your business."

Again, Black ignored him. "For me, it was the last option, except I joined the Navy. It was either that or go and live with an aunt who hated me. Sooner or later, I'd have ended up in prison for murder. Come on, which one was it for you?"

"Yeah, I was running. Happy?"

"From what? A girl? A guy? You get into trouble?"

"My parents. Well, my mother. Look, how is any of this relevant?"

I understood where Black was heading, and my hand involuntarily tightened around Ben's. Out of the corner of my eye, Sofia looked so tense a single touch would shatter her.

"Just humour me. What was bad enough that you'd sign up for hell?"

Ben chewed at a piece of skin on his bottom lip. Would he refuse to answer? I only knew his mother lied to him, not what about, and Mrs. Durham had been nothing but kind to me as a little girl. Whatever she'd done to upset Ben, it must have been serious.

A minute ticked past, then two, and finally, he came to a decision.

"If you want to know that badly, I'll tell you on one

condition."

"Which is?" Black asked.

"You help me look for my sister."

Shit. He knew. He bloody knew! Sofia looked like she was about to cry while Black's lips curved slightly in satisfaction. The manipulative bastard understood exactly what he was doing—arranging his pieces on the board and waiting for Ben to walk blindly into a checkmate.

"Agreed. Now, satisfy our curiosity."

I leaned into Ben to show some support, and his arm tightened around my waist. Please, let this turn out well.

"It happened on my eighteenth birthday. My father was on a business trip, and my mother had gone with him like she usually did. I'd stayed at home, but I didn't plan on being there for much longer. I'd spent two years waiting tables to save up some cash, and I wanted to go back to Sandlebury, convince Gus we were meant to be together, and take her somewhere nice." He glanced at me. "France, ironically. I'd seen the French Riviera on one of those travel programmes."

"I'd have gone," I whispered, and got rewarded with a smile.

"Only when I looked for my passport, I couldn't find it. Turned the damn house upside down, and that's when I found the birth certificates, one for me and one for my sister, although I didn't realise it at the time."

"What were the names?" Black asked.

"Benjamin and Sofia Darke."

Bloody hell! The fourth name Logan had referred to. Another set of BD initials.

"Did you ask your mother about it?"

"When she got back that evening. At first she was shocked, then she got defensive. Told me she'd taken me away from my real father so we could have a better life. Apparently, he used to hit her, and when I asked about Sofia, she said she couldn't cope with two kids, so she'd left her behind because she was his favourite. A daddy's girl, she said. That bitch left my sister behind with a violent asshole and didn't tell me about it for sixteen fucking years."

"What did you do? Did you look for her?"

"Of course I did. First I went for Gus, only I thought she knocked me back. Turns out *her* mother had a problem with telling the truth as well. And when I packed to leave home, I found my damn passport in my sock drawer, so I flew to America. The address Mum gave me for our old house didn't exist anymore. The whole street's disappeared under a shopping mall, and nobody in the area remembered me or Sofia or our parents. I spent every penny I had on searching, and when the money ran out, I didn't want to go home. I needed a new start."

"So you joined the legion?"

Ben gave a hollow laugh. "*Legio patria nostra.* Or at least until they fucked me over as well."

"We'll help with that."

"And with my sister. We had a deal. I can't sleep properly at night from worrying about what happened to her. I don't even know if she's alive or dead."

I longed to tell him, but I didn't dare to interrupt Black. He was a man who liked to be in complete control, that much was obvious.

At least he didn't keep Ben waiting long. "She's alive."

"What?" Ben went rigid as he stared at Black. "You know about Sofia? You know where she is?"

"I didn't come to England to help you. I came to help her. When Augusta's father hired Blackwood, your DNA tripped a flag in our system."

"Where is she?" Ben's voice shook with emotion. "Please, tell me where she is."

"Right here," Emmy said.

Time slowed down as Ben swung around to face her and Sofia.

"Ben, meet Sofia."

"Are you serious?"

Emmy nodded.

Ben stood slowly, as did Sofia, and before I could blink he had her in his arms, squeezing until she thumped him on the back to let go.

Even then, he didn't release her, just leaned back to get a better look.

"I don't... I can't... I've got no idea what to say," he muttered, and then both of them were crying.

Xav wandered in and took in the scene. "Someone told him, then?"

"Nah, Fia choked on a gummy bear and Ben's busy fucking up the Heimlich manoeuvre," Emmy said.

Xav gallantly raised his middle finger. "Fia, what's with all the tears? Isn't this supposed to be a happy thing?"

That earned him the bird as well. After a few minutes, during which Mika's "Happy Ending" played on repeat in my head, they finally loosened their hold on each other, and I scooched over on the sofa to give them both room to sit down. Ben kept one arm across Sofia's shoulders and tucked the other one back around my waist where it belonged.

"I can't believe it. The two girls I wanted most in my life, and they're both here with me."

"I'm not sure whether this is a champagne moment or not," Emmy said, looking at me. "It hasn't been an easy road to get here."

She was right; it hadn't. But if Angie were still here, I liked to think she'd have put her party frock on. And with all the difficulties surely still to come, I felt it was important to celebrate the small victories.

"Perhaps just one bottle?"

She raised an eyebrow at Xav. "Would you mind?"

He gave a brief nod and slipped out of the room. Ben couldn't take his eyes off Sofia, and when I studied them both together, I saw the similarities. Their dark hair. The colour of their eyes. The shape of their mouths. There were differences too—Ben's nose was straight while Sofia's had a cute little ski jump at the end, and Ben's jaw was a little squarer.

"I've finally found you," Ben whispered. "Tell me I'm not dreaming this."

"I'm really here," Sofia said, her voice croaky. "I've been terrified for the past few days in case Leroux got to you before we could. Emmy's sorry she shot you, by the way."

"I am?" Emmy asked. "Oh, yeah, right. I'm sorry I shot you. Look on the bright side—at least I didn't use a real bullet."

"You're Emmy Black?"

"The one and only."

"I always thought if you caught up with me, I'd end up in a body bag."

She threw her head back and laughed. "My

reputation precedes me. Seriously, though, I'm not that scary."

Xav arrived back with seven champagne flutes and two bottles of bubbly. "Ignore her—she is. I don't know where Gideon's gone, but if he doesn't come back, I'm drinking his share."

"I suspect he went to check on Roxy," Black said.

"What's with him and her?" Sofia asked. "He kept looking at her funny. Like he actually cared."

Emmy shrugged. "Dunno. He picked her up and carried her out of the bedsit, and she sat on his lap in the car all the way back."

Xav popped the cork on the first bottle, and Cristal fizzed onto the parquet floor. He poured, we drank, and before long, he'd headed out to fetch a third bottle. In between sips, Ben and Sofia spilled snippets of their lives and found they had things in common. They'd both travelled a lot, each spoke several languages, and neither of them liked ice cream, although I couldn't understand why.

"It's too cold," Ben said. "I'd rather have cake."

"Ice cream reminds me of things I'd rather forget."

"What things?"

"People."

"Not from your childhood? Were things okay at home? You know, when you got left behind? I always hoped Mum was right and our dad looked after you."

"Things...weren't good, and I hope that witch burns in hell."

Ben closed his eyes, and I began to regret drinking all the champagne. "Tell me he didn't hit you?" he whispered.

"No, he never hit me. He loved me. In every way a

grown man shouldn't love a little girl."

"Fuck."

"Until I was nine years old, I didn't realise it was weird for daddies to kiss their daughters goodnight with tongues." She spoke matter-of-factly, far less emotional than I'd seen her in the last few days.

Emmy was beside Sofia in an instant and wrapped her up in her arms. "Fia, stop."

"If I don't say these things now, I never will."

Ben swallowed, tension radiating from his body. "Did he...?"

"Put it this way, I was the only girl in high school who looked forward to her period each month, because it meant he'd leave me alone for five days."

Ben's fingers dug into my hip so hard it hurt, but I didn't say anything, not when Sofia was pouring out her pain beside us. The poor girl must have been bottling it up for years.

And Ben's fury leached from every pore. "I'll kill him. I swear; I'll kill him."

Sofia smiled, closing her eyes as she did so at some secret thought. "No need to bother. I already took care of the problem."

CHAPTER 30

AFTER SOFIA'S DRUNKEN...confession? Fantasy? Whichever, the party went a little flat.

"Do you really think she could have killed him?" I asked Ben quietly as we climbed the stairs to the second floor.

When Emmy had asked what we wanted to do about sleeping arrangements, I'd offered to share my room, and his eyes had glistened as he accepted.

"I don't know. She's my sister, and I don't know her at all. But with the company she keeps... Maybe."

A shudder ran through me. "I'm just going to pretend I didn't hear her say anything about it."

"That's probably for the best."

We reached the door to the room where I'd been staying, a luxuriously appointed double with its own bathroom and a view over the small but perfectly maintained garden at the rear. Only the second time I'd spent the whole night with a man, and I was going to do it in a virtual stranger's house.

"Are you sure about this?" Ben asked.

I nodded. Being with Ben was my only light in the dark maze I was lost in, and I needed him to guide me out.

"Three suitcases?" he asked when we got inside. "You've moved in permanently?"

"No, of course not. Dorothy just threw a few things together for me."

He didn't say anything, just chuckled.

"What's that supposed to mean?"

"I'll have to teach you to pack light before I get a hernia carrying your stuff." He yawned, then looked around the rest of the room. "You mind if I take a shower? I'm a bit... You deserve better."

"I don't mind what you look like."

"I do."

He still had pride.

"There are fresh towels in the bathroom."

As the water ran, I rummaged through my suitcases for a suitable nightie. Three suitcases, and all I had were flannel pyjamas and one comfortable old T-shirt. Oh dear. Did I dare to go naked? Or perhaps I could leave my underwear on? Mind you, I'd reverted to the white cotton for comfort after Ben left, so that wasn't much better. And I needed to brush my teeth, and my hair was a mess, and...

Ben walked out wearing a towel low around his hips, and my heart leapt into my mouth. He'd lost too much weight, but apart from that he looked so deliciously edible I licked my lips before I realised what I was doing.

"Uh, I just need a turn," I squeaked, then ran past him and closed the door.

Now what? In the dark with him in control, I hadn't been so worried, but today with emotions running so high? What if I didn't perform up to scratch? My hands shook as I squeezed toothpaste onto the brush.

In the end, I decided to strip out of my undies and put on the robe hanging on the back of the bathroom door. Not exactly sexy, but it gave me options.

I gingerly cracked the door open. "Ben?"

Nothing. Nothing but his steady breathing as he lay on top of the covers, still wearing the towel. I'd been thinking my dirty thoughts while the poor man was exhausted, and I felt terrible for it. What should I do? I didn't want to wake him, but I couldn't leave him like that. Luckily, the bed was a king, so I snuggled against his side, folded the duvet over both of us, and closed my eyes.

A soft kiss on my temple made my eyelids flutter open, and I woke to find Ben leaning over me. Or did I? Could I still be dreaming?

I reached a hand out and discovered three things. Firstly, I wasn't dreaming. Secondly, the towel had disappeared at some point during the night. And thirdly? Well, it seemed Ben was happy to see me.

He groaned as my hand connected, and I snatched it back. "Sorry."

"What are you sorry for? I've dreamed of waking up next to you since... Let's just say it's been more years than I should admit. You can put your hand wherever you like."

The robe had fallen open, and he reached down and pulled the belt away completely, then ran a rough hand up my side, hitting a ticklish spot that made me writhe against him.

"Good morning, *mon cœur*."

"Good morning, *ma bite*."

He burst into laughter. "You remembered?"

I did, and I felt extraordinarily proud. And my hand couldn't help wandering back to the object of my affections. The shaft was a contradiction as I stroked it, an oxymoron if you like—so velvety smooth yet so hard at the same time. A drop of pre-cum oozed from the tip, and I smoothed it around the head with my thumb.

With my eyes closed, I became Midnight's girl again. The one emboldened by the dark, eager to try all the things she'd read about but never experienced. Barely thinking, I stuck my thumb in my mouth and tasted him. His salty, sweet, earthy taste tingled on my tongue, and I wanted more. No, I wanted everything.

"Gus, I don't have a condom."

"I found a box in the nightstand drawer. I'm sure nobody will mind if we borrow one."

Okay, three. Ben flipped me onto my back first, and shattered me twice before his release warmed my insides. Then he helped me on top of him, where the sight of him underneath me as I found a rhythm and his hands gripping my hips as I rose and fell gave me the hardest, most delicious orgasm of my life.

"I'm a sweaty mess," I whispered afterwards.

"Wrong. You need to modify that sentence. Try 'I'm a sexy sweaty mess.' Or 'I'm your sexy sweaty mess.' Or maybe 'I'm your sexy hot mess.'"

"All of the above."

"In that case, we should take a shower."

"Together?"

"Dirty girls need help washing."

I rolled out of bed right away, a testament to just how filthy I was feeling. "What are you waiting for?"

"Bloody hell, you're hornier than I ever dreamed you'd be."

Him too. We got as far as the bathroom vanity, where I made the mistake of pausing to glance in the mirror. My hair was wild, and what was that on my neck? A bite mark? I bent forward to take a closer look, and Ben took full advantage of the position, pinning me in place with his hips as he traced my jawline with the tip of his tongue.

"On second thoughts, maybe we'll do it here. I like the idea of watching you watch me."

I gasped as he pushed inside me and grasped the marble edge of the vanity as he began to thrust. The image of him cupping my breast to suck on the nipple was the most erotic thing I'd ever seen. Move over *Fifty Shades of Grey*—Ben beat Christian hands down, quite literally, as his fingers skated over my stomach in search of my *chatte*.

A couple of rough strokes was all it took before I collapsed forward and almost knocked myself out on the mixer tap. Only Ben's quick thinking and quicker arms saved me.

"Careful, beautiful. I don't want another trip to the hospital this week."

"Sorry. Brain broken."

He silenced me with a kiss as he thrust harder, harder, then squeezed me tight against him as he came. We both stood there, staring at our reflections as our souls came back to our bodies. I certainly wasn't red-carpet ready, but it didn't matter. From my pink-tinged cheeks to my pert nipples to the gorgeous man pressed up against me, I'd never felt more beautiful in my life.

Ben lifted me into the shower. Whoever designed the house either had geriatrics or bathroom sex in mind because the double-width cubicle came complete with a seat at one end and several sturdy grab-rails. I tested the strength of one and looked at Ben hopefully.

"Nothing left in the tank, *mon cœur*. You'll have to give me a few minutes."

He sank onto the seat and groaned as he leaned back against the tile.

"I'm a little sore as well."

"Fuck. Did I hurt you?"

"No! I just feel...used, but in a good way."

"We need to take it gently."

"No, we don't. I can't get enough of you, and I don't care if I feel tender."

"But I do. Let's try something else instead."

Something else turned out to be him washing my hair and soaping every inch of my body while he peppered me with kisses. I was already in heaven when he dropped to his knees and showed me the importance of cleaning every last hidden inch.

"I love you," I gasped as he took me over the edge.

I could taste myself on his lips as he pressed them against mine. "Love you too, Augusta."

After that many orgasms, I was ready to collapse back into bed again, but a knock at the door made me clutch my hands over my bits even though it was still closed.

"Dudes, we've got work to do," Emmy yelled. "You can fuck later."

"Oh, shit," I muttered. "Do you think she heard us?"

Ben grinned. "Probably."

"How are we supposed to face them?"

"I'm never going to be ashamed of anything I do with you. Hold your head high, and we'll walk in side by side."

I looked down at my attire, or rather the lack of it. "Perhaps we'd better get dressed first?"

His smile faltered. "Yeah. I've only got yesterday's clothes."

"We'll get you some new ones. I could call... No, I can't call Dorothy. We'll sort something out."

"They just need a wash."

"I'll ask Ruth to show me where the machine is."

"You don't need to run around after me, *trésor*." He straightened the duvet, then bent down to pick up last night's condoms from the floor.

"We need to flush those. Emmy said... Well, she thinks that maybe Leroux stole the ones we used at midnight and used them to frame you for Angie's murder."

"I'd come to the same conclusion. There's no other way. The only girl I've been with since the Leroux thing kicked off is you, and when I jack off, I tend to do it in the shower."

A little of the tension I'd been carrying around with me seeped away. True, we'd never discussed exclusivity, but if he'd told me there was another girl involved, I'd have been devastated. But there was only me. And the thought of him touching himself in the shower with water streaming down his naked body made a mess in my knickers. Dammit.

Another soft knock interrupted us, and we both stared at the door.

"I'll get it," Ben said, doing up his jeans.

I tugged a T-shirt on as he let Sofia in. She hesitated to step over the threshold and held out a couple of carrier bags. "Here. I thought you might be short of clothes."

He took the gift with a quiet, "Thanks," but she didn't move.

"I'm sorry about last night. I shouldn't have unloaded all of that on you."

"Don't apologise. I'd rather know. I'm just sorry I wasn't there to stop him. If there's anything I can do to make up for it, just say the word."

"Until I got the call about the DNA match, I'd buried it, and I'll do the same again."

"Is that healthy?" I blurted, realising too late I shouldn't be listening in to a private conversation.

"It's better than it preying on my mind every second of every fucking day and night."

She smiled, and it chilled me to the bone.

Ben ignored the daggers coming from her eyes. "It can help to talk to someone."

"You think? My ex-employer sent me to a therapist once. I was so fucked in the head I didn't realise she reported everything I told her back to them, and they used that knowledge to their advantage. Damn it, I'm running my mouth again. Look, don't worry about me. We're here to sort out your problems."

"But—"

"Forget it. When you're ready, we're having a meeting downstairs."

She turned on her heel and disappeared along the corridor, her footsteps muffled by the thick carpet. I couldn't deny she scared me, but underneath her tough exterior ran a river of vulnerability. I got the impression a lot of people had hurt her, not just her father.

"She's not how I thought she'd be," Ben whispered.

"I don't understand her."

"Me neither, and I'm not sure anybody truly does."

CHAPTER 31

"WHY IS IT called Project Carbon, do you think?" I asked Ben as he held the door to the conference room open for me.

Xav's voice came from behind us. "Emmy's idea. It's because of the DNA, as in Ben's a carbon copy of Sofia."

Really? "They're not very much alike."

"They've got more in common than you might imagine."

What was that supposed to mean? I didn't get time to consider as Gideon walked up behind us, clutching a steaming mug of coffee. Oh, how I craved a cup of full-bodied roast, but we were already late.

I didn't miss Black's glower from the front of the room as Gideon took a seat next to Emmy. Sofia was already ensconced on the other side of her, and Emmy smiled as Sofia leaned in close and murmured a few words I couldn't make out.

Black flicked a switch, and the lights dimmed. "Shall we start? Forensics first."

When he spoke, everybody paid attention. He was a man of few words, and he didn't waste any of them. The way he moved struck me as, well, like a caged tiger full of pent-up energy waiting to be unleashed at a second's notice when the moment arose.

"We've got some reports back, and the lawyers have

evidence to work with now. We insisted the police examine not just the DNA from the semen in Angelica Fordham's body, but the rest of the sample. The cell walls within it show signs of damage, indicative of being frozen and thawed."

"Do you think that will stand up in court?" Ben asked.

"It's not going to court." Black spoke as if the matter were a simple fact.

"How do you know?"

"Trust me. And even if it did, the answer's yes. We've recreated the process under lab conditions with the same results."

"What, with a sample of—?"

"Exactly that," Nye said. "Emmy sent a memo round saying the first man to take the fruits of his labours down to the lab would get an extra week of paid holiday. Every toilet stall was full within seconds."

Gideon took a sip of his coffee. "*S'il vous plaît*, that is not an image I want in my mind."

Emmy grinned. "I, on the other hand..."

"Enough." This time Black treated both of them to a sharp look. "Forensics. The police have also reviewed all trace evidence at the scene and identified a single light-brown hair. The colour's a match for Leroux, but we'll need his DNA to test against. Renard?"

"I'll see what I can do. I also need to add another item to our agenda."

"Yes?"

"Leroux senior. He's been out of favour with the powers that be for a while now, and the incident with Guy didn't help. The xenophobic rhetoric he's been spouting is inciting tensions in Paris and the surrounding areas, especially around Strasbourg Saint-Denis, and it's been decreed that we do something about the problem."

"Such as?"

"Removing him from a position of power. My bosses haven't voiced a preference on the method."

Black glanced across at me, and I dreaded to think what he was planning.

"We'll take this outside the meeting." Still, he wrote the name Bertrand Leroux under Guy's on the screen, with a number two next to it. "Anything else?"

Gideon got up and walked to the front, then motioned to Black for his stylus. "May I?"

Black hesitated a second before handing it over, and Gideon's neat printing soon filled the screen as item number three: Roksana Bartosz.

Black raised an eyebrow, questioning.

"Leroux wasn't the only man to fuck her over."

"Elaborate."

"Roksana Bartosz was blackmailed, trafficked, and sold nightly by two animals thinking only of their personal gain. She spent last night scrubbing herself in the shower until her skin went raw, then crying into her pillow because two *bâtards putain* considered her life to be worth less than a car or a television. And right now, they're probably *un peu énervé* because they've lost a piece of merchandise, but tomorrow it won't matter to them so much because there are plenty more girls where she came from."

Silence fell as Black mulled over Gideon's words. His expression gave nothing away. Finally, he responded with a single nod. "Task number three is Roksana Bartosz."

Up until now, I'd been guilty of concentrating on Ben and his problems. His return, Angelica, our reunion, and the night we spent together. But he wasn't the only victim in this mess, and my heart went out to Roksana.

"Do you need me for this bit?" I whispered to Ben.

Black must have had superhuman hearing as well as his ability to intimidate and a weird sixth sense when it came to predicting people's actions.

"You've played your part, and I'm sure Roksana could use a friend."

Ben gave my hand one last squeeze as I slipped out of the room. I wasn't sure what to say to Roxy, but above all, I wanted her to understand that people here cared about her. Even Black in his own twisted way. I didn't know what item three on the board would entail, and deep down, I didn't want to know.

I found her in the kitchen with Ruth, staring into space as she ignored the bowl of fruit in front of her. She looked different. Not her eyes—they still harboured the same dark pain I'd glimpsed when Gideon helped her into the house last night—but she'd been cleaned up on the outside, and if you only glanced at her, apart from the scratches on her face, she was just another pretty girl who'd made her home in London.

"Hi," I said.

She took a few seconds to focus on me. "Hi."

"I'm Augusta. We haven't been introduced, but I'm staying here too. I'm Ben's..." What label did I put on it? Despite everything we'd done, it was too soon to call myself his girlfriend. "I'm with Ben."

"Then you're lucky. He's a good man."

Shit. I hoped she didn't think I'd come just to stake

my claim on him. "The best. But he's busy in a meeting so I thought I'd get some breakfast. Is the fruit good?"

She glanced at her bowl, which looked untouched, and shrugged.

"I can get you whatever you'd like, lovey," Ruth said. "Fruit, cereal, pastries. Or something cooked?"

"Some fruit would be wonderful."

Now I was here, I didn't know what to say. From what Gideon said, Roxy had been through hell, and any words seemed inadequate. "Do you have enough clothes? Toiletries? I've got spare I could lend you."

Even as I spoke, I realised how stupid I sounded. She was at least six inches taller than me and a heck of a lot thinner. My knee-length skirts would look like minis on her.

"I don't know."

Ruth put a bowl of mixed fruit down in front of me together with a pot of yogurt. "We've sorted all that out; don't you worry. What Roxy needs is a bit of company."

Really? She barely glanced in my direction, suddenly more interested in the bowl of fruit she was stirring. Ruth came closer and lowered her voice.

"She might not say much at the moment, but she knows you're there. Just be a friend to her, because I suspect she's got precious few of them."

I ate my fruit, and Roxy chewed a few pieces of hers before the spoon clattered into the bowl.

"Why don't you girls relax in the lounge?" Ruth suggested, and I nodded, forcing a smile. "I'll show you through."

"Good idea."

Roxy followed us silently, hugging a cushion to her stomach as she squashed herself onto the far end of the sofa.

"Any preferences on what we watch?" I asked, picking up the TV remote.

As I didn't have a clue what to say, perhaps a little mindless entertainment would help?

Her only response was a barely perceptible shake of the head.

I flipped through a hundred channels, searching for a suitable movie. A romance? Nope, that would rub salt into her wounds. Not a thriller either—too violent. I settled on *Billy Elliott* in the end. Surely that couldn't offend?

We'd almost got to the final credits when I felt her eyes on me.

"What's going to happen?" she whispered.

"What do you mean?"

"To me. What's going to happen to me?"

"I don't know."

"Will I be able to stay here tonight?"

After what Black and Gideon had said earlier, I couldn't imagine them kicking her out. "Of course."

She seemed to relax infinitesimally.

"Do you want me to ask the person who owns this place about the future?"

Another quick nod.

"I'll be back."

Now, where should I start? The conference room. I needed to find my way back to the conference room, and I could wait outside until Emmy came out. Technically it was Black's house too, but I was too nervous to hold an actual conversation with him in case he laser beamed me with his eyes or something.

Only when I found the home of Project Carbon,

after three wrong turns and an accidental trip to the gym, the room lay empty.

"Looking for Ben?" Emmy's voice from behind made me jump.

"You, actually."

"Yeah?"

"Roksana's nervous about how long she can stay here."

"As long as she needs. You want me to talk to her?"

"Please."

Except when we got back to the lounge, Emmy stopped at the door, and I bumped into her. Peering around the door jamb, I spotted a man seated in my spot on the sofa, his body angled towards Roxy as they talked.

Emmy took two steps backwards. "Gideon," she murmured. "Did Roxy say much to you earlier?"

"Hardly a word."

"Yet she's speaking to him. Let's leave them to it."

As we walked back through the house, she elaborated. "He knew more about her in the meeting this morning than anyone, which means he was talking to her last night as well. I think he likes her."

"Gideon? Really?"

She chuckled. "Yeah, I'm surprised too. But don't worry. He may be a cad, but he won't hurt her."

"I'm not worried. I just never imagined a man like him..." I trailed off because I didn't want to insult either of them.

"With a girl like her? Don't be fooled by his charms and the fact that his dress sense is sharper than James Bond's. He's a snake underneath, but he also understands people. He's got a way of digging out your thoughts without you even realising it."

I recalled Sofia's words from this morning, about her therapist taking advantage. "And how will he use that information?"

Emmy thought for a minute. "With her, I reckon he'll use it the right way."

Ben was in the kitchen with the other men and Sofia, sitting at the table eating a croissant. When he saw me, he held out an arm, and I stepped into his protective embrace.

"How are things?" I asked.

"Okay." He searched my face, a little wary. "We've made a plan."

Why did I get the feeling I wasn't going to like it? "Which is?"

"We know Leroux's in South London, but it's hard to get a bead on him. Gideon reckons his father's connections are helping him out."

"Bloody politicians."

"He's rotten to the core from what we've seen, and his son's out of the same mould. Anyway, we're going to try and draw Leroux junior out."

"How?"

"I'll ask a few questions of people we think he might know. Rattle some cages, that sort of thing."

The meaning of that dawned on me, and anger welled up inside. Anger at Black, who I bet came up with that stupid idea, and at Ben for agreeing to go along with it.

"They're using you as bait? That's your plan?"

"The longer he's out there, the more chance he'll hurt somebody else. I got close when he was with Roxy and look what happened—we got into a fight, and he stuck a knife in her thigh. He gave me the choice of going after him or saving her, and there was only one decision I could make. What if he tries that again?"

That sick bastard. "He might not."

"We can't take that chance. Black and Gideon both want him off the streets as soon as possible, and I agree with them."

"How did you find him the first time?"

"Women. Leroux can't keep away from them, and he doesn't play nicely. I asked around the red-light districts until I found an area where three girls had got hurt in the last month by a man matching his description."

"And then you found Roxy?"

"Five minutes too late. I showed a picture of Leroux around, and one of the girls Roxy worked with said she'd just left with him."

He clenched his fists, and the shudder that ran through him said he blamed himself.

"It wasn't your fault."

"He only came to England to find me."

"From what you've said, he hurts girls wherever he goes. If not London, it would have been Paris, or Strasbourg, or Cannes. How did he trace you to Sandlebury, anyway?"

"It must have been through my bank account. That's the only way I can think of. I went to the branch in town to pay my wages in every week or two, and he must have followed me back." He closed his eyes for a second. "I thought I saw him once, only for a second, but I figured paranoia was getting to me because he was supposed to be in the secure hospital. Gus, I'm so sorry I brought him into your life."

"Stop apologising. This was all on him." My knees weakened as I pictured Angie's body lying on that sofa, but I pushed the image away together with my tears. I could grieve later. For now, I needed to stay strong for Ben.

"I wish I'd done things differently. Been more careful."

"You can start now. What if this plan to find Leroux goes wrong and you get hurt?"

He reached out and cupped my cheek with his hand. "I've got people supporting me now, and they're the best in the world at this job. This'll be over before you know it, you'll see."

I sank onto his knees and pressed my lips into the crook of his neck. "I'm scared," I mumbled against his warm skin.

"Me too," he whispered back. "But this is nothing compared to the fear I felt when I thought I'd lost you."

CHAPTER 32

OVER THE NEXT two weeks, the crazy world I'd been thrust into the middle of became the new normal. Life at Albany House settled into a routine.

I didn't hear a peep from my mother, but Dorothy texted every day to check I was okay, and Father showed his newly found caring side by calling a couple of times a week, meaning I felt both guilty for lying to him and sad because I couldn't go home to visit.

"I've cut down on the trips abroad," he told me. "After all these years, I've decided to start delegating more."

"That's good. You've always worked too hard."

"Funny, I always thought the best thing I could do for my family would be to provide for them, but now...now I realise I should have given time rather than money." His breath hitched. "I just wish I could turn back the clock, Gussie."

Dammit, now I was tearing up as well. "You did your best."

"But it wasn't good enough. I know I can't make up for the lost years, but do you think we could spend more time together?"

What he was really asking was whether I'd move back home. "How about we meet up for lunch soon? In the next week or two?"

"I'd like that." Disappointment tinged his words. "Just call my sec...me. Call me when you've got some free time, and I'll be there."

"I will. How's Mother?"

"She's...difficult. I got her to speak to a counsellor, but after three sessions she refused to go back, and she's not happy about the men Blackwood have sent to keep an eye on things."

"What men?"

"They said there's a chance Davies might come back here."

Not Beau, but Leroux. Bloody Leroux. Why couldn't he do the honourable thing for once and hand himself in? Then I could start repairing the ties with my family, and I wouldn't need to spend the day on tenterhooks waiting for Ben to come...back. I almost said home. I was feeling more comfortable at Albany House than I had a right to.

We still hadn't spoken about the future. What would happen if—when—Leroux finally did get caught? Father hated Ben right now, and Mother didn't like him much before, so I could hardly move him into the annex with me to play happy families, could I?

And even if my family did accept him, I wasn't sure I wanted to move back to Shotley Manor. I'd had a taste of freedom now, and I liked it. Maybe Ben and I could rent a flat together? Sapphire's royalties were still coming in, and Angelica's death had resulted in a huge sales bump as the morbidly curious picked up copies of the books to see what all the fuss was about.

"Penny for them?" Emmy said, sitting down beside me at the kitchen table.

"Oh, it's nothing."

"Try me. I'm a good listener."

"I'm just thinking about the future. You know, where Ben and I can live. Once this is over, he won't have anywhere to go, and I'm not sure I want to go back home."

"Then don't. But don't make any hasty decisions. You can stay here for a while if you want."

"Really?"

"Ruth'll enjoy the company. Most of us will be heading back to the States as soon as we get Leroux. Black's feet are itchy already. I keep telling him to go home if he wants to, but he won't because Gideon's here. It's kind of sweet."

"I thought he seemed a little jealous at times."

"Yeah, but I can't complain. He cares. Besides, the pair of them are getting on better now Gideon's paying more attention to Roxy than me."

"I noticed they've been spending time together. Do you think there's something going on?"

"He likes her, that's obvious, but she's so far from his usual type he's confused as fuck. It's amusing to watch him dance around her."

"What's his usual type?"

"Straightforward. Independent. Convenient. Everything Roxy isn't, basically."

"Do you think anything will happen?"

She shrugged. "He's never been the relationship type in the past, not after... No, that's his story to tell. But with Roxy? Who knows."

"I thought you and him...?"

"Friends with benefits, that's all it was. Now just friends. We didn't spend our days gazing into each other's eyes and having deep and meaningful conversations."

"But he does with Roxy."

"He does." She sighed. "And sooner or later he has to tell her that her father's dead."

"Oh my gosh."

"She tried to call him, but apparently it's normal for him not to answer for days at a time. Poor girl. All this time she thought she was working to keep him safe, and he was already gone."

My eyes widened. "That's...that's..." I had no words.

"Sick? Abhorrent? Criminal? All of the above."

"The people who hurt her killed him?"

"We believe so. And Gideon looks calm on the outside just like he always does, but there's fury bubbling away in his veins. I can feel it building."

"What will he do?"

She shook her head. "I'm not sure, but I wouldn't like to be the man who trafficked Roxy right now."

"What about Leroux?"

"He's a sneaky son of a bitch. We get a snippet of information and then he goes to ground again. Gideon's been feeding misinformation through various channels, and we got so damn close a couple of days ago. The fucking bed was still warm."

"He's got to be running out of places to hide, surely?"

"He is."

"I hope you catch him soon. It's like being in limbo at the moment, and I'm going stir crazy."

"This is a posh prison, huh?"

"I'm sorry. I must sound so ungrateful, and there are so many worse places I could be."

"Just give us a few more days, okay? You're safe in

here."

"I know." Flipping heck, I was acting like a spoiled brat. I made a conscious effort to change the subject. "Ben and Sofia are getting on okay, aren't they?"

She smiled, wide and genuine. "They are. She's always been kind of solitary, but recently...first she met Leo, now Ben. I've never seen her this happy."

"Leo's her boyfriend, isn't he?"

"Yeah. He keeps threatening to fly over, but they're starting a business together, and somebody needs to run that."

"I thought she worked for Blackwood?"

"She does, but most of us have sidelines. It's always good to diversify."

Ben chose that moment to appear in the doorway. Despite the gravity of our situation, he'd begun smiling more, and somehow he managed to be focused yet relaxed at the same time.

"You look better," I said to him as Emmy grabbed an apple from the fridge and sauntered out.

"I feel better." He dragged a stool up next to me and pulled me in for a kiss before his arm slid down to my waist. "Working with this team is...I've been learning a lot. If I didn't have this arrest warrant hanging over my head, I'd be enjoying it."

"Blackwood's good at what they do, then?"

"The best. I never planned to stay in the legion forever, and they were top of the list of companies I wanted to apply to."

"And did you?"

He gave a hollow laugh. "Not after Leroux screwed up my record. They only take the best. I'd be lucky to get a job as a security guard in a shopping mall now.

But still, I'm enjoying working with Blackwood for the time being."

"What does Sofia do for them?" I'd spoken to her once or twice over dinner, but apart from that, she seemed to spend most of her time either in the conference room or out of the house.

He grimaced. "She's been cagey about that. She's working on something with Gideon at the moment."

"You're okay with that?"

"Yeah. Not that I've got much choice." His mouth spread into a smile. "I can't believe I finally found her. Or rather, she found me. We may be virtual strangers right now, but I'll do whatever I need to do to keep her in my life. And you, *mon cœur*."

"I just wish this was over."

"It will be, soon."

If I'd known what was about to happen, I'd have regretted those words, but I was blissfully ignorant as Ben took my hand and led me up the stairs for a lunchtime quickie.

He took away all my pain, all my heartache, all rational thought, with just a few simple touches.

And Leroux? He wanted to take away everything.

CHAPTER 33

"I'LL SEE YOU later, *trésor*."

Ben slugged back the last of his morning coffee and put the cup in the dishwasher.

"Don't worry, I'm not going anywhere." The words came out a little more resigned than I intended them to, so I quickly followed them up with a smile. He dipped his head and kissed me, leaving me longing for more as he disappeared out the door.

I was eating my cereal when Sofia came in a few minutes later, dressed in a pair of tailored trousers and a white blouse.

"You look smart."

She grimaced as she poured coffee into a travel mug from the thermal jug Ruth always kept replenished. "I have a meeting. A boring one."

I didn't want to pry, not when everyone here held onto their secrets like badges of honour, but Ruth bustled in and saved me the trouble.

"About Mr. Leroux, dearie?"

"Nothing that interesting. Leo wants me to sign a contract for gym equipment."

"Gym equipment?" I asked.

She flashed me a quick smile. "We're opening a gym together in Virginia."

Ah, that must be the diversification thing Emmy

was talking about. "I've always been too nervous to go to the gym. I'd only make a fool of myself because I don't have a clue how to use any of the equipment."

"We'll have classes as well. Or I can show you how all the kit works."

"What? Like, in your gym?"

"You'll be coming to visit, won't you? Both of you?"

"Uh, yes, I suppose. I hadn't really thought about it."

But hadn't I always wanted to travel? Maybe a trip to America could help me achieve the dream I'd given up on after Rupert died? A holiday or two with Ben by my side would be heaven.

"Well, the invitation's there. We've got plenty of space for you to stay."

As Sofia left, Roxy wandered in wearing a pair of jeans and a simple T-shirt. Even in those, she managed to look stunning, and with each day that passed, she became more relaxed around everyone. Of course, she still hadn't heard the news about her father, and I hoped when she found out it wouldn't send her back into the nightmare she'd clawed her way out of.

"Good morning." I always tried to sound cheerful around her.

"Hi." She peered at me from under long eyelashes as she took her spot at the end of the table, placing an eReader next to the bowl of fruit Ruth brought her. That was new.

"You like books?"

Her cheeks turned a pale shade of pink. "Gideon gave it to me."

"What are you reading?"

Her blush deepened. *Meet Me At Midnight.*

It was my turn to colour up. It always felt strange when somebody I knew read one of Sapphire's books, especially a story as personal as that one.

"What do you think of it?"

"It gives me hope that one day a man will want me for who I am and not who society thinks I am."

Of all the things she could have said, she chose the one that made me tear up. I reached out and curled my hand around hers. "He will."

Indeed, I suspected he already had.

With the house empty except for Ruth, Roxy, and the daytime security guard who lurked in the office off the entrance hall, I figured it was about time I tried to get some writing done for the first time since I arrived in London. After all, I'd have to earn money if I wanted a future with Ben because I couldn't count on my parents to support me.

My head was filled with possibilities as I took my MacBook out of my suitcase. Perhaps I could explain the situation with Sapphire to Petra and continue publishing under that name? Or I could pick a new pen name to go with my fresh start. Or maybe two—one for my historical romances and another for the contemporary stories I wanted to write but hadn't yet dared to.

I'd just sat down at the desk by the window in my room—no, our room—when my phone rang. Unknown number. Please, tell me this wasn't the police with bad news about Ben.

It was worse.

"Ah, the second Miss Fordham. How nice to finally speak to you." The only Frenchman I knew was Gideon, but this voice wasn't his, not with that cruel edge.

"Who is this?"

"The man you and your new friends have been looking for."

"Guy Leroux?" I whispered.

"*Mais oui.*"

"What do you want?"

"It's more a question of what *you* want."

"I don't understand."

"I'm here with your family. Do you want to see them again?"

"No..." I whispered it to myself, but he heard me.

"What did you say? *Non*?"

I came to my senses enough to answer. "You can't be there. They've got bodyguards."

"Ah, *oui*, the two idiots in the car outside." He tutted down the line. "I'd have expected better from Blackwood. They gave up without a fight."

My pulse pounded in my ears as my heart raced on ahead of my thoughts. He'd got my family? That man had my family?

He carried on without waiting for me to answer. "Your father, your mother, Dorothy, Mary, Bernie. They're all here. Although your mother's sleeping right now. She wouldn't keep quiet, so I had to encourage her."

"You...you bastard! If you hurt them—"

His laughter cut me off. "Again, that's up to you. Thanks to your meddling friends, my options are limited, and I need money. Your father has a safe deposit box, and I need you to bring me the contents."

"What safe deposit box? I don't know anything about it."

"No matter—he's told me what I need to know. The

box is in Harrods, and you're able to access it in an emergency. I'd class this as an emergency, would you not?"

My knees gave way as I slumped onto the chair in front of the desk. A vague memory came to me of my father many years ago, telling me he'd stored jewellery and cash away for safekeeping, just in case.

He'd never elaborated on the "just in case" part. I'd guessed at a problem with the financial system, not threats from a madman intent on destroying my family.

"How do I get it?" I whispered.

"I can't hear you."

"How do I get into the box?"

My mother might have been an irritation lately, but she was still my mother. And my father, and the household staff... I couldn't let anything happen to them.

"You get into your car, and you drive home. I'll leave the key and instructions in the front porch. You go back to London, you get the contents of the box, and you bring it to me. Then I'm gone."

My legs shook as I tried to stand. "I'm coming. Just don't hurt them. Please, don't hurt them."

"Augusta?"

"What?" I spat the word. I'd never hated anyone as much as I hated Leroux right now.

"You've got one hour to get here. If you breathe a word of this to anybody, I'll kill one of my companions. Who do you want me to shoot, Augusta?"

"How can you even ask me that?"

"Because we're a team now. We need to work together to resolve this problem and the clock's ticking. Who do you want to die first?"

"Nobody. I'll get the damn money, okay?"

Perhaps hanging up on him wasn't the best move to make, but I was so angry I didn't care. What gave him the right to come into my family's life and ruin it?

Calm, Gus. Breathe. I couldn't afford to get upset, not with my family being held hostage and so little time. An hour? Had that bastard ever tried driving in London traffic? And more to the point, how was I supposed to get to Sandlebury? I last drove my car to the apartment I was sharing with Emmy, and although I'd seen it in the underground parking garage here, I had no idea what she'd done with the keys. I could hardly ring and ask, could I?

Okay, think. London. I was in London, and London had cabs. I could get a cab. It wasn't like I was in a fit state to drive, anyway.

I shoved on a pair of trainers and grabbed my handbag. Now, all I had to do was get out of the house without being seen.

Thanks to the conveniently placed security office, attempting to leave via the front door was out. Instead, I crept through to the kitchen, praying Ruth wasn't on one of her baking sprees. As I peeped around the door jamb, I heard her humming to herself in the utility room off to the side. Thank goodness. A lucky break.

Only that luck didn't last. I soon found out that staying at a house belonging to the owners of a security company brought its own problems. The bloody place was so secure that nobody could get in, and I couldn't get out either. The pedestrian gate set into the wall next to the equally tall metal gates across the driveway didn't even have a bloody handle, just a keypad that I didn't know the code for. A shower of tears burst out unbidden. What the hell was I supposed to do?

I crouched behind a bush as the sound of a rumbling engine outside caught my attention, then held my breath, palms sweating, as the huge gates slowly swung open. A delivery from Ocado! The online supermarket brought fresh organic vegetables, a selection of ethically produced meat, and my flipping salvation. The delivery man pulled into the driveway while I ran out behind the van, searching both ways along the road for a taxi.

Hallelujah! A black cab with its light on. I flagged the driver down and leapt into the back.

"Where to?" the driver asked.

"Sandlebury. It's near Oxford." I rattled off the postcode.

"Won't be cheap, love." He glanced up at the mansion I'd just come out of. "Still, I suppose you can afford it."

For once, money had its benefits.

CHAPTER 34

"IS THERE A way around this jam?" I asked, bouncing my knees as the cab inched along the road out of London.

"Traffic's busy at the moment, love. Workmen dug through the water main on the A40, so everyone's using the side streets while Thames Water argues with the council about who's going to fix it."

Dammit, why today? What was wrong with this country and its infrastructure? Something was always breaking, and it was always somebody else's fault.

"I'd be quicker walking," I muttered.

"Aye, along this bit for sure," the driver agreed. The faded badge taped to the Perspex partition behind the front seats identified him as Darryl Butterfield. "Reckon we should get out and help them dig."

He turned the radio on, and a commentary on first the failings of the government, then the unseasonably hot weather, then the week's upcoming football matches was exactly what I didn't need as I sweated against the leather seats. In Albany House, with its thick walls and air conditioning, I'd been comfortable in jeans, but now I felt like I was about to expire from heat exhaustion.

My phone turned slippery in my hands, and every few seconds I glanced at the screen in case Leroux called again and I'd somehow missed it. Or worse, missed Ben.

"Going somewhere nice today?" Darryl asked.

"Not really. I actually need to pick something up and then come straight back to London. Would you be able to wait?"

"Aye, but I'll have to leave the meter running."

"That's fine."

Finally, we crawled as far as the M40 and traffic cleared. Darryl sped up to fifty-five, seemingly happy to trundle along in the slow lane behind all the lorries.

"If you can get me there by twelve, I'll pay you double," I told him in desperation.

"Why didn't you say so, love?"

He stepped on the accelerator, and a cloud of black smoke belched out behind us as he swerved into the fast lane. I thought the old taxi would rattle itself to pieces as he floored it past a couple of Audis and a Porsche.

"Used to race dirt bikes when I was a lad," he told me, seemingly oblivious to the BMW driver he'd just cut in front of making a rude gesture in the mirror. "Most weekends."

"Did you win?"

"No, love. I crashed more often than I finished."

I felt around my waist for the seatbelt and gave it a surreptitious tug. Yes, it was securely fastened. My attempts to save my family would all be in vain if I came to a nasty end on the motorway before I even got home.

The vehicle developed a worrying clunk soon after we left the motorway, but thankfully we made it to Sandlebury in one piece. Darryl slowed down as we approached the village.

"Could you drop me off a little bit down the road from my house?" I asked. "I'd like my visit to be a surprise." And I didn't want an innocent party to get shot if Leroux decided he needed another hostage.

"It's your money, lady."

I had him pull over in a lay-by two hundred yards from the entrance to our driveway, and immediately regretted it when I stepped out of the vehicle and my legs started to buckle underneath me.

"Back in a minute," Darryl told me. "I just need to nip back to that petrol station we passed and fill up."

"Please be quick."

What was I thinking? I wasn't cut out to be a heroine, no matter how much I might wish it in my books. But I was here now, and I had no choice. My whole body trembled as I walked along the grass verge towards the place where this whole sorry story had begun with Ben's arrival and my sister's death. I almost hated the place now.

The gates lay wide open, inviting, not like the solid barrier guarding Albany House back in London. Oh, how I wished I was back there, watching a movie with Roxy or sampling Ruth's afternoon cakes.

A click from behind made me freeze, and although I'd never seen a pistol in real life, I knew from television what the cocking of a hammer sounded like. I turned slowly, raising my hands in the air as I did so.

"Where's your car?" Leroux asked. I recognised him from the pictures Gideon had brought, only his eyes had a crazy gleam in them that didn't show up on a computer screen.

"I-I-I couldn't find the keys, so I took a taxi."

"A taxi? A fucking taxi? Which part of my instructions did you not understand?"

"You just said come and pick up the key."

"Yes, in your car."

"I told you, I couldn't bring my car. Now, give me the damn key, and I'll get your damn money."

He started laughing. "You really are as stupid as your sister, aren't you? It must run in the family."

"Angie wasn't stupid!"

"She was stupid enough to believe me when I told her I was a French baron looking for a lady to make my wife, and quick enough to let me fuck her." He reached out and ran the back of one hand down my cheek. "Wonder if sister number two is a better lay?"

I almost threw up then and there. Breakfast again threatened to escape as I fought from gagging. "What about the money? We had a deal."

"Don't you get it? There is no money. I needed a vehicle and a hostage, and thanks to you I've only got one of the two."

"What do you mean a hostage? What about my family?"

He grabbed my arm and twisted it so I fell into step in front of him with the gun poking into my side.

"See what I mean? Stupid. You honestly thought I'd take on Blackwood's bodyguards to get into your house? Your father's locked in his study, nobody would pay a ransom for the staff, and if I were you, I'd let me shoot your mother in a heartbeat." We got out to the road and he looked both ways. "Now, where's this taxi?"

"H-h-he went to get petrol."

"*Merde.* Why do these things always happen to

me?"

"Because you're a murdering bastard."

That got me an elbow in the side, and I doubled over, gasping. Leroux swore under his breath, babbling hate against women in general and me in particular until the sound of an approaching car made us both look up.

The sick grin on his face made my stomach clench.

"Looks as if my luck is changing."

He forced me into the middle of the road and held the gun to my head as a black Porsche Cayenne with tinted windows came around the corner. In the narrow lane, the driver had no choice but to stop or run us down as Leroux stood his ground.

Even then, I half wished they'd chosen to accelerate. If I died, at least Leroux would be out of the picture and this nightmare would be over. I closed my eyes, waiting, only to find the bumper three feet from my knees as Leroux shoved me towards the passenger side, gun pointed at the windscreen.

"I'm going to get in the back, then you will get into the front. If you try to run, I'll shoot the driver. Do you understand?"

"Yes."

I stood at the side of the car while he wrenched the door open and climbed inside. My feet told me to hightail it out of there, but I couldn't. My morals wouldn't let me cause the death of an innocent person because of a situation I'd created. How could I have fallen for his trick? Why hadn't I tried calling my father after Leroux phoned me?

He was right; I was stupid.

"Hurry up," he yelled, and I pulled the door open.

It was then that I got my second shock of the day.

Sofia's barely perceptible shake of the head warned me to stay quiet, and in any case, I was lost for words as I clicked the seatbelt on.

"Two pretty ladies." Leroux's wild grin in the mirror scared the crap out of me. "This has turned into my lucky day." He nudged my temple with the barrel of the gun and barked an order at Sofia. "Drive."

CHAPTER 35

SOFIA SHIFTED THE car into gear, checked the mirror, then pulled away smoothly. How did she stay so damn calm?

"Where are we going?" she asked.

"Dover," Leroux told her.

"Dover? I don't know where that is."

"South. Head south. I've got a boat waiting."

Her American accent got stronger as she gave a shrug. "I'm not from around here. Either you'll have to give me directions or I'll need to program the SatNav."

"We're not stopping." He jabbed the gun in my neck, then pointed it towards the dashboard. "You sort it."

Marvellous. Now, technology and I weren't a good mix at the best of times, but faced with four arrow buttons and a tiny joystick, I didn't know where to start. "Which button do I press?"

"I'm not sure. I've only had this car a few days," Sofia said.

Was it even hers? Or had she borrowed it from Black? After all, he'd been driving an identical vehicle on the night we found Ben. I jabbed each button in turn and wiggled the joystick, but I didn't get a map. Then...

"Uh, I think I've changed it to another language. Is that French?"

Leroux spewed a string of curse words and shifted forward to take a closer look. Sofia accelerated, and outside the window, the trees rushed by either side of the narrow lane. I wanted to ask her to slow down, but I didn't dare to speak in case I upset Leroux more than he was already.

"*Salope stupide*. You've broken it!"

"Sorry."

Hang on, why was *I* apologising? He was the one who'd abducted me at gunpoint.

He shifted the gun into his left hand and leaned between the seats with his right outstretched. So, he thought he could fix it? Good luck with that.

Before he tackled the directions, he took the time to peruse my body, then reached out and squeezed a breast, hard. I cut my eyes to Sofia. Had she noticed?

"Will you scream like your sister?" he asked, his voice husky. "Are you going to fight me? Because I enjoy that. Angelica gave me one hell of a ride. It was almost a shame I had to kill her."

Could Sofia hear? Leroux wasn't talking that quietly, but her eyes remained fixed on the road.

His hand reached between my legs, forcing them apart an inch. "Are you ready?"

I swallowed down the vomit rising in my throat and closed my eyes. For a moment, I wished he'd just shoot me and get it over with.

"Have you worked out where we're going yet?" Sofia asked.

Leroux swore under his breath and reached for the SatNav. That sick, sick bastard.

I stared at my lap, dreaming up all the things I wanted to do to him, starting with the removal of a certain part of his anatomy. And that meant I barely noticed when Sofia turned the wheel to the left. Only the bump as we left the road made me look up, just in time to see a low brick wall coming straight towards us. At the last second, she crossed both hands over her chest, and everything happened at once. The front of the car crumpled, the airbags went off, and Leroux's body sailed past into the windscreen with a sickening crunch.

For a few seconds, nobody moved, then Leroux groaned from his position sprawled across the bonnet. How was he still alive? His head and shoulders had gone clean through the bloody glass! Sofia was silent, still, and every part of me hurt as I unclipped my seatbelt and kicked at the door. Where was the gun? Leroux had been holding it when we crashed. And why wasn't Sofia moving?

The seatbelt had sliced into my shoulder, and blood seeped through my jumper as I stretched out one arm and then the other. Fire burned through my left leg, but I blocked it. Sofia. I needed to get to the driver's side and check on Sofia.

Except as I half climbed, half fell out of the car, Leroux began to claw his way across the bonnet. Blood was matted into his hair, and a flap of skin hung from his forehead with the white of his skull peeping through the crimson mess underneath. Breakfast rose up my throat, and by the time I'd dumped it at my feet, Leroux was on his. He swayed slightly, wild eyes staring from side to side, looking for... Shit! We both spotted the gun at the same time as the sun glinted off the barrel.

I dived forwards, but he shoved me out of the way.

"*Salope!*"

Presumably, that was meant to be derogatory, but seeing as I didn't speak much French, the effect got lost.

I grabbed his arm, but my fingers slipped on the blood and he barely stumbled. I tried again, digging my nails in this time, and he let out an animalistic roar as he swung a fist at me.

Oh hell, oh hell, oh hell. I wasn't cut out for this. I wrote romance, not thrillers. My knees buckled, and Leroux's knuckles whistled past and connected with a tree.

"Bitch!"

Okay, I understood that one. He went for the gun again, and I used the last of my strength to leap forward and kick it into a patch of stinging nettles. If he wanted it that much, at least he could suffer first. And so could I. His punch connected this time, and I fell into the dirt, trying to twist away as he wrenched my arms above my head.

"I will enjoy killing you, slut," he hissed. "But perhaps we can have fun first, yes?"

I scrabbled amongst the soil and twigs as he straddled me, using his weight to hold me down. Blood dripped off his chin and splashed onto my breasts.

"Get off me!"

"You owe me this. Your *copain* ruined everything."

Insanity leached from his glittering eyes as he used one hand to tear at my jumper. I tried to buck my hips and get him off, but Leroux was bigger than Ben and fuelled by evil. Tears rolled down my cheeks as panic and fear warred inside me.

And then a foot connected with his head. What the...? Leroux lurched to the side, but Sofia followed and hammered a fist into his nose.

Thank goodness. Thank goodness Sofia was awake, and thank goodness she knew how to hit properly.

I wriggled out from under Leroux as Sofia rained blows down on him, and he began to crawl, spitting curses with every exhale. My heart shuddered in my ears as I scrambled away, turning just in time to see Sofia shove Leroux onto his front and kneel on his shoulders. He tried to push himself up, but she flicked one foot out and stamped on his hand.

"Don't even think about it, you fucker."

Her slim fingers reached around his neck, tightening, and his struggles subsided as she pressed harder. Ten seconds, twenty, and he stopped moving.

"Is he d-d-dead?"

She didn't release the pressure. "Not yet. Compressing the carotid artery causes unconsciousness in fifteen to twenty seconds, but it takes two to four minutes for a man to die." She glanced at her watch. "We still have at least a minute and a half left."

Bloody hell. She really was going to kill him, wasn't she? My breath came in ragged pants while Sofia choked a man without breaking a sweat.

And do you know what? I was grateful. Grateful that she had the strength and guts to do what I couldn't. But I didn't want to watch, so I screwed my eyes closed and fought against the nausea still churning in my stomach.

Please, make it quick.

The cracking of twigs from behind made my eyes pop open, and Sofia groaned as an elderly couple emerged from behind the Porsche.

"Is everything all right?" the grey-haired man

asked.

"Shit," Sofia muttered, loosening her grip.

What on earth was I supposed to say? Nothing that could implicate Blackwood or Ben in any way, that was for sure.

"This man appeared in my driveway and took me hostage. Then he stopped that poor lady on the road outside and forced her to drive us."

The man looked doubtfully at Sofia, still sitting on Leroux.

"He didn't wear a seatbelt," she said. "I only just passed my driving test, and I got so nervous I forgot how to steer."

She followed up with a giggle, and the man's eyes widened.

"He went clean through the windscreen," I said. "We were just checking for a pulse."

Another car engine sounded, and all heads turned as Gideon and Roxy appeared. How on earth had they got here?

"Should we call the police?" the old man asked. "And an ambulance?"

Gideon stepped forwards and flashed an official-looking badge. "Inspector Renton, Oxfordshire Constabulary."

Where had his French accent gone? He stooped to look at Leroux, then straightened.

"We've been looking for this man for a while, and we just got a tip-off he'd abducted a woman at gunpoint."

"Really?"

Leroux coughed, and Gideon produced a pair of handcuffs. "He's been one step ahead of us until now.

Would you mind waiting back by your car? This is a crime scene now."

He smiled at the elderly lady, who beamed back at him.

"What did he do, officer?" she asked.

"Armed robbery. He's a very dangerous man."

Gideon snapped the cuffs on Leroux, then walked towards the old couple, arms outstretched to herd them back to the road.

"Finish it," he whispered to Sofia as he walked past.

Except Roxy got there first and booted Leroux in the nuts with one of her shiny black kitten heels.

"That's from me."

Another kick.

"And that's for Ben."

"Done?" Sofia asked, flexing her fingers.

Roxy's shoulders slumped. "Yes."

I tried to stand, to walk away because no matter what Leroux had done, I still didn't want to see a man die. But my knees liquified as I staggered forwards, and the last thing I saw before the trees dimmed was Roxy crouching beside me, eyes filled with worry.

A siren woke me, and as the world came back into view, I tried to sit up. Hands pushed me back down, and I focused on Roxy leaning over me while Sofia pressed on my leg. Hell, that hurt.

"What happened?"

"You fainted," Roxy said. "You've got a deep cut on your left leg, and you've lost some blood."

"Really?" I tried to see.

My black trousers were rolled up to my knee, but they just looked wet.

"Gideon had a first aid kit, so I've bandaged it. Please keep still."

"Leroux?"

Sofia's lips formed a thin line. "Alive. You took priority."

Dammit.

Branches cracked, and several overexcited paramedics ran into view. Sofia made the mistake of mentioning a stiff neck, and they strapped her onto a spinal board despite her protests. Then they tried to uncuff Leroux and do the same to him, but thankfully Emmy and Black arrived and took over the scene while Gideon ran crowd control. For once, I was glad about Black's imposing personality. He ordered everyone to stay back while he ensured Leroux was well and truly incapacitated.

Meanwhile, Emmy waved off the paramedic Sofia was arguing with.

"She doesn't need a bloody ECG."

"But—"

Emmy glared at him until he backed away, then wrapped her arms around Sofia, kissing her tenderly on the cheek. Odd. I'd never seen Emmy be quite so sweet. And with Emmy otherwise engaged, I attracted Black's attention once he'd finished with Leroux.

"You need to get to the hospital."

"I didn't even realise I was hurt so badly."

"That's the adrenaline talking. Once it wears off, you'll be sore as hell."

He held his hand out and someone placed a blanket in it, which he draped over my shoulders along with his arm. The paramedics wheeled Leroux past on a gurney, and even though his hands were now cuffed to the rails on the sides, I couldn't help shuddering.

"He touched me," I whispered. "While we were driving."

"I know. Fia turned the dash-cams on the second he stepped out into the road. We've got everything on tape, including his confession."

I sagged in Black's arms, and rather than lower me to the ground again, he picked me up bridal-style and carried me towards a waiting stretcher.

"Does that mean they'll stop looking for Ben?" I asked.

Black smiled, and it changed his face from dark and brooding to drool-worthy. I kept my lips firmly pressed together.

"Our legal team's working on it as we speak. He should be a free man by tomorrow."

It was over. It was finally over. We had Leroux, and Ben and I could be together out in the open. We'd have our future.

A faint "shit" escaped Black's lips.

"What?"

"Don't look now, but here comes your mother."

"Is it too late to wish I was unconscious?"

Apparently yes. She screeched even louder than the siren on the ambulance as she wobbled over on heels better suited to a sober person. Father stood behind, seemingly unsure whether to back her up or die of embarrassment.

"What are you doing with my daughter?" she demanded.

Black's grip on me tightened a smidgen. "She was in

a car accident."

Mother's head bobbled on her shoulders as she looked around. "Where's her car?"

"The man who killed Angelica kidnapped me and a friend, and then we crashed."

"Where is he? Where's Beau Davies? Because I want to give him a piece of my mind."

A piece of her mind? Good grief. "He's not here, and in any case, he didn't kill Angie."

"Of course he did. The police said so." She belted Black on the arm, but he didn't flinch. "I want that man in jail."

Father wrapped an arm around her waist, but she shook him off. "Carolyn..."

"Don't you 'Carolyn' me. These buffoons you hired are wasting their time and our money."

Father sighed and did his best to ignore her, never an easy task. "Are you all right, Gussie?"

"I will be once I get back to London."

Another wrinkle creased his brow. "We were hoping you'd come home."

I gave Mother a pointed glance, then looked back at him. Seriously?

"I know what you're thinking, but your mother's trying to change. We're on our way to a counselling appointment right now."

"She doesn't need counselling. She needs Alcoholics Anonymous."

"We need to take this one step at a time."

I took a deep breath. "Well, until she's managed a few more steps, like all twelve of them, I'm going back to London to stay with Ben."

"Who's Ben?"

"You know him as Beau."

A deathly silence fell, punctuated only by the rattle of Sofia's stretcher being loaded into the ambulance.

My father spoke first. "Do you mean to tell me there's something going on between you and that boy?"

I nodded.

Mother gasped. "But he's a criminal!"

"The only thing he's guilty of is loving me."

Father's nostrils flared in the way they always did when he got angry. "I'm ashamed of you. I never thought you'd stoop so low as to cavort with the help behind our backs."

"Well, if Mother hadn't sent him away nine years ago, we wouldn't have had to hide, would we?"

"What are you talking about?"

It all came spilling out along with my tears; the way Mother lied to Ben and coerced me into marrying Rupert, and how Ben came back for me because what we had between us would never die.

"You disgusting child," my mother said when I'd finished. "All the money we spent on your education, your lifestyle, your wardrobe, and you just throw it away on some thug?"

Support came from an unlikely source. Black.

"Ben Durham is a good man, and it's about time you learned that there are more important things in life than money. Like your daughter's happiness. I suggest you take a look in the mirror and realise you can roll a turd in glitter but it still stinks. And you..." He gave a sniff. "Don't smell so good."

Father looked as if he was about to swing for him. "How dare you speak to my wife like that?"

"Because you're not man enough to do it yourself."

"If you think I'm going to pay your bill after this…"

"Like I said, there are more important things in life than money. Think about that."

Father started yelling at him, but Black only smiled as he carried me into the back of the ambulance. Wow. He'd put it a little more bluntly than I'd ever dreamed of doing, but I wanted to give him a round of applause.

"Thank you," I whispered.

"Always welcome, Augusta. Sofia's family, which makes you and Ben family. We'll look after you both."

CHAPTER 36

INSIDE THE AMBULANCE, Black settled me into the seat next to Emmy's, then backed out to deal with the remains of his Porsche. Sofia was still strapped onto the stretcher, and she didn't look happy about it.

"Right, we're ready to go," Emmy told the paramedic.

"We can't take passengers."

She just looked at him, and after a few seconds, he backed away. "I guess we can make an exception."

Emmy squeezed Sofia's hand as the ambulance pulled onto the road with a whoop of its siren. "How do you feel?"

"Like I don't want to be in an ambulance."

"You need to get your head checked."

"It's fine. I've had far worse, like the time we drank cocktails in Chamonix and went skiing in the middle of the night."

"I swear those trees came out of nowhere."

"They did. Anyway, I didn't go to the hospital then."

"Yeah, but you had a headache for five days and moaned like hell about it," Emmy said.

"I'm not staying in overnight."

"We'll see. Gus, how are you feeling?"

I shrugged, but that hurt. "A bit stiff, and my leg really stings."

And do you know what else hurt? That Ben hadn't even phoned to check I was okay. I pulled my phone out of my pocket again just in case. Yes, I had a signal, and no, there were no messages.

"Expecting a call?" Emmy asked.

"I just thought Ben might have called after the crash."

"Oh, we didn't tell him. He'd have come haring right up the motorway. There are cops everywhere, all itching to arrest someone, and technically, he's still wanted for murder. We had enough to deal with."

"I suppose that makes sense."

"We'll break it to him gently later. Far better for him to see you're not badly hurt when we get home than worry him unnecessarily."

As usual, Emmy was right. Only two minutes later my phone *did* ring, and it was Ben. I considered sending the call to voicemail, but that would have been strange in itself considering I was supposed to be relaxing back at Albany House.

"Hello?"

"Where are you, *trésor*?"

"Why?"

"Because I brought sushi back for lunch only you're not here. Did something happen?"

"Uh, I just…" Emmy mimed eating with a knife and fork. "I just popped out for lunch with Emmy and Sofia. You know, girl time."

"So Sofia's with you too?"

"Mmm hmm."

"Don't tell her, but she's got a surprise waiting when she gets back."

"What kind of surprise?" And why did I have a bad

feeling about it?

"Her boyfriend's flown in to see her. Nearly gave me a heart attack when he introduced himself. Walking into him as I came out of the john wasn't quite how I'd envisaged us meeting, but he's a nice guy."

Oh, shit, shit, shit.

"What's happened?" Emmy whispered. "You've gone white."

I put my hand over the phone. "Sofia's boyfriend's turned up at Albany House."

"Fuck."

"Uh, Ben, our food's just arrived, so we'd better eat. Love you."

I ended the call as Sofia tried to sit up, but the straps across her chest wouldn't let her. "Get these off me!"

She scrabbled at the buckles and Emmy grabbed her hands.

"Relax. Just breathe."

"I can't. I promised Leo I wasn't going to do anything dangerous for at least six months. Now I've got cuts all over my freaking face."

"Maybe we could do something with your hair? You know, to hide the worst of it?"

"There's a massive bruise coming up on my hip too. I can feel it."

"Leo will forgive you. He's one of those understanding guys most women spend a lifetime looking for."

Sofia sighed and flopped her head back onto the stretcher. "Ouch. I know. I'm lucky in so many ways."

The two of us made a right pair when we walked into Albany House three hours later. The doctors had given us matching neck braces, I had a row of stitches all the way up my calf, and we both clutched bags filled with assorted painkillers and anti-inflammatories.

Ben and a blond man I took to be Leo were sitting in the kitchen, chatting over coffee, and they both leapt up when they saw us.

"Honey, we're home," Emmy said.

"What the hell happened?" Leo asked, raining kisses on Sofia's head.

"There was a slight problem with the car," she said.

"You had an accident?"

"No, I crashed it on purpose."

"Seriously, what happened?"

Emmy fetched the orange juice from the fridge and poured herself a glass. "She really did crash on purpose. But look on the bright side, Leroux came off worse."

Ben's jaw dropped. "You got him?"

"He's under police guard in hospital."

"What the hell happened?" Ben echoed Leo's words.

"You have to promise not to get mad."

"Why?"

"Promise."

He sighed. "Fine, I promise."

We headed into the lounge, where Ben wrapped his arms gently around me as Emmy recounted the afternoon's events. I'd been afraid he'd be angry at my stupidity, but instead, he kissed the corner of my lips.

"Please don't ever try to handle things on your own again."

That was a no-brainer. "I won't."

"Fuck, if anything had happened to you..."

"It didn't. Sofia found me in time. Uh, how *did* you find me?"

Emmy answered for her. "Roxy saw you leave in a hurry and called Gideon, then we tracked your phone. Sofia was the closest, so she arrived first. It was a stroke of luck when Leroux ordered her to play chauffeur."

"I'm not sure I'd describe it as luck."

"I would. If Sofia hadn't been driving, you'd probably be in Dover by now."

And that didn't bear thinking about. I shuddered, and Ben pressed his lips against my cheek. "It's over. Don't think about it. We've got the rest of our lives to live, and right now, you have to decide where you want me to take you on our first date."

"Anywhere?"

He looked down at the floor. "Well, not too expensive. I don't have much money until I get a job. Then I'll make it up to you."

"There's a job for you at Blackwood if you want it," Emmy said.

He slowly raised his eyes. "Are you kidding?"

"I never kid about work. Everyone's been impressed by your performance over the last couple of weeks."

"But I thought with my record from the legion..."

"Because you fought for people who couldn't fight for themselves even when it cost you everything? You're exactly the kind of person we want working for us."

"I don't know what to say."

I gave him a nudge. "You told me you always wanted to work there. Say yes."

"Are you sure you're okay with it?" he asked me. "I might be late home quite often."

"Follow your dreams. I followed mine, and look what happened."

Ben broke out the grin I loved so much. "In that case, I'd be honoured to work for Blackwood."

"There we go, sorted. Now, make sure you take Gus somewhere nice."

Pizza. A week later, four days after Ben's name was officially cleared, we went for pizza. Not posh Gregory-style pizza, but the cheap and cheerful kind with an all-you-can-eat salad bar and a menu in English rather than Italian. And I loved every second of it.

The stiffness in my neck and back had receded, the brace was gone, and I snuggled against Ben in the taxi on the way back to Albany House.

"Thank you."

"For what?" he asked.

"Everything. For coming back to find me. For giving me exactly what I needed."

"Part of me still wishes I'd stayed away. Then you'd still have your sister."

"Please, don't think like that. There was only one man responsible for taking her away from me, and that was Leroux. And Angie would have wanted us to be happy."

Now that Leroux was under arrest, my stress had

been replaced by grief, a darkness that threatened to consume me if I let it. But each day, Ben lit another candle and used it to brighten my way. I'd never stop missing my sister, but I'd take the time we'd had together as a gift, and now I needed to live life for both of us.

Ben kissed me softly on the lips. "You make me happy."

"Ditto, Mr... You're changing back to Darke?" Ben had been considering his surname for a few days now.

"It's a fresh start for both of us. Durant holds bad memories, and Durham doesn't feel right now I know the asshole who brought me up isn't really my father. Sofia said she hung on to her surname because it reminds her she can survive anything, and I feel I should show some solidarity."

"I think you're doing the right thing. Sofia's your family now."

"And you."

"Meet me at midnight?" I asked.

He looked at his watch. "How about eleven?"

"Mr. Impatient."

He nuzzled my ear, keeping his voice low so the cabbie couldn't hear. "You're lucky I haven't spread your legs right here."

"I love it when you talk dirty, Mr. Darke."

"I love it when you write dirty, Mrs. Darke."

My heart stuttered to a stop. "W-w-what did you just call me?"

"Only a matter of time, *trésor*." The taxi drew up outside Albany House, and Ben shoved twenty pounds at the driver. "Keep the change."

We both had our eyes programmed into the iris

scanner that opened the gate now, no need to use the keypad, and a quick glance was enough to gain entry. Ben picked me up, with one hand already sliding up my thigh under my dress as the front door swung open under his touch. I wrapped my legs around his waist, and when he pressed me against the wall in the hallway, I attacked him with my lips, my hands, even my teeth.

A cough sounded from nearby, and I twisted in Ben's arms to find Emmy and Black behind us. Judging by the amount of clothes they both weren't wearing, they'd had the same idea as we did.

"Oops. As you were."

I screwed my eyes shut, and Ben hastily carried me up the stairs.

We didn't lock lips again until the bedroom door was safely closed behind us, and then I tore at his clothing like Edward fricking Scissorhands. His shirt ended up torn on the floor, swiftly followed by my dress, bra, and knickers. He went to lift me onto the bed but ended up hopping around instead.

"What happened? Are you okay?"

"Trod on a fucking button. Get on the bed, *trésor*."

With pleasure. I threw myself backwards onto the thousand-thread-count sheets and opened wide for him. He didn't disappoint.

"I've been hard for you since dessert," he murmured. "With the way you licked that chocolate mousse off your spoon, I could hardly keep my hands off you."

Oh good—my plan had worked, then. "I don't know what you're talking about."

"I think you do." He ran the tip of his tongue from

my collarbone to my earlobe, then gently nibbled on it. "You're a little minx under that innocent smile."

"As of last week, I'm also a little minx on birth control pills."

When Emmy insisted I see the doctor for a check-up after the accident, I'd used it to my advantage.

Ben paused in his ministrations and met my eyes. "Are you saying what I think you're saying?"

"I don't want anything between us."

"Fuck, *mon cœur*. I can't wait."

"That's kind of the point." I could feel my wetness running down my thigh. "Woman on the edge here."

I didn't have to tell him twice. He reached between us, ripping one orgasm from me with his fingers as his cock nudged my entrance.

"Perfect fit," he whispered. "You were made for me."

With skin on skin, every sensation was heightened, and I barely lasted five minutes before he made me see stars again. His thrusts slowed, waiting for me to come back to earth again before he went for number three. Ben always had been an over-achiever.

Heat spread through me, mine and his, as we both groaned at the same time. Yes, my first date night with Ben was something to be remembered.

"Best surprise ever."

He dropped kisses on my hair afterwards while I used his shoulder as a pillow.

"Uh, I have another one."

I tilted my head back in time to see his eyes gleam.

"Really?"

"I started writing again today." It took some effort, but I rolled over and retrieved a few sheets of paper from the drawer of the bedside table. "Want to read?"

A smile spread slowly over his face as he scanned the pages. "A picnic? You want to go on a picnic?"

My cheeks turned a little pink, but I nodded.

"I think that can be arranged. After all, you're my favourite thing to eat."

CHAPTER 37

A WEEK LATER, Ben had introduced me to the delights of dining alfresco, and I saw the strawberry yogurt on the breakfast table in a whole new light.

"Are you looking at flats again today?" Roxy asked.

"No, we've already found one."

"The Camden place?"

"Yes."

Albany House had every luxury we could ask for but one: our own space. After we'd accidentally walked in on Emmy and Black in the hallway, Ben and I agreed we'd like a little place of our own, and once we'd viewed a couple of unsuitable properties, Emmy suggested the flat I'd originally shared with her in Camden. Turned out she owned the whole building and rented it out. We planned to move in once we got back from visiting Sofia in Virginia, and Ben would start his new job soon after that.

The planets must have aligned or something, because after weeks of hell, good things were finally clicking into place. I had Ben, the freedom I'd secretly craved, and at least two orgasms every night. Even my father had phoned to apologise, although we both acknowledged we had a lot of bridges to mend.

"How about you?" I asked Roxy. "Are you staying on here?"

She nodded. "They said it's okay, and I feel safe for the first time in two years." She gave me the shy smile I knew drove Gideon nuts. His tongue practically hung out every time she turned it on, although she seemed oblivious. "I'm going back to medical school in the autumn. Black helped me to arrange it."

"In Poland?"

"There's nothing left for me in Gdansk."

Her smile disappeared, and I knew she was thinking about her father and the man who'd taken her from him. The man who forced her into this position in the first place. He still lived there according to Ben. Gideon had broken the news of her father's death a few days ago, and she'd sobbed in his arms for the whole evening.

"You're staying in London?"

"I've got a place at UCL, starting in September."

"Congratulations!" I slid off my chair and gave her a hug, which she returned hesitantly. "You'll make a wonderful doctor. Plus, if you're staying here, you won't be so far from Gideon."

Oh, now she went pink. "He's been very kind, but he's going back to Paris soon."

"It's only two and a quarter hours on the train."

"That might as well be a lifetime away. At the moment, I'm scared to go as far as the university, and besides, he hasn't asked me to visit."

"He will."

"I don't think so."

My phone rang before I could point out just why she was wrong in that assumption. I was expecting Ben, who'd gone into Blackwood's office for orientation, but instead, I saw an unknown number calling. My heart leapt into my mouth, and I forced myself to swallow it down again. It couldn't be Leroux. Leroux was still under arrest in hospital.

"Hello?"

"Miss Fordham?"

"Yes. Who is this?"

"Sergeant Nash from the Metropolitan Police. I'm afraid I've got bad news."

Not Ben. Please, say Ben was okay. "What is it?"

"We've had a security breach, and Guy Leroux has escaped from the hospital."

My knees buckled, and I landed on one of the kitchen chairs with a bump. He was kidding. He had to be. "Is this some sort of sick joke?"

"Afraid not. I'm aware he came after you personally last time, and if you'd like, I can arrange protective custody."

"I'm not going into custody."

The phone slid out of my grasp as panic welled up inside me. *Breathe. Just breathe.* Leroux couldn't get me in here, not with the security system and the guard by the front door.

"Ma'am?" The policeman's voice crackled.

"I'm here. Thank you for letting me know."

"If there's anything we—?" he started, but I'd already stopped listening.

Ben. I needed to call Ben.

"Are you okay?" Roxy asked.

"Leroux's escaped."

"Holy hell."

My fingers were shaking too much to dial Ben. Twice, I tried and failed, but before I could hit third time lucky Emmy wandered in, whistling.

"Leroux's escaped," I told her, ashamed of the quake in my voice.

"Yeah, I know. Have we got any chocolate milk left?"

"Did you even understand what I said?"

"Leroux's escaped. Not surprised really. The security at the hospital was atrocious."

"He's on the loose! What if he hurts someone else? What if he vanishes again?"

"Relax, would you? Dammit, no chocolate. Strawberry milkshake will have to do." She upended the carton and took a slug. "Don't tell Black I did that. I always tell him off for not using a glass."

"How can you act so calm?"

"Because we're a step ahead this time. When Leroux was in the hospital, I snuck into his room and planted a tracker in him."

"You what?"

"They're tiny nowadays. The long-range ones are about the size of a kidney bean."

"How on earth did you plant it inside him?"

"I look good in a nurse's uniform. Black wanted me to keep it on with a pair of heels while... Too much information?"

I closed my eyes until I'd regained control of my ragged emotions. "Yes, too much information. What's going to happen with Leroux? If you know where he is, can't you tell the police so they can arrest him again?"

"They had their chance. We'll do this our way now. Just know that you don't have anything to worry about."

Worry? Of course I was going to worry. By the time Ben ran in twenty minutes later and gathered me up in his arms, I was cursing my mother's genes as I fought to stay away from the vodka bottle.

"He's got out," I sobbed.

"I know. We'll fix it; I promise."

"But how? Emmy says she knows where he is, but she won't tell the police."

"The police have already let him go twice—once in France and once in England. And he's still getting help from his father."

"I hate him. I hate both of them. They tried to take everything from us, and they tore my family apart. What if they decide to have another go?"

"Blackwood will handle it." His brows knitted together before smoothing out again. "They want him out in the open because it's easier to make him disappear that way."

An icy cold wave broke over me. "That's what they plan to do? Make him disappear?"

"Would you be upset if they did?"

I thought about it. Guy Leroux didn't have a scrap of goodness in his body, and he'd made a misery out of lives the world over. Quite honestly, I had more affection for a wasp than for that bastard.

"I hope he rots."

Nobody spoke another word about Guy Leroux. Ruth cooked up a feast of French delights for supper, and I managed to eat a few morsels while everyone else left in the house laughed and joked. Ben, Black, Emmy, Sofia, Xavier, Gideon—even Roxy managed a smile.

Ben tried his best to take my mind off the situation

that night with three more creative orgasms to add to my collection, and I slept more soundly than I ever dreamed I would. Maybe I could get through this after all.

The next morning, I found a new guest at the kitchen table, and when she looked me up and down with eyes that threatened to suck out my soul for closer examination, I had to suppress a shudder.

"Gus, this is Ana," Emmy said.

"Nice to meet you," I lied.

"Likewise."

"Are you here on holiday?"

"Work."

She didn't speak again, and over the next two days, I barely saw her or anybody else as they plotted and schemed in the Project Carbon conference room. Or the war room, as I'd taken to calling it.

Then, on day three, I walked into the hallway and found a pile of luggage.

"Is somebody going on holiday?" I asked Emmy as she dumped a green canvas duffle bag onto the floor by the door.

"We all are, sort of. Are you packed?"

"What for?"

"I thought you and Ben were taking a trip to Virginia?"

"I just assumed that with the Leroux thing, it was cancelled."

"Don't let him dictate your life, Gus. Forget that bastard. Go pack, enjoy your break, and Fia will join you in a week or two."

So I did, even though the atmosphere in the house left me nervous as hell. One by one that afternoon, we all departed from Albany House, except Roxy, who had tears in her eyes as a town car pulled up outside the front door. Emmy slung a bag over her shoulder and headed towards it, followed by Gideon with a pair of suitcases.

"You're going with Gideon?" I asked her, quietly so Roxy didn't overhear.

"He bribed me with pain aux chocolat and mille-feuille."

"Black doesn't mind? I thought he wasn't keen on Gideon."

"Work's work, and he's eased up with the attitude since he realised Ren's into Roxy. Well, not into her yet exactly, but he sure as hell wants to be."

"He hasn't told her that."

"Because he's an idiot. Hopefully, he'll come to his senses before she gets sick of waiting."

"Perhaps you could give him a nudge?"

"Kick up the backside, more like, and he'll probably still dither." She gave me a quick hug. "Enjoy Virginia."

Flipping Gideon. He kissed Roxy once on the corner of her lips, almost chastely, then rode away in the car with Emmy. The Mercedes turned out of the driveway, and he didn't so much as glance back to the steps where Roxy stood with a single tear rolling down her cheek. My heart ached for her. Why did men have to be so difficult?

Ana was next to leave, and I breathed a welcome sigh of relief as she and her black aura climbed into a cab. Xav walked off towards the Tube station, and that left Sofia and Black.

"Are you going somewhere nice?" I asked her as she hefted her suitcase out of the door.

"Vietnam. The sun's calling."

Black picked up her case as well as his own and dumped them into another waiting town car, much to my surprise. "What, both of you?"

"If Black doesn't annoy me so much that I throw him out of the plane on the way."

"Isn't that...?" The words slipped out before I could stop them. Black and Sofia were taking a holiday together?

"Weird?" She smiled, only with resignation, it seemed, rather than mirth. "No, it's work."

Oh, hell. Not Leroux?

"Hang on. You're not planning to—"

She blew me a kiss. "Have a nice break. See you soon, and remind Leo to call the pool cleaner, would you? I forgot."

Then they were gone, leaving me standing with Ben. His arms gave me strength.

"Aren't you worried? I mean, she's your sister."

"Yes and no. I'll always be worried about her, but I know her better now, well enough to know that I can't stop her if she puts her mind to something, and well enough to know she can look after herself. Come on, *trésor*, let's go inside and finish packing. We've got a flight to catch."

He leaned down to kiss me, then took my hand. I followed.

I'd follow him anywhere.

EPILOGUE

THE LONDON EVENING Standard, England, 6 August

Part of Sidwell Gardens in Clapham remains cordoned off today following the discovery of a body in the exclusive development.

Police have not confirmed the man's identity, but locals who voiced their shock at his death named him as Janek Antol. A source confirmed he's the same Janek Antol who was acquitted of trafficking underage girls to the UK three years ago to work in a network of illegal brothels.

Officials remain close-lipped about the suspected motive, but *The Standard* understands an empty safe was also found in the upstairs bedroom with the body. A robbery gone wrong? Or did Antol's alleged wrongdoings finally catch up with him?

Le Monde, France, 6 August

Parliament has been left reeling today following the shocking suicide of nationalist politician Bertrand Leroux at home in Paris. A source says the note found with the body voiced his disappointment in his son, who, according to documents leaked two days ago, was convicted of the rape and murder of a citizen of Chad while serving overseas with the Foreign Legion, as well as the rape of her 10-year-old daughter. Guy Leroux was released early from a secure hospital before killing a second woman in England, being re-arrested, and subsequently escaping. His whereabouts are currently unknown, but police have warned the public not to approach him if seen.

Bertrand Leroux's death marks the end of a turbulent year for the politician famed for his recent outbursts against Muslim refugees and his campaign to reduce overseas aid payments. Opinions on the streets of Paris suggest little sympathy for a man who once boasted he drank more than the GDP per capita of Denmark in wine every year. "He was a vile human being," said Helene, 24, while 36-year-old Philippe expressed his dissatisfaction with a voting system that allowed Leroux to serve as a senator for so long.

Senator Leroux's ex-wife could not be reached for comment, but if the assault charge she once brought against him before it was struck out by antiquated inviolability laws is anything to go by, she's most likely raising a glass tonight.

Fakt, Poland, 6 August

According to emergency services, a gas leak is the likely cause of the explosion that rocked a four-bedroom house in Gdansk late yesterday evening while neighbouring properties remained untouched. Fire crews battled through the night to bring the flames under control following the blast just after 11 o'clock.

A police statement said the body of one

unidentified male was found on the ground floor, and nobody else was thought to be in the house. The gas supplier would like to reassure the local community that an investigation is underway, and they are continuing to monitor the situation.

Thanh Niên, Vietnam, 9 August

The identity of a man washed up on the beach in Phu Quoc yesterday remains a mystery. The deceased, found wearing navy blue shorts and a yellow T-shirt, is believed to be a foreigner, but no overseas citizens fitting his description have been reported missing, and no ID was found on the body.

According to a local official, the body is believed to have been in the water for several days, attracting the attention of local marine life, which is making identification difficult.

Anybody with information is requested to contact the police.

WHAT'S NEXT?

The Blackwood Elements series continues in *Rhodium*...

Rhodium

Lawyers. Stefanie Amor's had enough of them to last a lifetime. One left her heartbroken, the other left her in bed and did a runner. But as the witness in a murder case, she's got no choice but to cooperate with defence attorney Oliver Rhodes, a great white shark who gets his kicks from chewing up lesser mortals and spitting out their sorry remains.

Oliver has two passions in life: money and winning. Stefanie's a shiny new toy he's not supposed to have, pretty to look at but so easy to break. Playtime's fun, but what happens when the game isn't a game anymore?

More details here:

www.elise-noble.com/rhodium

And if you'd like to see more of Emmy, you can find her story in the Blackwood Security series, starting with *Pitch Black*.

Pitch Black

Even a Diamond can be shattered...

After the owner of a security company is murdered, his sharp-edged wife goes on the run. Forced to abandon everything she holds dear—her home, her friends, her job in special ops—she builds a new life for herself in England. As Ashlyn Hale, she meets Luke, a handsome local who makes her realise just how lonely she is.

Yet, even in the sleepy village of Lower Foxford, the dark side of life dogs Diamond's trail when the unthinkable strikes. Forced out of hiding, she races against time to save those she cares about. But is it too little, too late?

****Warning****

If you want sweetness and light and all things bright,
Diamond's not the girl for you.
She's got sass, she's got snark, and she's moody and dark,
As she does what a girl's got to do.

You can get Pitch Black for FREE here:

www.elise-noble.com/pitch-black

If you enjoyed *Carbon*, please consider leaving a review.

For an author, every review is incredibly important. Not only do they make us feel warm and fuzzy inside, readers consider them when making their decision whether or not to buy a book. Even a line saying you enjoyed the book or what your favourite part was helps a lot.

Want to Stalk Me?

For updates on my new releases, giveaways, and other random stuff, you can sign up for my newsletter on my website:
www.elise-noble.com

Facebook:
www.facebook.com/EliseNobleAuthor

Twitter: @EliseANoble

Instagram: @elise_noble

If you're on Facebook, you may also like to join Team Blackwood for exclusive giveaways, sneak previews, and book-related chat. Be the first to find out about new stories, and you might even see your name or one of your ideas make it into print!

And if you'd like to read my books for FREE, you can also find details of how to join my advance review team.

Would you like to join Team Blackwood?

www.elise-noble.com/team-blackwood

END OF BOOK STUFF

Welcome to my random musings, which may or may not contain typos... Okay, so I'm not entirely sure what went through my mind when I was writing this book. Sorry, Mum. It just kind of happened. Originally, it was just going to be a little novella about Augusta and Midnight, then Gregory appeared, and Ben became Mr. Darke, and somebody had to die because somebody dies in nearly all of my books. I just can't help it. Even books that are mostly funny like Nothing but Trouble end up having a dark side.

You may have noticed I really struggle to conform to genre expectations too. I read all the craft books, those ones that tell me the rules like the hero and heroine must meet in the first chapter, that backstory can't be in chunks, that I shouldn't mix first and third person, that I should have a dude with a bare chest on the cover if I want to sell books, but then heart overrules head and I end up writing whatever I want to. I write because I love it, and I love my characters. I'm just thankful that people choose to read my books. Trev the horse is thankful too, because it means I can afford to buy him bananas and oranges and those little treats that smell like coconut.

Anyhow, Carbon... I loved writing this book because I got to use characters from all of my Blackwood series

—US, UK, and Elements. Since the original Black trilogy, I've tried to keep all my novels self-contained so they can be read as standalones, but I also like developing Blackwood into a bigger world and finding out what characters from earlier books have got up to. Or, in Emmy's case, what trouble she's managed to get into now.

So, what's next? In Elements, it was going to be Rhodium, which pairs up with White Hot in the main Blackwood Security series. I've already written the first draft of both of those. But now there's Gideon and Roxy, and I'm super curious about what's going to happen to them, so I might write their story too. What do you think? Let me know :)

My next book out will be Joker in the Pack, the first book in the Blackwood UK series. I wrote that a few years back now, and even won an award for the unpublished version. That one's all edited and scheduled for release at the end of July. If you want to see more of Nye, that's the book you want ;)

If you'd like to hang out with me and be the first to hear Blackwood news, you can find me in my private Facebook fan group, Team Blackwood. Cover reveals and teasers get posted there first, plus I run exclusive giveaways in there.

Thanks for reading, huge thanks if you've written a review, and I hope to see you soon!

Elise

As always, I need to thank my team because I couldn't get these books published without you. First up, my beta readers—Terri, Jemma, Quenby, Harka, Jeff, Renata, Helen, Lina, Musi, David, Stacia, and Nikita.

Abigail Sins for the cover. Amanda Ann Larson for editing. And finally, Emma, John, and Dominique for proofreading.

OTHER BOOKS BY ELISE NOBLE

The Blackwood Security Series
For the Love of Animals (Nate & Carmen - prequel)
Black is My Heart (Diamond & Snow - prequel)
Pitch Black
Into the Black
Forever Black
Gold Rush
Gray is My Heart
Neon (novella)
Out of the Blue
Ultraviolet
Glitter (novella)
Red Alert
White Hot
Sphere (novella)
The Scarlet Affair
Spirit (novella)
Quicksilver
The Girl with the Emerald Ring
Red After Dark
When the Shadows Fall
Pretties in Pink (TBA)

The Blackwood Elements Series
Oxygen

Lithium
Carbon
Rhodium
Platinum
Lead
Copper
Bronze
Nickel
Hydrogen (TBA)

The Blackwood UK Series
Joker in the Pack
Cherry on Top (novella)
Roses are Dead
Shallow Graves
Indigo Rain
Pass the Parcel (TBA)

Blackwood Casefiles
Stolen Hearts
Burning Love (TBA)

Blackstone House
Hard Lines (2021)
Hard Tide (TBA)

The Electi Series
Cursed
Spooked
Possessed
Demented
Judged (2021)

The Planes Series
A Vampire in Vegas (2021)

The Trouble Series
Trouble in Paradise
Nothing but Trouble
24 Hours of Trouble

Standalone
Life
Coco du Ciel (2021)
Twisted (short stories)
A Very Happy Christmas (novella)

Books with clean versions available (no swearing and no on-the-page sex)
Pitch Black
Into the Black
Forever Black
Gold Rush
Gray is My Heart

Audiobooks
Black is My Heart (Diamond & Snow - prequel)
Pitch Black
Into the Black
Forever Black
Gold Rush
Gray is My Heart

Printed in Great Britain
by Amazon

56857270R00213